Beyond the Walls

Alice Westcreek

To my sister Lisa, thank you for continuously being the worst example a little sister can look up to.

I

My parents love each other more than anything in the world. Whenever my father moves, my mother moves with him. They are like magnets, constantly together, never apart.

Because my parents love each other they had me, and twelve other kids. Yet they only ever looked at each other. It was as though the rest of the world wasn't important to them.

We didn't live in a hateful home. Just one that didn't really care that much. The only time I saw my family as my family was when my sister, who was twelve at the time, was found dead on the side of the road after being missing for ten days. It felt like that was the only time my mother was able to see beyond the bubble she and my father lived in. As though that was the only time she cared.

We buried Katha in a dark, wooden coffin on the top of a hill nearby our run-down house and moved on. Everyone went their own way again, worrying about school, about their future, about themselves.

I sat down next to her gravestone, with my back against it so I could look down the hill and keep an eye on the kids playing. A few times a week a military vehicle would drive by the road next to our house because we lived relatively close to the fence.

The kids always took great interest in it, and sometimes got too close. I did not want to get lectured by some random sergeant again.

After the Blood War, the world was nearly destroyed. Nuclear and biochemical warfare was the way to go, the way to wipe out your enemies and in return, be wiped out yourself.

It is still unclear to this day what exactly happened. The first bomb everyone sends is to the nation's government. There really was no way of knowing which country set it all off. Who was to blame for the many deaths?

It didn't really matter anymore. No one had the resources to wage war on other countries. There was now a clear divide in the world. Us versus them. Really it was all just a game of chance. I read in a history book that there were plans before the war to create a wall in the United States, but they wanted to put it on the southern border. They never built that though. Ours circled the entire kingdom. I had only seen paintings of it, and my teacher once drew it on the board, it was so high up into the sky that you can't even see the top, with barbed wire and electricity to keep them out.

"Hello sister," I said to the blue sky above me. It was quite unusual for the weather to be this nice. Most of the time we just get a bunch of rain, sometimes even snow. "Do you want to talk?"

I liked Katha when she was alive, she wasn't as stupid as the other kids. She didn't run into soldiers, she didn't scream for attention, she just looked around with big, blue eyes, never really sharing what she found so mesmerizing.

"Tomorrow is the day." I continued, tearing out some grass and laying it on my lap. "My interview is tomorrow." Inside the fence we have a system in place, a system that is supposed to help everyone, but it had some serious flaws. There was an option to take an interview. Any teenager who could not get an apprenticeship could try their luck there. The interview decided where you will work for the rest of your life: doctors, military, engineering, hunters, teaching, politics or the worst of all: factory.

Factory really was just a collective name for everything that was left. Originally these people did actually work in the factories. But now they can also be bakers, farmers or even garbage collectors. It all depended on how well you did in your interview. I was nervous as all hell. The thought of having to spend the rest of my days on a farmer's land somewhere caused my stomach to turn into a knot. I couldn't do that, not for the rest of my life. Farm hands especially have it the hardest. It's heavy work, and it doesn't pay well either. But running wasn't exactly an option either. Desertion, even just from a farm, is punishable by death.

"I don't know what to do." I admitted freely, now that only the birds and the sky could hear me. I heard of people crossing the wall into the unknown, but if I get caught I'll die, if I don't get caught I could also very well die because I hardly know what's beyond the wall. It seemed like I was stuck. I had put all my hope into finding an apprenticeship, but no one would take me. Even in the city it was hard for kids to stand out, we had no chance here in the countryside.

I had asked my parents about the interview, and my teachers. We also got an official book about it, even though that one was only ten pages long.

Supposedly we are getting interviewed by the leaders of the seven workplaces. That, however, hasn't happened in hundreds of years. They now send representatives to do their jobs for them. I heard that the military sees these interviews as a punishment for when an officer misbehaves, and only sends those out. I guess it would be pretty boring to do, just sitting around listening to hopeful teenagers for one day. They must have forgotten what it is like.

"I am scared, Katha." She was should have done this last year. She could probably have been a doctor or a teacher. She was smart and observant, it's what the teachers wrote about her in her notes. Mine said different things. My fourth-grade teacher wrote down that I had trouble focusing, which was only partly true. I could focus, just not on things that I found boring. My fifth-grade teacher said that I was too energetic, and my seventh-grade teacher said that I was smart, but behind on the rest of the class because of 'external factors'. She was talking about my home situation without pointing it out. I never had time to do my homework properly. Seventh grade was when my brother left. It was when more and more weight started coming down on my shoulders.

I stayed up there for quite some time, saying small things to the gravestone. I informed her how the rest of the family was doing, how her best friend got placed in the factory last year and on the state of the world, which I didn't know either, but I just guessed it was pretty much the same as when she died. Nothing ever really changed around here.

I only went down when I noticed my mother leaving the house and looking around her playing kids. I did not want to get scolded for being lazy. I got up, brushed my fingers over the stone one last time and went down the hill.

Instead of her usual scowl, she had just gotten home from her job as a factory worker, today she smiled when she saw me.

"How was your day?" She asked me. It caught me off guard. She never asked about anyone's day, unless something bad happened and she wanted everyone's accounts on it.

"It was fine." I answered. We obviously didn't do anything in school. It was only hugs and goodbyes. Even though we were all from the same region, the chances of getting placed together were very slim. There simply weren't enough jobs around here.

We walked inside the house. My parents shared a bedroom upstairs, but the rest of the kids slept downstairs. There simply wasn't enough space for everyone, most of us slept on the floor, covered in blankets.

"So, tomorrow." She said, looking at me as though this was the first time she really saw me. She walked around me, lifted my arm and touched the small layer of fat underneath it and mumbled small words to herself. She sighed and crossed her arms over her chest.

"Where do you want to be placed?" She asked me. I hadn't even given that a thought before. I just didn't want to get placed in factory, that's all. Military was also a hard one to succeed it, but I could rise in ranks there if I worked hard enough. All the workplaces had the same rule: If you don't succeed, you get put into factory. Even if I did get lucky and get picked, there was still that possibility.

"I don't know," I admitted. "Maybe military."

"You wouldn't last there," She snapped at me. "You're too skinny. Your grades were good, you could be a teacher."

We heard a kid crying outside, which wasn't that much of an uncommon sound around here. She glanced out the window, revealing the tattoo on the side of her neck.

Tattoos were only used as a decorative form of art outside of the fence. Inside, it was to show your rank. Each workplace had their own symbol. The teachers had two dots, the doctors one round ball cut in half. The factory workers had the most simplistic one. A filled in square. A large one too, if someone failed this tattoo needed to cover up their previous one.

My mother's tattoo covered up her short-lived military career. She got kicked out on the first week for being too lazy. Maybe that's why she snapped at me.

"Your brothers," she was still looking outside. "They all got placed in factory. Weren't even tried somewhere else first." Her eyes followed the children running around. "They get enough money for themselves only." A lot of the economy came down to trading, seeing as no one in the factory made enough to buy everything they needed to survive. The only place where they could spend their salary was in the Union stores, which sold the basic life necessities. I finally saw where it was going.

"If you get placed somewhere else you need to send money home." She wasn't asking, she was telling. "You'll get extra. Keep what you need and send the rest to us."

"Why?" It was a shitty thing to ask her. But I needed to see her panic. To see if she thought of her kids at all. It never looked that way to me. She slept on a bed, we didn't. She even slept there when we were all down with the flu. And when Arthur broke his leg. She didn't care, she saw us as a burden.

"Because your father is getting weaker," Her eyes remained focused on the outside, but her tone got venomous. "I give it two years max before he can't work no more." More crying came from outside, yet she remained still. "I can't support the family by myself. You brothers can't do anything right. But you," she finally turned to me. "Your grades were high, the teachers liked you, the town folk knows you. It might be enough."

The thought of sending money back home was confusing. On one hand, I wanted to make sure my siblings didn't starve to death, I kept them alive for too long just to see them die when I leave. On the other hand, I can't know for sure if she will use the money for them.

"I guess we'll have to see where I get placed." It was all I could say to her.

2

The only way to keep my hands from trembling was to clutch the fabric of my skirt tightly. I didn't want to look how I felt: incredibly nervous.

My mother was right though, my father did come home looking paler and paler each day. He didn't work in the local factory like her, he was a farm hand. Soon he won't be able to do anything but sit at home. They will all starve if that happens. Or worse: She could start selling children.

Slavery here wasn't the same as it was beyond the wall. Here it was civil, almost. If they got sold as a child, they will get the option to take the interview when they reach the age of nineteen. After that people can only go willingly into slavery, most often used as a way to avoid working as a foot soldier or really horrible factory jobs. They work as maids and cleaners, but usually only in the larger cities.

"Derbi, Anthon." A man dressed in military clothes shouted the name across the courtyard. I had to get up at four this morning, just to make it here on time. I walked for six hours, without a companion to talk to. I had been worried about getting lost, but there were plenty of other teenagers going the same way. They were just as silent as I was, it felt like a death march.

People my age filled up the courtyard. I hadn't seen most of them before. This was the centre of the region, some had to come from even further away than I did. Most people talked nervously to each other, others like me did not. I just watched as more people went in looking nervous and coming out looking like they'd seen a ghost. Safe to say, I was terrified.

Anthon Derbi exited the room a lot quicker than the people before him. He walked over to his friend, who was lounging against the wall next to me.

"The hell did you do?" The friend was grinning, giving Anthon a quick smack on the back as a greeting.

"They started asking their questions." He was laughing too now. "I just said: 'I'm gonna be honest with you, I am only interested in the hunters.' Then I turned to the bloke and said: 'So what do you want to ask me?'" Anthon was an idiot, that much was clear. An idiot who was definitely going to be working for the factory.

The hunters were a group of elites. They were originally a branch of the military, but when they also started taking on the role as ambassador, they got promoted to being their own workplace. They knew how to fight, how to plan battles against the radiate rebels and how to actually win them. The hunters never picked anyone from this region, especially girls. We were all just simple factory folk around here.

Three more people got called in. I listened in on Anthon and his friend, who was clearly lying to make himself feel better. There was no way that the hunter 'looked at him with appreciation on his face'. I was already annoyed by him, someone who was smart enough to become a hunter would definitely also be.

My thoughts once again shifted to what I would do if I got placed into factory. Everyone in the courtyard came from a factory background, it was rather obvious. Most, if not all of them, had holes in their unwashed clothes and looked underfed. I'd like to think that if I got placed in factory I would be brave enough to climb the wall.

What was beyond the walls was both a mystery and as clear as day. There were people there. They are called radiates. Their part of the old country hasn't been purified of the radiation yet. The life expectancy on that side of the wall isn't very high. Though I learned in school that it wasn't per se because of the radiation poisoning or other health problems. It was because of the lack of food and medicine, which turned people against each other.

The mystery part came in with rumours. Apparently, there were monsters out there. People as tall as trees, men and women with four heads and long claws. I thought most of these were just made up to keep us inside, but when my teacher showed us an old photo of a skeleton with three heads, I was prone into believing.

"Thorne, Julia." The man shouted. With numb legs I moved from my spot, clenching my skirt again. The man just looked at me with blank eyes and showed me to the correct door. He must think I am just another teenager, I straightened my back, took a deep breath and entered the room.

No one bothered to decorate it or by the looks of it clean it up either. There were several cobwebs in the corner of the room and it smelled like old socks that should have been thrown away years ago.

There was one large table, with seven people behind it. Across from it stood a single chair. Most of the people behind the table were still talking to each other, so I just closed the door behind me and sat down. I folded my hands in my lap. Hopefully, they would stop shaking that way.

Even if it wasn't for the tattoo in their necks, it was clear who was who. On the far-left end of the table was the factory recruiter: a small man with a constant look of desperation edged on his face. He was quietly reading my file.

Next to him were the teacher and the doctor, who were in some sort of discussion. They could also have been flirting, the doctor smiled and tugged a piece of her blonde hair behind her ear, while the teacher was desperately trying to hide his red cheeks. In the dead centre of the room was the military man. He could have quite possibly been the largest man I had ever seen. He had a stern look on his face and was fully decked out in his military uniform. He didn't look like he was here because he was being disciplined. He looked like he was about to do it to the rest of the room.

The politician and engineer were also talking, but they were very openly talking about me. The politician said something about technical skill to the engineer while pointing at the paper. I hadn't received the highest of scores for the subjects related to engineering, like physics and the time we all had to fix a lamp and I ended up electrocuting myself. But I did get high scores on my presentations and verbal exams, so maybe politician could work for me.

And finally, the hunter. He did not look at the paper, nor was he talking to someone else. He just looked at me. He didn't wear his official uniform, unlike the rest of the room. I caught his dark brown eyes for a second before my attention got pulled to the centre of the table.

"You are Julia Thorne?" The military man asked, his voice loud because he undoubtedly uses it to shout at troops.

"Yes, sir." I answered. Always speak with two words to a superior, I thought to myself. But only moments later I was thinking that maybe it came off as being a kiss ass, which I also definitely didn't want to be. My heart was beating loudly in my throat.

"You have quite the grades here." His eyes glanced over my file. Learning always came natural to me. If I found it interesting it stuck in my brain, if it wasn't it would slide right off me. Which is probably why my physics grade doesn't quite match the rest of the report card. "Your teacher said you were a little behind your class," the teacher added. "Why is that?"

"I have a lot of younger siblings. I needed to take care of them after school and couldn't do my homework on time." I answered, I could literally see the interest fall on his face, so I quickly elaborated. "Eventually I found a way to do it on my way to school." I seemed to have redeemed myself a little.

They asked me about more things. Why did my teacher write down that I had trouble focusing? Was I currently engaged or married? Did I know how to wire a lamp? One by one the people at the table asked me questions, sometimes more than once. I found my nerves cooling down, I just had to tell them the truth. They would find out if I lied and then I would definitely get sent to the factory.

"What is the worst injury you ever sustained?" The hunter asked, cutting off the teacher who was just taking his time to set up another question for himself. The hunter hadn't talked the entire time, he just looked me over. It made me feel incredibly uncomfortable like he could see right through my clothes. His voice was heavier than I expected, he looked so tiny next to the military giant.

"Two broken ribs and a laceration to my arm," I said, rolling up my sleeve a little to show him the white line across my forearm. He raised one of his eyebrows, showing me that I needed to tell more. "I was pushed aside by a military convoy when I went to get my sister. I fell onto a piece of metal."

It wasn't what the military man wanted to hear, but I simply couldn't lie. One of the doctors had probably written it down somewhere. The hunter didn't give any inkling that my story was good or bad, he just went back to staring.

The teacher asked his final two questions and suddenly I found myself outside again. The air felt a lot warmer and more welcoming than before I entered. But the man had the same blank stare and didn't allow me to savour the moment before calling the next name and ushering me away.

The walk back home felt like it was only an hour, I was deep into my thoughts about things I could have said differently and things I shouldn't have elaborated into at all. I didn't even notice the large abandoned buildings that were swaying dangerously in the wind as I passed them. Before the bombs fell, the city I had to walk through had been thriving. It was now entirely out of use until the government found a way to fund the rebuild of it.

Rebuilding the world was a slow process. After the bombs fell it was all about survival. Nations were started on the ashes of the old ones, but it took years for people to figure out how to survive without all the luxury items they were used to. American cities like New York, Washington DC and Los Angeles were all nuked. But so were other cities like London, Berlin, Seoul and Moscow. Radiation became a bigger enemy than any other nation used to be.

It took a long time for America to recover. But gradually people united under one leader, James Alexander. He helped clean up the first city from radiation and named it the new capital: Vancouver.

Closely after that followed Seattle and after that Portland. His land and population started growing and his grandson finally put a name to it: The Union of Nations, but most people just call it the Union.

My siblings welcomed me home. They were all eager to hear the questions they asked me. I could tell my parents were listening in on the conversation, but neither of them said a word to me.

That night I laid awake as the raindrops fell heavily onto our wooden roof. I heard soft snoring all around me, but I couldn't seem to fall asleep myself. I kept tossing and turning, retucking the pillow and trying to find a better angle to lay at.

I got to lay near the oven tonight, as a final goodbye gift from my siblings. It was the best place in the house because it was the warmest. The fireplace often went out early into the night, and it wasn't a very safe place to sleep, but the oven kept its heat for longer.

I couldn't go to the factory, I just couldn't. Slaving away on a warm field somewhere wasn't what I wanted to do with my life. I wanted to get chosen, I needed to. I could help people as a doctor or as a teacher. I could protect them as a soldier, I could get very rich as a politician.

I always thought politicians were just for show. We had a royal house, a king who decided what happened. The politicians are supposed to be the voice of the people. Citizens should be able to come up to them and say their complaints. But other than the guy yesterday, I had never seen one over here. They just didn't care that much.

I could make a pretty good politician, I thought to myself as I turned around once more. Though I don't think I could live with myself knowing that people out there are starving while I am getting loaded. Maybe I could use that and actually change something.

I started to slowly drift away. I could do any of them. I could electrocute myself every single day, as long as I don't get placed in factory.

3

It was a rare occasion for us to all leave the house at the same time. More often than not one person was sick and stayed home, or it was a day off and my parent worked while the kids stayed home. Today showed how long it had been, it took twenty minutes to find the key that locked the front door.

Thankfully this time we didn't have to walk to the city. We would hear the result in front of my old school.

I tried to enjoy the last few moments I had with my siblings, knowing that the chances of me seeing them again were very slim. People need to go wherever the government sends them to. The jobs around here were slim, only field workers and local factory workers lived here. Most of the jobs were in the city. There was one day of the year when people were allowed to have a day off to visit their family, but especially during the years that I would be learning or training I simply wouldn't have the time for it.

I could feel my heart beating in my throat as the school came in sight, the school that I had spent twelve years of my life on. I hadn't always liked it, but I never thought I would miss it.

On the steps in front of the school stood the seven people from yesterday, they were all talking together, except for the hunter, of course, he stood about a metre away from them, gazing at the people in the crowd.

My sister fussed with my hair, caring a lot more about it than I did. It always got so frizzy once you touch it too much, I just put it in a braid or a ponytail. Besides, they weren't gorgeous blonde locks like the girl next to me, who was crying her eyes out and hugging her brother. Mine was just dull, brown hair that never worked with me.

I hugged all my siblings, whispering in their ears to look after each other. I shook my father's hand and had a brief moment of eye contact with my mother. I wouldn't really miss them, I just hoped they could take care of the rest.

I took my place in the line of students who were at the front of the big crowd of families. I smiled at Francesca, we were always put together. The teachers preferred to keep things alphabetical in the classroom, so Thorne and Tor were put next to each other. She looked about as scared as I felt. Her grades weren't that good, I knew that, but overall she was much more social and outgoing than I'll ever be. Maybe the teachers were smart enough to write that down in her file.

"Silence." Said the same man who ushered us into the room yesterday. He nodded at the people on the steps as the crowd instantly hushed.

Several kids came out of the school, dressed in different coloured tunics. Every class gets to send in one person, usually the one with the best grades, and read out the keywords of the workplaces. I even got to do it once, when I was six, I studied the lines for weeks because I struggled with the word 'integrity'.

"Seven places to work, seven places to change the world." The oldest started, his voice low but still filled with tension, this wasn't something to mess up.

"Teachers," one of the girls, who was in a pink tunic, said. "Wisdom, passion, patience." All of our past teachers were watching through the classroom windows, there was no one to say the words with the little girl besides the teacher from the interview.

"Hunters," a boy said, his tunic black just like the hunter's clothes. "Loyalty, strength, perseverance." The hunters said the words along, though he only whispered it.

"Military," it was a small girl dressed in blue who said this. "Resilience, dedication, power." This time more people talked along with it. The man on the stage spoke with her, completely drowning out the girl's voice.

"Politicians," next was a boy dressed in red. "Knowledge, honesty, empathy." The only person to say it with him was on the stage. There were no politicians around here. They were all up in the big cities.

"Engineers," the girl seemed sure of herself that said this, her voice echoing over the square. "Truth, trust, improvement."

"Factory," the boy started, though the entire audience saying it along drowned out his voice. "Happiness, effective, impact." I could say it along too, better than any of the other workplaces. The quote was in our house, my parents had referred to it a hundred times when they scolded us. Happiness, effective, impact. The keys to life.

"Doctors," the last girl was the oldest, even though I got to do this one when I was younger. "Integrity, caring, humane."

"Seven places to work, seven places to change the world." The boy concluded. The crowd clapped, though they weren't very enthusiastic about it. Most people came from big families here and had seen this happen a dozen times already. No one really cared for the ceremonial part, it was the part that came after that really mattered

"James Alexander once said that when he thought of the future he did not once think of the clean cities, the peace or the everlasting prosperity. He said he only thought of the children. Our current king, King Avon, fully supports his ancestor in this philosophy. The future belongs to the children of today." The military man said, clearly having memorized his lines as he said them without any form of emotion on his face besides concentration. "You have all done a marvellous job at raising these kids, at teaching them how to become prospering adults. And now in return, they will make the world a better place." Though he paused, no one in the crowd dared to clap.

He grabbed the piece of paper from the teacher and put on a pair of old, battered looking, reading glasses.

"I will read out your name and workplace, then proceed to move to the right bus." He said to the crowd, before hiding his face behind the paper.

"Genevieve Hops, factory." He started. With a bowed head Genevieve moved over to the bus that had the word 'factory' painted on it. I was so nervous, I didn't even notice that the buses all already had people in it, the kids who came from the towns near us.

There weren't many people in my class, my fears seemed to be true. Everyone got sent to factory so far. Most of the people didn't even seem to mind it that much. They all came from generations of factory workers; it was in their blood.

"Francesca Tor, factory." Francesca gave me an encouraging smile and left me, the factory bus was almost entirely full already, but there was a new, empty one behind it. I took a deep breath.

"Julia Thorne," I saw a small smile tug at the corner of his mouth before he gave me my life changing verdict. "Military."

I wanted to cry. I was so happy. I was getting out of this hell hole. I could go make something of myself! My family wouldn't starve, Sure I might die fighting radiates, but everything beat working the fields, even an early death.

With a big smile on my face, I walked over to the military bus. In the back of my mind, I knew that military was the easiest to get into besides factory, but I didn't care. If I worked hard enough, which I definitely will, I could move my way up in the world.

This bus was also nearly full, maybe it was because some of these people took up two seats, they were that big, but it didn't matter to me. I was living on cloud nine.

I sat down the second row from the front, at the window seat. I could see my family. Most of the younger kids were crying, they didn't understand what was going on when I was saying goodbye. My mother made eye contact with me. She didn't need to say it, or to sign it. I could tell by the look in her eyes. Money.

I wasn't surprised, though I will send it to them. Whatever I can spare. I knew I wouldn't get anything in my years as a cadet. I didn't know how fast I could progress, but I was dead set on working the hardest that I can.

They rounded off the ceremony. No one else got into the military, but there was one girl in my class, Elisabeth, who got to go to engineering. Seeing as she was the one who eventually fixed the lamp for me, I thought it fit her.

The military man entered the bus and plumped down on the row in front of me. Right on his heel followed the hunter, who sat down across the aisle from him. The bus slowly took off, taking it's time to drive over the many bumps and potholes in the town road before reaching one of the main roads.

Infrastructure was not something the Royal family paid a lot of attention, or money, to. Everything in the capital had already been build up and was being well maintained anyway, that was the only thing they saw of their land. All their money went to expand their land, and not taking care of what they already had.

It took about an hour for me to fall off my happy cloud and realize what was going to happen: I was going into the military.

I would be training for months, maybe even years, before making the choice: Inside or out?

Should I stay inside the wall and spend the rest of my life dealing with bar disputes or should I go beyond it, and encounter the monsters I was so frightened of?

They would probably make us choose fast. The fighting you need to know for breaking up drunks versus getting shot at is vastly different. The environment we'd have to deal with was different.

I got the strange sensation that someone was watching me. I tried to shrug it off and play it off as a girl thing, I didn't see a lot of women as I entered the bus, but then they'd only be able to see the back of my neck anyway.

I looked up to see it wasn't any of the military guys who were looking, it was the hunter. Now that I was closer to him, I could see he had a scar from underneath his eye all the way down to the corner of his mouth, causing his lip to get tugged down a bit.

Eventually, I just turned my head back and looked out of the window. I don't know whether he looked away or kept looking at me the entire ride to the next town.

It was a small one, just like mine. I looked up as the two of them exited the bus. The hunter didn't look at me anymore. He had on a stern face as he exited the bus and greeted the province mayor, who looked like he ate everything I had eaten in my entire life in just one day.

I watched the next ceremony play out. There were only six students here, but only one of them got assigned to the factory. Three got sent to us. The first two sat together, but the last guy was forced to sit next to me. He was huge, much like everyone else on the bus, with long, blond hair that reached his lower back. The other two boys had a similar hairstyle, I guess it was in fashion here.

The hunter and the military man sat down again, and the bus started moving. This time we didn't take any small roads, only wide ones, ones that survived the Blood War.

"So how did you get dragged into this?" The military guy asked the hunter.

"Gunshot to the knee," he said, pointing to his right knee. He did keep it at an awkward angle into the isle of the bus, I should have noticed. "Headquarters figured I was the man for the job." The military man nodded.

"Beyond the wall?" He asked. I saw the boy next to me tense up, clearly also following the conversation. Most people around these parts were pretty superstitious and thought of the wall as their protector. As something they should not talk about.

"Aye," he just answered. "You?"

"Wife had a kid." The military man said. "I do this, I get to spend the next four weeks with the little one." The hunter nodded his head. He had been beyond the fence and got shot in the knee. At least he didn't get eaten by the monsters. The guy looked so confident, even with his knee messed up.

I decided to put it out of my head and focus on the big question for the rest of the trip: Inside or out?

4

The bus ride was fourteen hours. Most people fell asleep around the eighth hour, seeing as it was the middle of the night, but I remained wide awake. I couldn't sleep, not when we could be arriving any second. I did not want my first impression to be of a drooling girl who talks in her sleep.

The base we arrived at was still active during the night. It was a large compound, with six large halls for training, sleeping and storage. The forest surrounded us on all sides. It felt like it was a little world on its own.

There were still people outside training and guarding the fence that surrounded the compound, even though the moon was already high up into the sky. They eyed the bus as it rolled through the gate, probably remembering what it was like to be in our position.

They told us to line up outside. A few hours ago, another bus had joined us while the other six left. From all over the country cadets had rolled in. There were a total of twelve busses already parked.

"Welcome to home base." It was a female voice who spoke, but I was in the back, I could not see what she looked like. It gave me a small spark of hope though. I had only seen two other girls in the bus, both looked even more fragile than I was.

"You will all sleep in barrack four." I saw her hand signing which way to go. "Do not cause a commotion. You will find fresh clothes when you are woken up tomorrow morning. Enjoy your sleep, you'll need it."

So boys and girls did not sleep separately. A part of me had already been preparing for it. It didn't matter that much. There were too many people around for something to go down. Besides, I would scream my lungs out if it did.

As the people started to move towards the barrack, I spotted the hunter talking to the woman. I only caught a few words, but it looked like he was staying here too.

Curious.

I was tired as all hell, I didn't stop to think about a whole lot of other things. I found a nice unoccupied spot in the corner of the room and laid down on the mattress. It felt kind of weird, I had never slept on one before. It felt like I was lying on a cloud, and that I was just waiting for the fall back down to earth.

A loud sergeant woke us up the following morning at the crack of dawn. He used a metal pipe to slam against someone's bed, waking us all up in an instant.

We received clothes which were nothing like I had ever worn before. The pants and top were tight but made of stretchy fabric so I could move around in it. I never got to have these kinds of clothes. We didn't have a seamstress around for miles, but we did have a fabric shop we traded wheat from the field behind our house with.

My mother and I didn't really know how to sow, everything was loose and flowy. All the girls wore skirts because they were the easiest for us to make.

The cafeteria was huge and filled to the very last seat. It was easy to spot the cadets, we were the only ones struggling to keep our eyes open. My body felt sore from the mattress, which was a rough start to what would turn out to be an even rougher day.

We ate some sort of stew, though no matter how hard I tried I could not discover what was actually in it. Eventually, I decided that it was probably best not to know. Some of the cadets had started making friends, but I wasn't one of them yet. In a sort of silent way of understanding, most of the girls wound up sitting together. It seems like there was already a clear divide in the small group. There were girls who were already built like they had been working out for years, and the girls who looked more like me, happy to finally have something to eat.

On the wall next to me was the only form of decoration the military had put up, a large banner that read: 'resilience, dedication, power' I knew that every workplace was obliged to put the words up, but it seemed like the military rather just did it one time than the millions of times the factory did it. The factory my mother worked in had the words in every room of the building.

Another sergeant came and fetched us for the training. We were all brought into one of the large halls. Large mats, training dummies and other equipment filled up the room.

"My name is Sergeant Honnis," the man had dark skin and wore the standard, navy blue, military uniform, completed with the hat that covered his bald head. "I will be your drill sergeant for the next week. After that, we will decide whether you go to the wall, to the cities or another workspace." My mother must have been standing in a hall like this when she heard the same thing, not knowing that a week from now she'll be forced into a life where she does the same things every day in an assembly line. I was determined to show that I did belong here, that I wasn't lazy.

"We will begin with dividing you into different squads." The man spoke low and fast, not really caring for any reaction we may have, like the girl next to me who by the looks of it did not know she could lose her place here.

He started calling out the names that belonged to which squad. There were twelve squads, with each about twenty people in it. I was a part of squad number two. There was thankfully another girl in it, though she was hardly recognizable as one. She was as tall and wide as most of the boys.

"Squad one and two will be starting with running today." He said, signing someone over. He looked like just another drill sergeant, only he was solely focused on the running exercises.

There was a path in the surrounding forest that we had to follow. It wasn't wide enough for us to comfortably run next to each other, especially on our first day here, so we all ran in one long line. We started off at a steady pace. It wasn't too hard for me to keep up. I quite liked running. The wind in my hair, the sense of freedom, the feeling of strength. That was only the first five minutes of course.

I was getting more winded by the second, but we went on relentlessly. The instructor ran beside us, sometimes picking up more speed to check up on the front or slowing down to watch the back for strays. He ran next to me for a few minutes.

"Take bigger steps." He instructed me. "Breathe through your mouth, not your nose." I followed his instructions immediately, even though he went on to someone else. It didn't help much. Maybe breathing through your mouth is easier when you have already done it the entire time, and the bigger steps almost made me step on the heels of the cadet in front of me.

We were about halfway through the trail, I was pretending not to feel the stabbing pains in my side, when someone fell. He was near the front of the line, people behind him started falling over him because they were not able to stop in time.

I jumped aside into the grass to avoid the large group of winded cadets lying in the dirt. Instead of asking if they were okay, the drill sergeant started yelling at them to get up. I was so thankful. I finally got to take a few good breaths.

It took some time to get the line back in order. One cadet tried to convince the sergeant that he broke his arm, which gave me even more time to recover. By the time we started running again, I was breathing normally.

The second part was harder though. As an extra obstacle there were small hills we needed to run over. My legs felt like they were on fire, and my lungs wouldn't mind me stopping either. But I pushed on, I wasn't going to be a part of the list of people the sergeant yelled at. I needed to prove myself. I wasn't lazy.

I was damn near going on my knees when the ending came in sight. The path curved to the left, and suddenly we were by the fence again, except there wasn't a gate to go through.

"Anyone who can cross this fence in less than one minute will get a ten-minute break. Others do lunges." The sergeant said, setting the timer on his stopwatch. I didn't know what lunges were, but by the look on everyone's faces, they weren't something I was interested in doing.

The fence itself couldn't have been higher than four metres. It seemed a pretty straight forward climb, but I wasn't experienced in it. My older brother yelled bloody murder at me when I tried to climb the school building to get my shoe back, which a bully had thrown on the roof. That was over ten years ago, and I hadn't dared to climb since.

"Three, two, one. Go." The sergeant counted down. Everyone scrambled to get up the fence the fastest. I hooked my fingers as high as they could go in the fence and started my climb. My legs ached but the fire to prove myself hadn't gone down. I needed to do this, it's only a damn fence.

My way of climbing seemed to be working. I kept on hooking my hands through the wires and pulling myself up, there simply wasn't a place to put my feet.

"Forty seconds passed." The sergeant warned. One guy made it across, he was looking back at us with boredom in his eyes. I was almost at the top, from there I would go down as fast as I could. I just needed to make sure not to get stuck on-

The guy next to me had swung his leg over the fence, kicking me harshly on the back of the head. The surprise of it all got to me, and I accidentally let go of the wires. I fell on my back, the wind getting knocked out of me.

I scrambled to my feet, desperate to try again. But the sergeant's loud voice said: "Time." I was on the wrong side of the fence.

Luckily, I wasn't alone. There were four other people. One had fallen like me, the other three simply did not make it in time. My head hurt from where the guy had kicked me, which had caused me to faceplant into the fence. He was on the other side of it, looked at me like I was the one in the wrong.

I sent him the dirtiest look I could muster. If it wasn't for him, I would have made it. I wouldn't have to do whatever these lunges were.

Lunges were horrible, that's all they were. My knee had to touch the ground or it didn't count and I'd have to do it all over again. We had to circle the fence back to the main gate, doing lunges.

It took about an hour, mainly because if I fell over or did it incorrectly, I'd have to start over again. My legs were on fire, I was itching to sit down and maybe get some theory lessons.

But I was wrong.

After we went through the gate, we were immediately ushered back into the training hall. There we got reunited with our squad. They were practising punches and kicks.

We were given the same instructions they had. Put your feet a little apart. Pull your left shoulder back as you punch with your right hand. Make sure you don't break your own hand on impact.

I was starving. It had not been long since we ate breakfast, but the amount of exercise I already had to do had burned up all my energy. With each punch I threw I had to tighten my stomach, it only started hurting more and more

"You won't get anywhere punching like that." Sergeant Honnis said to me. I had been in a trance, I didn't even notice him standing behind me. "You don't have any strength in your upper arms yet. We'll train them in the next few months. For now, you should get more strength from your shoulder and stomach."

I stepped aside as he showed me how. I had just been standing still and punching, he now twisted his body a lot more to get extra momentum into the punch. He hanged around me for a few more minutes, until he was sure that I got it and moved on to the next person, who was already beating the dummy half to death.

What I had noticed were the people from the interview. Though I still didn't know the hunter's name, I had heard through gossip that the military man's name was Colonel Grenin. He still looked as frightening as ever, they were both making their way through the cadets.

I kept on punching the bag, not stopping when the pair walked straight by me to look at the boy next to me. Hunters didn't take in women. I was punching to impress Colonel Grenin. Hoping that he would see that I was good enough.

My head had started to hurt from where the guy kicked me, I could tell it had started to bruise and swell up, but I ignored the pain as best as I could. Besides, I hardly felt it compared to my empty stomach.

Lunch came around when the sun was at its peak. It was a rare occasion at home to eat two full meals in a day. Though I was happy that they switched that up here. If I got too hungry at home I would eat an apple from the tree behind our house. But I couldn't imagine going through more exercises on an empty stomach.

We got a slice of bread and some stew, which I happily dug into. Our squad sat together. Most of them were like me, absolutely starved. While there were also four from the capital region, who looked at the food with distaste.

"More stew?" The guy who kicked me in the head said, crossing his arms over his chest. "I'm not eating that. They can get me something else."

"Good, go on a hunger strike." The only other girl said to him while shoving a piece of bread in her mouth. "See if they care." I stifled a laugh. The guy looked like he had never been made fun of in his life. The fact that I laughed rubbed him the wrong way.

"What are you laughing at, bitch?" He said to me, puffing out his chest in an effort to look bigger. "You couldn't even climb the fence."

"I could have if you would have watched your damn legs." I answered him, calmly taking a sip of the stew. On the inside, I was absolutely freaking out. I never really cursed at someone. Nor did I go around picking fights. You learn not to do that pretty quickly if you have three older brothers. I knew I needed to stand my ground however, I couldn't let him walk over me this early. I needed their respect.

"You were in my way." He said.

"You took up half the fence." I answered. The guy opened his mouth to say something hateful back, I could see it in his eyes, but slammed it shut when he saw the drill sergeant heading our way.

"Squad two?" He confirmed. A few people nodded in response, thankful that the confrontation had been stopped. "You will receive muscle-building exercises for the rest of the day. Report to Sergeant Jof in hall three."

He didn't say anything to me for the rest of the day.

5

I woke up the next morning painfully sore. Everything hurt from the blow to my head to the bottom of my feet, which were covered in blisters. It wasn't until I swung my legs of the bed that I noticed how much my muscles were aching.

I still wanted to prove that I wasn't lazy, but I wasn't even sure of that myself. All I wanted to do is morph into my mattress and stay there forever. However, the punishment for being late was a death run for the entire squad. Which meant that we would have to run laps until you either collapse or throw up. It wasn't something I wanted to experience.

I had to drag myself out of bed, each movement hurt. I was glad to see that I wasn't on my own with that. By the looks of it, most cadets were hurting. I took the little extra time I had to clean up my face. I hadn't had the chance to shower yet, that would have to be tonight, so the best I could do was quickly rinse off.

I got a little surprised when I saw my reflection. I had heavy, dark circles under my eyes from all the tossing and turning I did last night.

What was more prone was the deep purple bruise on my left cheekbone, from when my face had hit the fence. It had swollen up so much that it was covering a part of my eye. I carefully dabbed it with a wet cloth, hoping the swelling will go down soon.

It looked like I had been in a fight, which wasn't the case. The guy just kicked me and I fell because of it. I wasn't even looking to fight him for what he did. I hoped he felt the same way.

We started the morning off with a run again. It was the same trail, but this time there were no breaks. No one was dumb enough to fall. My legs were positively screaming after the first two minutes.

But I stuck it out. After a while, I felt like this would be my death run. Like I would collapse right now. But the fence soon came in sight and I was not doing lunges today.

"Anyone who can cross this fence in less than one minute will get a ten-minute break. Others will do lunges." He repeated the same thing as he said yesterday. We all spread out over the fence again. This time I made sure I wasn't near anyone, especially the asshole who had kicked me.

"Three, two, one. Go." The sergeant counted down. I used the same technique as yesterday. I hooked my fingers as high as I could get them and pulled myself up. Sadly for me, yesterday I didn't have aching muscles. It was definitely harder, but before he said the forty-second mark, I was on top of the fence.

I thought I would just jump down, but I was beginning to second guess that decision. It looked a lot higher from up here. I felt a wave of panic wash over me. I could not be the loser who is too scared to jump down the fence.

"Ten seconds left." The sergeant warned. I quickly swung both legs over the fence and hooked my fingers in it again, so I could slowly climb down. It helped, but I could tell by the sergeants face that time was running out for me.

"Time." He said, as soon as my feet touched the ground on the other side. There were only two people who hadn't made it this time. Both of them hadn't made it yesterday either.

Someone bumped harshly into me as I turned around to enjoy my well-deserved break. It was the asshole from yesterday.

"You got lucky." He hissed at me.

"What's your problem?" I asked him after regaining my balance and following the rest of the squad.

"People like you who don't belong here." He answered, picking up his walking pace so he could walk beside his friends. Great, I was making enemies before I even managed to get any friends.

The guy was well liked in the group, but I still hadn't heard him introduce himself to anyone, so I didn't know his name. I decided to name him fish face because his eyes were bulging out of his skull and he constantly looked confused about everything.

I did belong here. And even if I didn't, I would make sure no one could tell. I was not going to spend my life in factory.

After lunch, we all went back down to the hall to train, where we were met by Sergeant Honnis. He guided us to one of the barracks that had been revamped as a classroom.

I sat in the far back of the room with the other girl, whose name was apparently Elska, beside me. We hadn't had any deep conversations yet. But there was still a bit of comradery between us girls. We were severely outnumbered. It helped if we stuck together.

"This afternoon we will be teaching you combat theory." The sergeant said. Fish face groaned loudly. He clearly didn't get into the military because of his profound intellect. "How well you do in this classroom could determine your future ranks. We don't want a general with the IQ of a toddler, so try to keep up." It gave me a spark of hope. Learning was easy for me. Maybe I could find some job that did not involve getting shot in the knee, but more the planning side of what troop goes where.

The lesson was quite easy. The sergeant told us about the different ranks in the military, how to recognize them on the uniform they wore and what types of jobs they did.

It became clear early on: If you want to make it big in the military, you have got to go outside of the wall, not inside. The chances of getting a higher rank were much slimmer inside. You were far more likely to become the small town peacekeeper.

I would try to go for the wall. I had always been kind of curious what was beyond there. Whether it would be complete devastation or more like in here, fragile but rebuildable. I had never even seen a radiate before. I know that most of them are savages, but a boy in school once told me that there were also normal ones, who just wanted to live their life out there.

I was so thankful for the lesson we received. Not only was I able to answer a few questions, but I also got to sit and relax my sore muscles for longer than ten minutes.

The rest of the class didn't feel the same way. Elska was the first out of the door once he said we could go have dinner, but that may have also got something to do with her stomach growling for the past two hours. The rest of the squad all jumped up too, eager to get out of the hot classroom.

I was the last to leave and followed the group back to the cafeteria. Much to fish face's pleasing, there was no stew. We got to eat mashed potatoes and vegetables, loads of them. Everyone was happily chatting away with each other, speaking of the exercises we did today and where everyone came from.

"What about you?" Elska kindly asked me. To keep yesterday's argument under wraps no one had bothered asking me so far. I smiled back at her.

"Countryside," I answered. "My parents are both factory workers."

"Mine both military." She admitted. "They started my training about the same time I could walk, so they'd be certain I'd make it here."

"Well, it paid off." I said to her after chewing down a piece of tomato. "You barely get winded from the exercises. I am already tired for tomorrow." Elska laughed loudly.

"Just don't rest in between the exercises. That will make it worse." She gave me more advice. How I could punch harder, how the running would be easier, even how to climb the fence. I was finally starting to make a friend.

That night I got to unwind my muscles in a hot shower, another thing I had never done before. We always washed with as little water as we could, we had to buy it from the store to make sure it didn't have radiation in it. We lived too close to the wall, we could never be too careful.

Here it was different. The water came from a river nearby and any bad bacteria or radiation were immediately filtered out of it. They even had boilers to heat it up. For a few minutes, I felt like I was in paradise as the water hit my sore muscles.

Paradise did not last, however. Like anywhere else on the base, men and women are treated equally. We slept in the same barracks, we showered in the same room. Several other people came in to shower. Most of them I had never seen before, they weren't in my squad, but they were all other cadets.

I noticed how some of their eyes lingered over to me for too long, even after I had grabbed a towel. I wasn't a prude. I had kissed a boy before, much to my brother's outrage. But kissing behind the school building and being ogled while you are naked is a completely different thing.

I had the rest of the night off, so after drying off I put on some exercise clothes, they were the only ones given to us, and started exploring the base. There were many halls and barracks I didn't dare go inside, fearing that I might accidentally stumble into some general's office. I just walked around a bit.

The compound was large, but it turned out I had only seen a small fraction of it. Behind the hall I trained in was something resembling a town square. There was a library, a church and even a post office.

There weren't many religions left. We called all of them the old beliefs. In history class, we were told about the holy wars that used to go on before the bombings. Afterwards, no one cared about the colour of your skin or which holy book you believed in. They were just wondering if you were going to steal their things.

Most people nowadays in the Union believe in a mix of all different believes. I don't know what radiates believe in, but I've been told they worship ordinary things like water and food seeing as it is so hard to get out there.

My heart jumped at the sight of the library. I loved reading, but there was only one library in the next town over, where I had finished reading all the books a long time ago.

It was absolutely beautiful on the inside. Much like most other places in the compound, this used to be a barrack for the soldiers to sleep in. The base had become the main training area for cadets, and not so much for housing all the soldiers. They had turned some of the barracks into different things. Like the classroom I was in today.

It wasn't the biggest library in the world, but it was more than enough for me. I did not recognize any of the titles, but most of them were related to the military in some way or another. I let my fingers brush over '*Military strategies of the twenty-second century*', '*The art of war*' and '*Once an eagle*' before finally picking up a random book on the shelf and reading the back.

I hadn't heard of the 'renowned' guy before, but detailed reports were hard to come by. They weren't exactly top survival priority after the first bombs felt. I held the book to my chest as I continued to glance over the other titles.

There weren't many other people in the library. There was a guy behind the counter, who looked old enough to have written all of the books by himself, two men in uniform who were going over some old looking maps, and in the corner of the room I spotted the hunter.

He had a cup of something next to him as he was reading a book, looking totally relaxed in the wooden chair. He flicked over to the next page and sighed, before looking right at me.

I have got to stop making awkward eye contact.

I kept my eyes solely focused on my feet as I made my way over to the librarian. I was allowed to bring it to the sleeping quarters with me, as long as I left my squad number and in which barrack I slept.

I didn't dare to glance over at the hunter again, those guys gave me the creeps. It's like they know what you're thinking. They'd know if you ever do something wrong.

The book turned out to be a bust. The detailed reports were all just guesswork, and the renowned guy just repeated everything they said in the fake reports in the first place. I guess it made sense, why would they print the real reports out and put it in a library no cadets ever willingly attends?

For the third day in a row, we started with the morning run. I used some of Elska's tips and actually did not find it as horrible as I did yesterday, though it still wasn't my favourite thing to do. Especially because today we went on a different path, which meant that we would be running side by side. At first, I thought fish face was just trying to mess with my head when he stood beside me, but then the sabotaging started.

He tried making me trip three times but failed. I managed to either jump over his foot, or regain my balance pretty quickly, without holding up the line. He also tried slowly pushing me off the track but was quickly called out by the sergeant.

We stopped at the same place we stopped at for the last two days: The fence. There were some things that just did not make sense. Why go for another path but make sure we end up at the same stretch of fence to climb over? Why make us do the same thing for the same reward when the largest part of the squad can already do it? Surely they did not just make us do it for the two people who failed.

"Anyone who can cross this fence in less than one minute will get a ten-minute break. Others will do lunges." He said the exact same thing. It was like he was a robot, repeating the same thing over and over again. It didn't make sense.

We spread out over the fence. The sergeant was preparing his stopwatch when I noticed something. Near where he was standing, where he had been standing on the exact same spot as the last two days, there was a weird dent in the fence, like someone had been shoved into it on the other side.

No one wanted to climb over right next to the sergeant, so getting closer to it wasn't a struggle. I was really hoping that I was right.

"Three, two, one. Go." The sergeant counted down. Instead of taking a running start like the others did and jumping on as high as I could, I moved closer to the ground. I was right, there was a weird dent. It wasn't because someone had been shoved into it, the fence itself was broken.

I could easily move the wire aside and crawl through it before any of the other people were even on the other side of the fence. He said to cross the fence, not necessarily climb over it. I was praying I was right, and that I had not pissed the sergeant off.

It took about ten more seconds before another person stood next to me. It was the same guy who had won for the last two days, I think his name was Teryn. He had seen what I did and looked at me like I was far beneath him. Like I had cheated. But come to think of it, maybe he looked like that all the time. I hadn't exactly seen him smile either.

Today there were four people who did not make it. One of the cadets who did not manage to do it yesterday was standing proudly beside me today. But the other person failed again, along with some cadets who had been struggling through their run too. It was clear that the muscle ache had started to take its effect.

"Cadet Thorne." The sergeant said. For a split second, I realized I messed up. I had been a smart ass. I had bent the rules, which the military obviously isn't overly fond of. "Was the only one to notice a very clear disturbance in the fence. I said cross. Not climb over."

I didn't know whether I should smile or not. I got praised by a superior, but my squad were taken down for it. The only person who send me a nice grin was Elska.

"Thorne, you are excused from climbing the fence. The rest of you will climb the fence and do lunges until the ceremony next Sunday." The sergeant ordered. "If one of you fails to climb the fence. All of you, not you Thorne, will do a death run." Everyone immediately glanced over to today's failures, who were all as pale as snow.

This hadn't made me more popular in the group. I was the bitch that caused everyone to do lunges, maybe even a death run. I was the only one enjoying a small break.

At least they didn't have to do lunges all the way around the compound. They only had to do them for about fifteen minutes before jogging back in. I got a lot of filthy looks my way, and I could see several heads turn to me when the drill sergeant explained what we would be doing today.

We would start our fight training. On each other.

Though Elska and I tried, we weren't paired off together. It was Teryn who would be my partner for the day. He did not seem to hate me as much as fish face, but we were very far away from becoming best friends.

Teryn was tall, though he wasn't quite as tall as I was, and had black hair that covered his forehead and the top of his eyes. He had a freckled skin and very thin lips, which were constantly pressed in a disapproving frown.

The sergeant showed us the correct way to bring someone to the ground. This technique was mainly used on civilians who caused a disturbance, the goal was not to injure them but to disorientate them. At first, we learned different ways of landing, which ones hurt and which ones hurt slightly less. Once he figured we could do that. The real fun started.

Teryn allowed me to go first. I grabbed his shirt with my right hand and put my left hand under his left arm. I had to turn my back to him and throw him over my shoulder. Which looked a whole lot easier when the sergeant did it.

"Put more force behind it." Teryn noted as I tried for the third time and failed. I nodded and did what he asked. I had been holding back a bit because I don't think my reputation can take it if I accidentally injure one of our top squad members as well. But he was right. Three days of training did not cause me to have Elska's muscles. I needed to get momentum in there.

I grabbed his shirt again and quickly turned. Teryn finally lost his balance and I threw him over my shoulder onto the mat. The wind got knocked out of him, which is supposed to happen, but he did not get injured.

After that, it was his turn. He threw me over his shoulder within seconds, clearly not having the reservations I did. As he let go of my shirt, I noted how his eyes darted upwards, before returning to me.

I followed his gaze and found the hunter. It clicked in my head, he was scouting out military cadets to join the hunters. Teryn would make a good one, he had been on top of everything since we got here.

"Do it again." I whispered to him as I noticed how the hunter glanced over to us. Teryn and I had a brief moment of eye contact, he looked like he was trying to see if I have ulterior motives. My only motive for helping Teryn is in the hope that maybe he could put in a good word for me, should fish face try to confront me again.

I quickly got up and let Teryn throw me to the ground again and again. Until the hunter left the hall.

"Do you think he saw it?" I asked him, after getting up from the last time. My back and butt were sore from all the falling, and I wasn't completely sure whether or not I would be able to throw him over my shoulder again.

"He would be blind if he didn't." Teryn said, before glancing back at me. "Thanks. I owe you one."

We weren't treated with another theory lesson after lunch. Instead, we got to do push ups, sit ups and other horrible things, with a new drill sergeant constantly shouting in my ear when someone did something wrong.

I got called out for lagging behind the rest. The sergeant's payback for that was that I had to do ten more minutes of jump roping. I didn't mind it that much, anything was better than lunges, I used to jump rope all the time with my siblings at home. It almost felt like I was back on the meadow behind our house, trying to continue on longer than everyone else.

Thinking of my siblings made me feel homesick. I wanted to go back to the time before my brother had to do his interview. When everything was nice and simple and I did not have to think twice about whether or not people like me. They were my siblings, they were stuck with me.

My brothers would have fit in here. They were always trying to prove to each other that they were stronger. I don't understand why they got factory and I got this. They weren't dumb like fish face either. Maybe it-

"Thorne! Are you trying to show off?" My thoughts got disturbed by the drill sergeant shouting in my face. I had been doing the jump rope exercise twice as long as I was supposed to do.

"No, sir." I quickly answered, but it didn't look like it was enough for him. He kept on looking at me with wide eyes, he looked like he could be related to fish face. "I just got distracted, that's all."

"You get distracted out there, you get you and your squad mates killed. Is that what you want Thorne?" It was like the sergeant was incapable of talking on a normal sound level. He was shouting everything loudly into my face. I could see every line in his face as he tried to look as intimidating as possible. Maybe it would have been if I hadn't been quite a bit taller than him.

"No, sir."

Elska and I walked to dinner together and sat down at an empty table, away from our squadmates. I hadn't exactly made myself popular today. Sure, I was now one of the top people in the squad, but I had made sure the rest of the squad would suffer for it.

"My dad told me that a soldiers alliance is defined the moment he sees true combat." Elska said after I brought my worries to her. "Once we're further into our training, they'll see you as more of an asset."

"Tell that to fish face." I mumbled into my soup. Elska started laughing loudly.

"Fish face? You mean Djorn?" She laughed. "I can never unsee that now. Thanks, Julia."

So his name was Djorn, not fish face. I had heard the name pop up a few times, but never directly at him. I glanced over to where he was sitting. His entire table was occupied, whereas mine was completely empty beside Elska. People were laughing, Djorn even slammed his hand on someone's shoulder blade, which created another fit of laughter.

A few tables over I saw Teryn. He was completely alone. There were only two other people at his table and they were on the other end of it, away from him. I hadn't seen him made any friends either.

He was completely focussed on the training. Now that our squad did not sit together anymore at lunch, he was even more alone than I was.

I was going to invite him to sit with us, I really was, but the moment I wanted to propose it to Elska he got up and left the cafeteria, having already finished his meal. Maybe tomorrow.

I returned the book to the library and called it an early night. I was exhausted from the physical exercises, but even more so mentally. I never thought I would feel homesick. Back in our old house, I was the oldest of the siblings after my brothers had left. I was the one they went to for advice or help. Here I was a newbie. And an unpopular one at that.

I wasn't disturbed anymore by people walking around the sleeping area, occasionally even knocking into my bed on accident. I had gotten used to it over the last few days. It was never truly quiet here like it had been quiet in the countryside. There was always something going on here.

I'll admit, I wasn't expecting this though.

It must have been far past midnight already. I felt someone wrap their hand around my waist and drag me out of my bed. I was still half asleep, so all of the minimal fight training that we have had completely slipped my mind.

It was too late to start shouting. A large hand was covering my mouth. I still felt like this was all a dream. I couldn't think straight.

Obviously, I fought the guy as hard as I could. He had one, strong, arm around my waist and his one hand over my mouth. It had to just be one person. I tried kicking him in the balls, but my leg just wouldn't bend that way. Instead, I hooked my leg around a random person's bed, hoping that the shaking would wake him up.

It didn't. Before I could even try again another person came in and grabbed my legs. I was left defenceless.

There was a small alley between one of the barracks and the exercise hall. Especially in the dark, it was hard for anyone to see what was going on in there. It was the perfect place to rape someone.

The hand got replaced by a piece of dirty cloth that they tied around my head. All the alarm bells in my head were now going off, and I was finally wide awake. But they didn't try to push me to the ground like I thought they would. Instead, they shoved me harshly against the stone wall. I didn't have time to prepare for it and hit my head against the bricks.

There weren't just two people, there were six. Even if I had Elska's or Teryn's strength, I could never take on six at a time. But when they stepped closer to me, and the moonlight hit their faces, I knew I wasn't going to get raped.

They were my squadmates.

"This is how it's gonna go down Thorne." Djorn stepped forward. Of course, he was their ring leader. I knew I had pissed them off with the fence thing, but I didn't know I did it to this point. The point that they wanted to beat me up in an alley.

"From now on, you will fail." He said, taking another step towards me so that he was only a few inches away from my face. The moonlight caught something else. In his hand was a knife from the dining hall. "Every exercise we do, every theory lesson we have. You will fail or be on the middle ground." He pressed the knife in my cheekbone. "You're a little bitch. You have been since the start. There is no way in hell any of us will let you get a higher position." I started talking back at him. Trying to persuade him to take the mouthpiece off. I could tell that I was getting under his skin by talking through his little monologue. Eventually, he ripped it off.

"I crossed the fence. I didn't do shit to you." I spat.

"You don't belong here, Thorne." Someone else said. "Everyone can see it. You're not strong. You're the konsi of the group."

The konsi, a bird which was typically found in the northern part of the kingdom, was a bird that often faked its own death when a predator came too close. Sadly, falling from the sky while pretending it's dead often leads to actual death. Nowadays the konsi was used as a way of setting a wrong example, so the rest of the class, or in this case the cadets, could see what was the right thing to do.

It would make sense. I wasn't strong. I didn't gain any points from my 'the military shoved me aside' story. Maybe they did only accept me because I am the konsi.

"You just got lucky with the fence." The guy continued. "And now someone else will be the konsi because you're suddenly amazing."

"The rest of us worked hard to get here." Djorn said. I did not see the punch coming. I was too focused on the blade. He hit me hard in my gut. I doubled over in pain. I felt like my dinner was gonna come up.

"Cool it Djorn." Someone whispered from the back. "Just scare her, we can't leave a mark. They'll see it. Start askin' questions."

"She won't say anything." He sounded so confident about himself. Another blow. This time to my face. I felt pain radiate out of it, spreading across my face as I tried to keep the men in focus. "You snitch on us. We'll come back with a sharper knife."

He was right, I wasn't terrified now, he probably couldn't even stab me with that knife, the blade was made for putting butter on toast, not for doing any physical damage. However, if he got his hands on some of the training equipment that they just left lying around...

He hooked the back of my knee, causing me to lose my balance and fall to the ground. He kicked me in the stomach, twice, before turning to the rest of the group.

"Any of you want in on this?" He was smiling. I could tell. I tried fighting the tears, but it seemed like the only logical reaction to what was happening. I couldn't fight, I couldn't do anything but clutching my painful stomach. Most of the people looked like this wasn't what they signed up for, all except for one, who took a step forward.

I don't know why they invited him. He hadn't been able to even climb the fence yet. But he looked more than willing to take that out on me. He kicked my face. I felt the warm liquid of blood coming down my nose and pour over my mouth. He went in again, but a loud voice disturbed him.

"What's going on over there?" The voice was heavy. Judging by the size of his silhouette, he was either an officer or a sergeant. The guys immediately bolted out the other side of the alley. I knew I needed to do the same. I couldn't snitch on them without making my life a living hell in the military. If I didn't they could make a notation that I got caught fighting.

I used the wall as support and got up. I needed to move faster, I heard footsteps coming after me. With every step I took, I could feel my stomach clutch together painfully. I could feel the blood practically pouring out of my nose. I needed to move faster.

"Julia." The voice was much more familiar now. I turned around and saw that I was wrong. It wasn't an officer who spotted us, it was Teryn. He didn't seem all that startled by the blood, he just put his arm around me so I could lean on him and led me back to the barrack.

We went straight for the bathroom. It was entirely deserted because it was the middle of the night, so it gave us some privacy.

"Djorn?" He guessed. I didn't answer. Would this be qualified as snitching? I just looked down at my own, blood stained, hands. I saw Teryn nod from the corner of my eye. "Just sit tight okay. I'll get a sergeant."

"No." I quickly stopped him. "I just need to get cleaned up. I'll be fine."

"Julia, you need medical attention." He said, picking me up and placing me in front of the mirror.

My cheek was still pink where he punched me, and my lips were painted dark red by my own blood. Nothing compared to the pain in my stomach however, and he hadn't even seen that yet.

"Your nose is probably broken." He stated. "I saw them kicking you. The doctor needs to look you over."

"I can't." I said. "They'll ask me what happened. They could kick me out for being too weak. I didn't fight back." It sounded like a good excuse in my head. Teryn seemed to buy it. He walked over to one of the bathroom stalls and got a roll of toilet paper. It took some time for it to stop bleeding. Eventually, Teryn concluded that my nose probably wasn't broken.

"I fell face first onto the sidewalk when I was eight," he said, pointing at his own nose. "My mother threw a fit. The bone got mended quickly enough in the hospital, but it hurt for days."

"Right, you grew up in a city?" I remembered hearing something about that during dinner yesterday. Talking helped, it made me forget the pain for a while.

"Calgary." He answered. "I was happy I got sent here though, and not further south."

"I thought this was the only cadet training base there is?" I asked back.

"This is the only one solely training cadets. There are four more bases." He explained. When he saw me looking at him oddly he elaborated. "My mom's a teacher, my dad's a doctor. I grew up around maps and information."

It wasn't that uncommon for teachers and doctors to get married. Factory workers usually marry factory workers, but the rest of the workplaces tend to mix a lot. The engineers work together with the doctors to create better medical equipment. The teachers learn some medical training from the doctors in case something happens in their classroom. They'd be happy to marry one of the higher workplaces, no one wants to degrade their rank. Even if it was all unofficial.

Teryn left to go back to sleep shortly after that. He offered to take the empty bunk next to mine, but I refused. I knew I wasn't going to sleep anymore tonight.

Instead, I settled for a hot shower where I stayed until my hands looked like they were about a hundred years old. I spend the rest of the night hiding away in the bathroom, fearing for what was to come the following morning.

6

The next few days were awful. It felt like I had only gotten awful days since I arrived here. I wanted to believe that things will get better, but after getting slammed into a training mat for the hundredth time by someone who was definitely a part of the people who beat me up, I was getting sick and tired of it.

I could only hope that after the ceremony we would be doing different things. It just looked like we were doing the exact same things over and over again here. With occasionally a little bit of theory lessons in between.

I did what the guys asked. I stayed in the middle, but I never failed something. Even with my painful stomach. I couldn't let myself do that. I wasn't going to get kicked out of the military because of them.

The ceremony was tomorrow morning. It was when all of the cadets would hear if they have to work for another workplace, realistically meaning only the factory, or where they got placed. Inside or out.

That night I met up with Elska and Teryn. We didn't know whether or not this would be a goodbye party. Elska was extremely good in all the exercises but practically falls asleep during theory. Teryn was succeeding at both, with him it was just a gamble if it would be the wall or the hunters. I felt like I was playing between inside the walls or factory.

"You'll make the wall." Elska reassured me.

We found a quiet place in one of the barracks and even managed to steal a bottle of beer, which we had to share between the three of us. I had never tasted alcohol before. But after a quick sip, I realized I never wanted to again. It tasted awful.

"Not after the beatdown." I said, passing the bottle along to Teryn. I quickly wanted to change subjects. I still haven't told them who was responsible, even though they both guessed it correctly. He wasn't exactly hiding it from anyone. "I think Teryn will get into the hunters. You're strong enough."

"That was your plan all along wasn't it?" Elska asked. Teryn shrugged, taking a big gulp of the beer.

"My parents wanted me to follow their footsteps. I was training for the military all along." He admitted. "I didn't exactly aim for it. I just wanted to get the highest position possible."

"Which is a hunter." I added. "The guy looks at you all of the time. You'll make it."

"He was looking at everyone." Teryn countered. "You as well. Especially after the stunt you pulled with the fence."

I had never even considered the hunters as a possibility, and I wouldn't start now. They didn't accept women. It was as simple as that. It wasn't some sort of sexism. Everyone knew the hunters often find themselves on the front line of battles. They needed to be extraordinarily strong. Men are just more often physically build stronger than women.

"As long as it isn't factory." I just said to them.

We laughed and drank that night, but not too much so we wouldn't get up in the morning. My night was happily undisturbed. Though it seemed like we were woken up even earlier than usual.

We were given special clothes for this event. They were somewhere in between workout clothes and something a little bit fancier. But they were definitely far from a uniform. We wouldn't be allowed to wear that anytime soon.

I tied my boring, brown hair back in a ponytail and followed the nervous group of cadets to the dining hall. Elska and Teryn were already there, eating in silence.

"Good morning." I greeted them. Teryn just nodded at me while Elska started an entire word vomit. She wanted to let me know she appreciates my friendship even though she would definitely be send to work in factory for the rest of her life. She didn't even seem to hear my protests to that statement and instead went on to another vomit of how she believed in both me and Teryn.

Teryn had finished three bowls of stew, I had barely finished mine and Elska had left hers completely untouched. Outside the bell rang three times. We had learned early on that two means incoming friendly, three means generals calling the cadets and four means incoming enemy. We all knew that today we were meeting for the ceremony.

Everyone was quiet. It seemed like even Djorn was feeling a bit anxious. Several other squads joined ours. They were going squad by squad. Sadly for us, they did it as a countdown. We were second to last to enter the hall.

We watched as several people entered the hall in large groups. I overheard some people questioning the people who came back out. He said that the people going to factory were entering the busses on our right, and the ones who were going to the wall were going to the busses on our left. Only the people who got signed to inside the wall were staying here in this compound for the time being.

We slowly watched the busses fill up. Factory received many defeated cadets. Some completely broke down in tears after they exited, they needed to be dragged to the bus by other unlucky cadets. I never thought so many people would get sent away. I had heard rumours before among other cadets that the military was accepting less and less cadets each year, simply because they didn't get to fight the radiates as often anymore under king Avon's peaceful reign.

"They'll go to the farms," Elska announced. "My dad told me. The factory sees that the military thought they were strong enough to fight. So they think they're strong enough to work as a farmhand." I thought back to my mother. She told us the stories about when she worked in the field. It was where she met my father. After she got pregnant, they stationed her behind an assembly line, never returning to the field.

I wasn't going to the factory. I had decided that. If they were to send me there, I would try to cross the wall. Finally, our squad got called in. My heart was thumping loudly in my chest. I tried to look calm though. I didn't want to embarrass myself in front of the main officers of the compound.

Their uniforms were heavily decorated with all sorts of medals and ribbons. They were all also quite a bit older than any of the sergeants I had seen so far. They stood in an impeccable straight line next to each other. The hunter had followed suit and joined the straight line. His black clothes immediately gave him away though. Military uniforms were always dark blue in the Union.

Someone else who looked out of place was a factory worker, dressed in the grey clothes I had grown up with all my life. He was slouched over and tried his best to stand in line, but he was slightly off. His block tattoo was especially large, he must have been tried somewhere else first.

They had changed the rules a few years ago. Before, they tattooed the people the moment they hear their workplace. This, however, resulted in a lot of cover-ups, so they changed it to after one trial week. You could still fail after, but at least the Union wasn't wasting that much money on ink anymore.

They told us to form a line outside. I was positioned as one of the last, while Elska and Teryn were closer to the front. I felt confident in their future careers. They had shown hard work to all the sergeants, never once complaining about anything. Besides, the busses outside seemed to almost be full. I myself am pretty sure that one of the empty seats is reserved for me.

"Welcome cadets." One of the generals started, his face wiped clean of any emotion. "For the past week, you have been given an example of what your life with us in the military will look like. Are there any people here who would like to forfeit and work in the factory?" It was a common courtesy to ask, but realistically, who would want to give this up? No one moved an inch, even the people who have had a rough go of it, and the general continued.

"Your sergeants have spent the last week assessing you, seeing if you are what we need you to be. Or if you have what it takes to become just that." He spoke in a monotone voice, he had remembered all his lines and got to do it ten times before even reaching us.

"I will call out your name and say either foreign, domestic or relocate. After the line is finished, everyone that is being relocated can stay, to hear where you are being relocated to. The rest of you can go to the proper bus or to the dining hall." His eyes shifted to us for a second to see if anyone was too dumb to understand what he had said. Again, no one dared to move a muscle.

"Derian Dormea," he read out. "Domestic." He called out more names, but I honestly could not remember which one belonged to which person. That was until he reached "Kory Fenchillik," the asshole who could not climb a simple fence but liked kicking me when I was down.

"Relocate." I wanted to cheer. I wanted to smile but I managed to keep my face in check. There was still a possibility that I would be working with him for the rest of my life. Maybe I'd beat him up a little before climbing the wall.

"Teryn Dendillion," the guy in front of me was the size of a mountain, so I could not see Teryn or any of the other cadets, but I could imagine him standing there with his back straight, much more ready for what was about to come than I was. "Relocate."

The giant in front of me got shocked by this. But I knew this was a good thing. They would never let the top squad member go unless a hunter was taking him. The general obviously did not let any of us celebrate and moved on to the next name.

"Djorn Visch," he said. "Foreign."

They couldn't have picked a worse person for the job. They shouldn't even have relocated him to the factory, they should have bumped him right down to the criminals who were cleaning up radiation outside the wall.

He moved further down the line of people. Until he reached "Elska Hornbick," my heart started fluttering again, same as it did for Teryn. "Relocate"

What? They didn't let Elska in? They must have made a mistake. Sure, she wasn't the brightest but she did the exercises they wanted her to do without hesitation. Maybe she got chosen to become a hunter too? I had to cling to that hope.

I heard more names called, recognising a few as part of the group of cadets who attacked me. Most of them got to stay but were going to domestic. There was only one other who got relocated.

"Julia Thorne," he read out. "Relocate."

That was it. I would have to cross the wall. My life inside here was over. I refused to live a mundane factory worker life. I had learned enough, read enough books from the library to know a little bit about life beyond the walls. Hopefully, it was enough for me to survive out there until I learn more. That is if I find a way across.

I wouldn't get to see my family again. Sure, I had prepared myself for that anyway. But there was always United Day. The day where everyone has a day off to visit family. Both my brothers had opted not to. But I still could have. I heard military even gets more time to make the trip.

But I wasn't military anymore.

The rest of the line went by quick. And all of a sudden half of the room left. Out of the twenty-one cadets in our squad, there were nine who did not make the cut. We closed ranks again, and I found myself right behind Elska. She glanced back at me for a second, giving me a sad smile.

Maybe there was hope. Maybe even if I would have to work as a farm hand I could do it with Elska. It could be better. And if it wasn't, I would ask her to leave with me. Though I doubt she'd do that to her military parents.

"This does not mean the end of the line for you." The general said. "There is glory to be found in the other workplaces as well." His eyes shifted briefly to the hunter before turning back to us.

"Kory Fenchillik," he read out. "Factory." That wasn't a major surprise. This time I could see Kory slouched over, avoiding eye contact with the factory worker at all costs. Another person got called for the factory, before reaching Teryn.

"Teryn Dendillion, hunters." Elska and I smiled to each other, breaking the line briefly. I mean what were they going to do? Send us to the factory? At least one of us got what they wanted. The hunter himself still seemed unmoved by it all. But he was looking at us at least, one of the other generals was staring longingly out of the window.

"Elska Hornbick, factory." My heart fell. She didn't deserve this, she did everything they asked and excelled at it. I didn't have time to get over the news though. My heart was thumping loudly with anticipation for my name to be called. Maybe I was an exception. Maybe they thought my thing with the fence showed intelligence, I could be a teacher.

"Julia Thorne, hunters."

My mind went absolutely blank. My legs felt numb. He hadn't just been looking at Teryn, he had been looking at me too.

Elska did not look at me. I know what she must be thinking. We could maybe have gone somewhere together. Maybe if I hadn't distracted her she would still be in the military.

The hunter met my eye. Was that a smile playing at his lips? I couldn't tell. I couldn't tell if I am supposed to be happy. Didn't he know I got attacked and didn't even fight back? I wanted to prove I wasn't lazy, but I never thought they would place me in the hunters!

"Thank you for giving it your all." The general said. "Help make our kingdom the greatest in the world." His eyes shifted to me. "Wherever that may come from."

Elska did not look at me or at Teryn as she turned around and walked away to the bus. We were left in the big hall, completely unsure of where to go.

The hunter walked off the stage and signed us to follow him. Teryn and I exchanged glances. Everything was so confusing. I know I am supposed to be happy, so why did I feel so bad? Maybe it was because Elska deserved to be here. Not me. They could have gotten out names mixed up? Though I think the hunter would have called that out already.

"Aren't there any more hunter cadets?" I whispered to Teryn as we were leaving the hall.

"No. Just the two of you from this base." The hunter answered loudly. We left the hall immediately. When we got outside, we had to walk by the last squad who were waiting to get called in. I could feel some eyes on me, on the both of us. But I kept my back straight.

This was something to be proud of. It was something I would have never seen myself doing. I hadn't dared to hope for this. I still couldn't bring myself to realize what was happening.

I would be training to become a hunter. The elite of the elite. Alongside with someone who is already my friend, so I wouldn't even be alone like I feared I would be.

Djorn had stopped outside to talk to the other cadets who were still waiting. He glanced over at us when we exited the hall. I wish there was some way to always remember this moment. His bulging eyes followed by a hateful stare. I flipped him off with a smile on my face.

Even if I get kicked out tomorrow, at least I got that.

The hunter was limping a little bit, probably from the bullet to his knee he spoke about earlier, but kept a steady pace. He brought us to something resembling a bus, but it was a lot smaller and painted bright yellow.

There were still plenty of seats to choose from inside. Teryn sat down across the aisle from me while the hunter sat down in front of me.

"So, introduce yourselves." The hunter said after turning around and looking at the both of us. Teryn and I were both at a loss for words. "I know quite a bit already. But it's always good to seek some confirmation." He looked at Teryn, probably telling him to go first.

"My name is Teryn Dendillion." He simply said. "My father is Daniel Dendillion, he's a doctor in Calgary. My mother's Askashia Dendillion, a teacher."

"Where did you learn how to fight?" The hunter asked. Outside trees were rapidly passing by. The driver drove much faster than the previous bus driver had.

"Books mostly." He answered. "I practised in my room and with my friends." The hunter nodded, sizing Teryn up with his eyes. He already has a good, strong build. More importantly, he had a constant resting face of 'get out of my way' which definitely fit the hunters very well.

"And you?" The hunter finally turned to me.

"I am Julia Thorne." I said, trying to keep my voice from shaking and showing him how incredibly intimidating I found all of this. "My parents are both factory workers." There really wasn't much else to say was there. I could tell him about my brothers, but why would that even matter? "I never really fought until I came here." The hunter cracked a small smile, just enough for me to see that the joke landed.

"Do you have any questions for me?" He asked us. About a thousand, I thought to myself. But when I saw that Teryn wasn't going to answer, I settled for just one.

"Where are we going?" I asked him. It seemed to be the most urgent thing right now. Sure I wanted to know why he chose me, but a part of me is scared that I am the konsi again. Sometimes ignorance is bliss.

"Hunter headquarters." He responded. "You'll be meeting your mentor and your fellow trainees."

We had to drive for most of the day. There was only one toilet break, which was a lot easier for the guys than for me. We drove through a mountain range and passed quite a few lakes. It's funny how I spend nineteen years on the same spot, taking the same road to the same place over and over again, and it seemed like I was seeing the entire country in just a few hours.

We were silent the entire way. I wanted to ask Teryn what he thought about Elska's placement, but I didn't want the hunter to listen in on my worries.

Hunters get a high salary because they take a lot of risks. So sending money back home shouldn't be an issue. I just don't know when I should be expecting to get paid, but I hope it was soon. Maybe it was the time I got to spend apart from my family, but I remember my father as damn near falling apart.

We drove for hours on end, but the driver did not seem to mind. I don't think he even got out of the bus for the pee break. We finally arrived, just before dinner time.

It was nothing like the military compound. The only thing that the two had in common was a long fence, stretching around the area. Inside of it was one of the largest buildings I had seen in my life. It looked like a giant block, with a few windows carved in it. I counted at least nine floors, but it could also have a basement.

The only people outside were two guards, who were completely useless. They got dispatched from the military, guarding the small gate that allowed entrance onto the compound. They quickly scrambled together as they saw the small bus approaching but looked positively bored out of their minds before.

They opened the gate after a small chat with the driver and peering through the windows. The bus took us right to the front door but left as soon as we got out.

"This will be your home base, should you make it." The hunter told us as we walked up the steps to the front door.

Inside the smell of freshly baked bread was strong, along with something spicier. Really we just had to follow our noses, to find the rest of the hunters.

The cafeteria was minuscule next to the one of the military. There were five long tables. One was fully filled with food, while the others occupied the hunters.

"Grab some food and sit over there." He pointed the table out to us that clearly had the cadets on them. I shuffled awkwardly behind Teryn, who also looked uncomfortable for the first time in his life, to the food table. I had been absolutely starving since the afternoon, but I had to refrain myself from loading my plate full. First impressions matter, and I wasn't about to let mine be that I was a glutton.

We sat down at the table. The other tables were all busy greeting the hunter who brought us here, though some of them were just eating quietly. I could tell that there were a few eyes on me, and probably Teryn also. It felt much more personal here than the military had been. There the sergeants didn't even eat with us, they had their own private little canteen for that.

I looked around our own table. Most of them seemed like Teryn: big, buff and intimidating, though I doubt any of them were taller than me. They weren't as big as I had seen in the military. They could probably still move around quickly.

There was only one other girl here. She had piercing blue eyes, which were focused solely on the food in front of her, and bright, white hair. There was something off about her. The guy next to her had noticed too and moved further away from her.

There were fifteen of us, already counting in Teryn and myself. Though I knew that there would probably still be people who get cut out as we train. My father had worked with a man who kept repeating that he was close to becoming a hunter, though he had been kicked out over twenty years ago.

I didn't understand why he was so obsessed with telling that to everyone, it wasn't like he made it. But now I got it. He had to survive a week in the military, and then probably months of training here just to get kicked out. I think I'd be the same mess of a person after all of that.

7

Like in the military, all the cadets slept in the same room for the first night. Though the way the room was laid out, it made me wonder if this was our permanent sleeping spot. It looked more makeshift, they hadn't even bothered taking out the training equipment.

Breakfast was a quiet affair, though the older hunters were already here. Teryn broke the silence by muttering a 'good morning' to me, but other than that, we enjoyed our, fresh out of the oven, bread in silence.

They took us to a classroom. I hadn't seen a lot of the building yet, but it looked like it was built before the bombs fell. There were many rooms, some converted into work-out spaces, others resembled closer to a classroom like I had known it in my old village. Just a bunch of chairs with desks and a place for the teacher to stand and explain things on a chalkboard. It wasn't the supersonic things the military used like their smartboard and chairs that had wheels on them. The horrible sound of the chair scraping over the floor felt more like home.

The chairs were spread out over the room, not in clean lines at all. I sat down on one near the wall, with Teryn a little behind me. The hunter who brought us here seemed to have left already, it was just a bunch of strangers standing in front of us now. I hoped that I was just feeling a little bit paranoid, I thought I kept catching them staring at me in particular.

"Welcome." One of them said, shutting the other ones up immediately.

They were all standing a little bit behind the man who spoke, he was clearly in charge or at least taking the lead. He was tall, but like most hunters not taller than I was, with a bald head and a thick beard that shielded half of his face from us.

"My name is Dorian Felthove." He said. "Inside this base there is no need for titles, But we obviously require you to treat your superiors with respect."

The man was looking around the room, his eyes lingering for a moment on the girl with white hair before continuing. "For the next few years you will be trained in all the needed principles to become a hunter. You must pass all of them, there are no retries." He glanced over at the people behind him. "To ensure that you do make it, you will be personally trained by your mentor. There is quite a bit of rivalry going on, so I suggest you make them proud."

He pulled up a stack of pages from the table. "The people who recruited you as military cadets kept detailed reports about you." This didn't surprise anyone. It was obvious that they followed us around once we sparked their interest. I could only hope that he hadn't seen me getting beaten up. "I paired you off with a mentor who I thought would suit your needs and strengths best. Again, no retries, so you better get along." His eyes glanced over the page in front of him.

"Devin Smis." He called out. Devin was tall and lean, but definitely already had some muscle on him. His black hair was spiked in every direction like he hadn't bothered to check it in the mirror this morning. "Your mentor will be Antheas." He pointed him out of the lineup. Antheas still seemed pretty young compared to some of the others in the line, but smiled kindly at Devin.

"Teryn Dendillion," he read out next. "Is paired off with…" Apparently, Teryn had two pages written about him, Dorian had to flip the page over to read it.

"Greyson." Greyson was the second tallest out of the group and looked like he was somewhere in his fifties. He had a stern face and didn't smile at Teryn, or even acknowledge his presence.

"Athena." The man read out next. This girl had a near book written about her. She didn't look faced by this however, and just stared ahead until he found the name he had scribbled on the paper. "Ferik Howers." Two of the hunters glanced towards Dorian for this decision, which was about all the shocked reactions we would be getting. Clearly, they didn't agree, but no one commented.

He read out more names, while I was desperately trying to remember which name belonged to which face. I would, hopefully, be staying here much longer than I had been in the military. I wanted to learn their names, but when they finally reached mine all I could remember was Teryn and Athena, because she was so odd.

"And finally, Julia Thorne." He said, pulling up my papers. I also had quite a lot of pages written about me. A lot more than Teryn or any of the other guys, but less than the other girl. "Your mentor is Alder."

Alder had deep-set, light blue eyes and black hair that just reached over his shoulders. He had an oval face, with very high cheekbones and a slightly crooked, broken nose. Though many of the other hunters had that as well. He had looked pretty intimidating before, but when he saw me he gave me a small smile, which softened his features immensely.

"You will spend the rest of the morning getting to know your mentor, in the afternoon you will get to know the other apprentices and after dinner you will be receiving your tattoos." Dorian concluded. The room shifted once he left. A few of the older hunters exchanged quick comments before shaking hands with their apprentice.

"Welcome." Alder said as he shook my hand. Somethings at least never change. I had been the tallest back home, and back in school, by the looks of it that would not change here.

We walked through the building in silence. It seemed like that was what the hunters preferred over anything, silence. Alder did not glance back to see if I was still following him, he just assumed I was. Eventually, we made it all the way to the top floor. Where we walked to the end of a long hallway into one of the rooms.

It was clearly a living room. There was a couch and a comfortable chair as well as a dining table. There were two more doors, but they remained closed.

There were four chairs around the dining table. I sat down in front of Alder and watched in silence as he scanned the pages of the report on me. They were all typed out on a typewriter but had red, handwritten, annotations surrounding it. On the last page, someone wrote 'Alder' in large, blue letters.

"I was hoping I'd get you." He said, still looking down at the page. "You got brains and fire according to old Norton here." Fire. He thinks I have fire in me. I want to prove myself, that's true. But I don't know if I had really shown any 'fire'. He must have not seen me after I got beaten up. "Of course, *you* were a little bit of a surprise, but we'll work with it."

Why would I be a surprise? Didn't he just read an entire folder about me?

"So." He said. "There are currently thirty-three hunters in active duty. We only accept Recruits every five years, so you got pretty lucky."

"If I had been one year younger, I wouldn't have been picked at all?" I asked him.

"No, you would have spent five years at the military training base before being selected to train even more." He explained, his voice was low and heavy. I'd hate to see him angry. "Most of the other apprentices were already a few years in."

He explained more about the hunters and what would be expected of me for the next few years. I would be training for a long time first. If they are convinced that I am capable of holding my own in combat I would shadow Alder on his missions. But that was only if I made it. He told me that usually at least half of the recruits get laid off or get forced to resign because of injuries they sustained during training. He also quietly added that sometimes people lose their focus while on a mission and die, even though they were only simulations of missions.

"Now we need to know more about you." He said. "Where did you grow up?"

"Countryside," I said to him. He kept on looking at me to tell more so I did. "My parents are factory workers. I have twelve siblings, three of them are already working for the factory and one died when she was little." I was thankful that he didn't press on about Katha, I never really liked talking about her anyway. We just preferred to sweep things under the rug in my family.

"You got high grades." He stated.

"I like learning." I answered.

"That's good. We can use that." He mumbled, paging through the papers that got written about me. He was going through them too fast for me to be able to read what it was saying. So I had to settle for just answering his questions.

"I'm not going to lie Julia." He said, shutting the folder and moving it aside. "This is not an easy place. Things are going to get rough. People you know will die. You might die. There is no dishonour in saying you don't want to go through with it."

"I do want to go through." I answered immediately. Who in the right mind would trade in this life for the factory? Sure it might be dangerous, but at least every day would be different. I wouldn't have to work the same assembly line for fifty years before living off a pension that won't cover any costs.

"Good." He said. "Now there is this asshole here, his name is Greyson, he has been training recruits since I joined. He always gets the highest ranked recruit in the end." He smiled at me. "We are going to break that long-lasting victory, it will especially hurt because you are... y'know, a girl."

"Greyson got Teryn as his apprentice." I doubtingly said. "I've seen Teryn train, I don't think I could beat him. In anything."

"There are more principles than just fighting." Alder explained. "Being able to fight is important, but just doing that won't get you accepted into the hunters. You need to be clever for that."

I could be clever. But could I realistically beat Teryn? He was smart too, and he had the advantage of being raised by two smart parents. Coming to think of it, nearly every other apprentice looks like they could beat the shit out of me.

No, I was going to do this. I had to.

Alder was nice enough, though I could tell that there was something off about him. He kept on making small comments about me 'being a surprise' and 'working around it'. Eventually, I was just left convinced that I was a konsi again. Only I could stop myself from being kicked out as a bad example, I just needed to do everything perfectly.

I ate lunch with Alder in his room, which was apparently the room he had taken me to, and he showed me to mine, which was directly across the hall from his.

It did not have a living room like Alder's had, but I did get my own bathroom with a shower, which was more than I could have hoped for. It also had the hunter's words 'loyalty, strength, perseverance' written on the wall next to my bed, to make sure I'd always see them.

That afternoon we were meeting the other apprentices. It did not take long to figure out that they were not the happiest bunch of people. Most of them leaned against the walls of the room, eyeing everyone who came in but talking to no one.

"Hey." I greeted Teryn. "How's your mentor?" He was across the room from us, speaking to the other hunters. It seemed like the man was incapable of smiling, even when the rest of them burst out in laughter.

"Alright, I guess." He shrugged, looking at him from the corner of his eyes to check if he was listening in on us. He clearly wasn't, he had just started telling a story to the other hunters. "He's pretty uptight. Told me he would skin me alive if I stepped outside the lines."

"He sounds..." I noted how he glanced over to us. "Lovely."

I told him a bit about Alder, and we discussed the book that had been written about me by the hunter. We could only speculate what was in it, even though Greyson had discussed what was in Teryn's in great detail.

"The hunter saw the attack." He said to me. "Made a detailed report about it too. I'm guessing he also put that part in yours."

"He saw it and didn't stop it from happening?" I could definitely have done with less of a beating. It would have made my week a lot easier. I still had the bruises on my stomach, but much like the bruise on my face they had faded to yellow and green and weren't as sore anymore.

"Maybe he wanted to see how I reacted." Teryn quickly dismissed it. We were waiting for the final few people to come in. Everyone had the chance to change their clothes too. We all went from the military blue to the hunter's black clothes. Though the clothes weren't as different as the ones we got in the military, these just have short sleeves.

Finally, Athena and her mentor walked in. I finally got why I thought there was something off about her. "Radiate." Teryn whispered beside me.

Athena's right hand was entirely covered in tattoos, along with some that went about halfway up her forearm. I had no idea how she had managed to hide that, but I guess no one really looked at her up close, or they just got distracted by the white hair. This time she wasn't hiding it. She confidently marched up into the room and leaned against the wall. She was pretty, but not in a conventional kind of way. Her kind of pretty looked more dangerous, like even looking at her for too long would cause death.

I had never seen a radiate in real life. I knew that occasionally the government allowed a few inside the wall in return for helpful information, but none of them would ever bother settling in my old town. I didn't even know they got to do the interview, I just assumed they got sent off to work in factory or cleaning up radiation with the criminals.

"I think we are complete." Dorian had returned. Alder explained to me that he was in charge of the overall apprenticeships, but usually left most of it to the mentors to figure out. Only if there were any real problems then he would step in. Or like today, he would make sure there were no immediate fights between apprentices trying to prove their worth to each other.

"Each and every one of you got chosen because you stood out from the crowd." Dorian said, after ushering us all to stand in a circle. "The common misconception about us hunters is that we know everything, and will win a fight from anyone, no matter their size."

His eyes slowly made their way down the circle. "Obviously, that is incorrect. Why make a genius train his muscles when his mind is worth so much more?" He looked me in the eye for a few seconds before continuing. "We expect you to be well-rounded, that's true. We expect you to be able to defend yourself. But most of all, you need to work well in a team."

"Hunters never work alone. Teamwork is the core of our organisation." He continued. "We will be your family. Your friends. Should you make it of course." I glanced over at Alder, he was leaning against the wall near the door. One of the other mentors whispered something at him, which caused a small smile to break out on his face before he looked back at the circle of new recruits.

"The following years you will be trained and tested in various aspects of our trade." Dorian said. "I advise you all to make friends, not enemies. You will be partaking in simulations of missions together. But also against each other."

I needed to focus on training my mind. I could spend every living hour training and I'm sure I would never match up to Teryn or any of the other guys here, they were all the size of mountains already. Besides, they probably expected to become a hunter, unlike me who still thought this must all be a dream.

"Today, we keep it simple." Dorian said. "Starting from this end. Introduce yourself."

One by one everyone talked a little bit about themselves. Most of them preferred to keep things short. They told us their name and what they had previously done. Teryn and I couldn't really do that, we were the only ones who had only spend one week in the military, so we just said where we were from instead. Finally, it was Athena's turn.

"My name is Athena." She spoke with a slight accent. "I don't have a last name. I am from Doneégara, which is beyond the fence." This surprised no one of course, everyone had seen her tattoos. It was only the older hunters who gave any sort of inkling of interest towards her.

No one liked the radiates. They were savages. They were either trying to freeload off the Union or they were against us, making them rebels and enemies. Not a day goes by that there isn't some rebel attack against the wall or the Union soldiers beyond it.

No one really liked Athena to begin with. Why would my brothers get sent to work in horrible conditions when someone like her gets to be here? Her 'I don't really care' attitude also definitely wasn't helping.

"Well," Dorian said after the Athena had introduced herself. "I hope everyone remembered that. Like I said, this is your family now."

8

The air that night was different than it was before. The hunters weren't completely silent or talking loudly together, there were only hushed whispers. It felt like death himself was about to walk through the door.

That was only partly true. Someone important was going to walk through the door, but it wasn't death. Though he undoubtedly caused it many times.

Jack Alvarez was an intimidating man. He had deep lines edged into his face and a constant scowl. His arms were entirely covered in scars, some large like the one I had from my run-in with the military convoy, some as small as papercuts. There were already some grey streaks in his black hair, he was the oldest out of all the hunters I had seen so far.

The hunters were the only place where the apprentices were tattooed by the leader of the workplace, something that would have intimidated the hell out of me even if I hadn't seen Jack Alvarez come through the door. I understood why they were silent, this was a man you did not want to piss off.

One by one we got called into the room. Those who entered didn't return, though we did hear something like a party going on downstairs. There were loud voices and laughter, accompanied by the sweet smell of properly cooked meat.

Nero got called in next. When he walked to the door, he made sure to roughly bump into Athena. She regained her balance quickly and didn't go face first like I would have done.

"You okay?" I asked her after he had entered. She was rubbing her shoulder with her tattooed hand. I could make out a dragon, and something that looked like a flower, though I had never seen that particular one before.

"Yeah." She just said. Teryn had been the first one to get called in. I really didn't know any of the other ones yet, I was struggling to remember their names enough already. Though I still believed in the companionship among girls, even if she's from beyond the wall. I didn't want to admit it to myself, but I thought she was the most interesting person out of all the other apprentices.

"Julia." I said, holding out my hand for her to shake. She eyed me suspiciously but shook my hand anyway.

"Athena."

I didn't really hate Athena for entering the Union. I would have probably done the same thing if I was in her position, though it still sucked that she took the apprentice position over someone who had been born in the Union. I didn't exactly trust her either though, how could they be sure that she wasn't a rebel?

"So, you're from beyond the wall?" I asked her. We were the only two still left, accompanied by one of the mentors who called the people in. He was watching our conversation play out but didn't join in.

"Yup." She said, staring ahead of her and not meeting my eye.

"What's it like out there?" I asked her.

"Hell."

I had no way of responding to that. Athena didn't seem to be a woman of many words, and even though I wanted to know more about what was beyond the wall I really didn't feel like this was the time to push on. Luckily for us, Nero didn't take long to finish. There were two knocks on the door, the mentor glanced over to us.

"Athena." The mentor said. "You're next."

Of course, I was last, that was just my bad luck. Athena calmly entered the room and left me with the hunter.

I didn't remember his name, but I was starting to see a pattern between all the hunters I had seen so far. Most of them had broken noses and a lot of scars, though not as many as Jack. The hunter in front of me had a scar on the right side of his nose that went all the way up through the beginning of his eyebrow.

Athena took a lot longer than Nero. The voices downstairs had grown even louder. The smell of food was making my stomach ache, I was so hungry. But finally, about twenty minutes after she went in, there was a double knock on the door.

"In you go." The hunter just said, rising from his spot against the wall and walking away to join the feast downstairs.

My nerves were flaring up inside of my stomach. I wiped my sweaty palms on my black pants and opened the door.

The room was small and poorly lit. There were a few windows, but the dark sky outside only let in some moonlight. There were a lot of candles, mainly centred around a table that was set up in the middle of the room.

Closer to the window stood Jack Alvarez, he was wiping away some blood he got on his hands. On the kitchen sink next to him were a knife and a small bowl with some black powder in it.

"Lay on the table." His voice was heavy and low, fitting his appearance perfectly. I understood why he was the elected leader, I wanted to listen to him immediately.

I climbed onto the wooden table and laid down on my back. I saw the moonlight reflect on the blade as Jack picked it up. Like it had reflected on the blade Djorn had threatened me with.

No, I wouldn't think about that now.

There was a chair next to the table that Jack sat down on. He put the bowl of powder down and placed the chair right next to my face.

"It will hurt." He warned me tilting the knife so I could get a better look at it. It had a short leather-bound handle. The blade itself was curved into a pointed end. It looked like it got sharpened recently. "Tilt your head to the other side."

I did what he told me to do, though my instincts told me to get the hell away from the scary man with the sharp knife. I stared into the darkness of the room, wondering how the hell he was supposed to tattoo me, the candles did not give enough light to see things clearly.

"Best to talk through the pain." He said. "Ask anything."

Anything was a tempting option. I had so many questions floating around in my head that I wanted to hear the answer to. Were there truly monsters out there? Was I the konsi? Why did he bother tattooing all the apprentices when half of us won't even make it? But of course, there was one question that boomed out over all of them.

"Why me?"

The blade pierced my skin for the first time. He was right, it hurt like a bitch. "Because Norton likes to break the rules." He said. I could feel the blade move around on my neck, but the pain numbed my ability to pinpoint exactly where it was. "We don't accept women, but we made an exception for Athena because of her skill level. Norton saw this as a way to push his agenda through and recruited you." I only needed to move a little bit to the side and the sharp blade would cut through my throat and kill me. A very comforting thought to have. "He didn't mention you were a female in his report. So I assumed you were a man. We all read your file and agreed that you had potential."

"No one knew I was a girl?" I gritted my teeth and spoke through the pain. Tears were threatening to form in my eyes, but I could not allow myself to cry in front of him. Not after hearing that I am only here because of someone else's agenda.

"We didn't." He confirmed. He grabbed some of the black powder and rubbed it in the fresh wound. It felt like it was numbing the pain almost, even though he roughly rubbed it in.

"If you were a male, you would have been accepted anyway." He went on to cut into my skin again. I tried to deflect the pain by digging my nails into my arm. It helped a little bit, even if it was just to shift my thoughts.

"So, am I getting kicked out?" I had to ask, though it was hard not to sound bitter about it. Why bother tattooing me if he clearly doesn't approve me being here? He was the leader after all, one word and I was gone. I couldn't really pinpoint where the knife was cutting anyway, he could have been drawing a large square the entire time.

"No." He simply said. "You got the benefit of the doubt. Don't waste it."

He rubbed the black powder in again while his words sunk in. Athena was here because she was a badass who already knew how to survive and how to fight. I was here because the recruiter wanted women to be a part of the hunters too.

Once again, the blade sunk into my skin. I kept my eyes shut and tried to breathe as normally. I knew what the mark of a hunter looked like, I had seen it on all of the people here. There were three teardrops, in the form of a triangle. It was a relatively simple tattoo, that was easy to cover up if need be. Why did it hurt so much?

"I have a mission for you." Jack said, finishing off the final teardrop with the blade. A mission? This must be some sort of test. "Keep an eye on Athena. If you see anything that even slightly hints at her being a rebel, report it directly to me. Only to me."

"How am I supposed to contact you?" Please tell me he's not staying here to watch us train.

I did not want him to give me the benefit of the doubt only to inevitably watch me fail over and over again.

He retrieved something from the pocket of his jacket and handed it to me. It was an old device that no one ever used anymore. It was smaller than an apple. When I flipped it open it had a small screen and an even smaller keyboard to type on. On the back were panels that looked a bit out-of-place on this old of a device. It was new technology, which generated energy from light and wind. If neither of which was around, it would turn the device on standby, making it unable to be used.

"Contact info is in there." He said. "Use the code 284433662."

I was wondering how the hell I was supposed to remember it, when I glanced back at the keyboard. It only had numbers on it, the letters were smaller. The two was where the letter A was, from there it was easy to figure out that it was just the corresponding numbers to her name.

"And if she's not a rebel?" He rubbed the powder in one last time.

"Then don't let anyone catch you with that." He nodded towards the device. I was starting to think that maybe this wasn't just a test that he gave out to everyone. If he did, I'd have to watch my step. One of the other apprentices might have a similar device with the mission to watch me.

Jack washed my blood off his hands at the sink again, as well as the blade. He easily flipped it over, so that his hand was wrapped around the sharp edge and the leather-bound handle faced me.

"Your knife." He said. I grabbed the handle carefully, so I wouldn't accidentally cut him, and inspected it again, it looked like it had never even been used. I felt Jack's eyes on me, and I thought I had to make some amazingly smart comment on it, but I came up blank.

Eventually, he stopped staring at me, and I stopped staring at the knife. He made his way around the room to put out every candle with his fingertips until he reached the door.

The walk down to the cafeteria was highly uncomfortable. I didn't feel like I should be walking next to the leader. I was completely focussed on not accidentally tripping over my own feet and making a fool out of myself. He laid his hand on the door to the cafeteria but did not open it yet. They were still laughing and talking loudly inside, someone even got a guitar by the sounds of it.

"Do not disappoint me, Julia." He said without even looking at me and swung the door open.

I was immediately completely thrown off. Jack opened the door and confidently marched right in, while I stood there glued to my spot trying not to get hit in the face by the door. The laughter seemed to die off a little when he entered, the guitarist missed a beat and seemed to have lost his confidence, much like I had.

Don't disappoint him. Right. I glanced over at Athena, she was talking to her mentor in the corner of the room. Neither seemed very pleased with each other. She caught my eye for a split second and I immediately glanced away, hoping that I didn't look too guilty.

Teryn was talking to the other apprentices, I stumbled my way over to them. Teryn caught my eye and actually smiled at me. I don't know what was in his cup, but I'm guessing it wasn't water.

"Hey Julia." He greeted me. "You look like you've seen a ghost."

"Something like that." I just said, it seemed like the small device had somehow gotten four times heavier. As though everyone could see it in my pocket and I had already managed to fail my first mission.

"The guy is intimidating as hell right?" Arlo said. I remembered him from the introduction round, mainly because he is from Vancouver and said that he has trained in the military for years.

"Definitely." I said. I still hadn't seen my own tattoo yet, but the ones around me were all identical. It seemed like Jack had tattooed dozens of apprentices before and could do it in his sleep. Teryn's neck wasn't as red anymore, though it still looked sore.

"We were just talking about what kind of training we would be doing." Teryn said. "Whether or not it will be similar to the military."

"Strength-wise probably." I said, looking around the circle. Teryn and Arlo were both already buff, but the other guy-I think his name is Ethen-was a lot skinnier, like me. I was the tallest out of all of them, though the difference in height wasn't that great.

"Probably less combat focussed." Arlo's voice was pretty heavy, though he seemed like a schoolboy after talking to Jack. "Maybe more self-defence. We won't fight in an army formation, like the military."

"No, we just have to plan them." Teryn said, drinking deeply from his cup. I excused myself from the conversation to go over to the table filled with food and pick out my dinner. I never realized how little we got to eat back home until I was faced with the food here and back at the military. I knew that we had less than average, but I thought it had been enough. I was starting to get worried about my siblings. Were they smart enough to get apples from the tree? Did they make sure the little ones had enough to eat?

"It looks good on you." Alder appeared next to me, interrupting my thoughts. I raised my eyebrows at him. "I'm talking about your tattoo. Jack's a pro." I brushed my fingers against my freshly tattooed neck. It felt sore, like someone had just punched me again.

"You thought I was a guy." I said as I poured some water in a cup. "That's what you meant with 'working around it'." Alder grabbed a piece of bread from the table and put it on my plate.

"I did." He confirmed. "You caused quite a commotion when you walked in here. Norton has been sent to the Darkfort because of it."

"The Darkfort?" I asked.

"Alexandrem Military Fort." He said, leaning against the table. "Doesn't really roll off the tongue though, so we nicknamed it the Darkfort. Sounds more mysterious y'know."

"Why did he have to go to a military fort?" I put some vegetables on my plate as well as chicken and more bread. I was absolutely starving.

"The hunters claimed it as their own. It's our base outside of the fence." He explained to me. "This used to be the same thing before the fence expanded. A good thing too, they used to train people outside the fence. Loads of deaths before they even reached service."

"What will happen to Norton?" I felt bad for him. Though he used me to push his own agenda through, he was the only reason why I was here. He could have gone for Elska, she'd probably be better than me as well, but he chose me instead.

Jack really hadn't answered that. If I was a guy, I would be good enough too. But good enough with what? I wasn't strong and Norton saw me getting beat up. The only thing I had going for me was my grades, which didn't even mean that I was smart. It just meant that I could remember the right things to write down on a test.

"You look worried." Alder commented, not answering my question. He had grabbed a glass with some weird brown liquid in it. It looked like Teryn had been drinking that too.

"I am worried." I admitted. "I haven't done anything that proves I belong with the hunters. I don't know what Norton saw in me, but I am not strong or smart. I won't make it." It came out as more of a word vomit than it was supposed to be, but I did stop myself from talking about Athena. Alder didn't even seem all that surprised about my little outburst.

"You have what it takes to make it." He reassured me. "Your file had to go through seven people before you even arrived here. They all thought you have what it takes, and I will personally make sure you become one of the first female hunters." He grabbed another glass with the weird liquid and handed it to me. "Drink it up, it'll give you some courage for the rest of the evening."

I took a big gulp from the liquid, which was a mistake. It burned all the way down my throat and tasted like it was made of something that was supposed to be cleaned with, not digested. It was nothing like the watered-down drinks I had with Teryn and Elska. Alder laughed as I coughed and coughed.

"Sorry kiddo, should have given you a warning." He hit me on my back until tears rolled down my eyes.

I wouldn't say that they let their hair down that night, I don't think the hunters are capable of that, but everyone did seem to enjoy themselves. I once even saw a small smile tug at the corner of Jack's mouth.

I didn't mingle too much with the older hunters, more with the apprentices. Most of them seemed nice enough, though they were all quiet and more observant. The brown liquid did really seem to help them in letting loose. I heard it was called a 'kitty cat' because the feeling of it going down your throat feels like a cat trying to claw its way back up there.

I didn't drink it, I thought it tasted horrible, but the rest of the people did really like it.

No one needed to be carried out, but there were several people who stumbled their way out, instead of walking.

Jack wasn't one of them. When it was far past midnight and the first few people left the party, he said his final goodbyes to our mentors. He only glanced back at us one last time. We made eye contact, but without saying it out loud I knew what he meant.

"Don't disappoint me."

9

The hunters preferred the mornings as early as the military, though it was an improvement to get woken up by Alder pounding on my door rather than some sergeant with his metal pipe.

"Breakfast in ten." Alder shouted through the door. I heard his footsteps go further and further down the hall before the silence returned. I wanted to take a shower first, but when I entered the bathroom and noticed my reflection in the mirror, I decided against it.

My tattoo was still just a bunch of scabs before it would heal with black lines. I didn't want the water to accidentally open it up and ruin the tattoo, so I settled on throwing some water in my face.

The bruise on my face had disappeared fully. My stomach was also clear of any bruises, it was only the right side of my ribcage that still looked a little green.

The clothes we received weren't as different as the ones from the military, maybe they were a bit looser, but that could also be because they expected a guy, not a girl. Especially my shirt fit loosely around my chest.

I looked odd in the black clothes, it wasn't a colour I ever wore back home. The cheapest fabrics were always the colour of mud, amplified by the fact that they always got dirty and we didn't really have any proper tools to clean them. The black almost made me feel stronger. Almost.

I made it down in time and saw that everyone was sitting with their mentor, so after grabbing my bowl of stew I sat down in front of Alder.

"Morning." He greeted me, not taking his eyes off the paper he was reading. Most mentors were preoccupied with something while they were eating. Some had papers laying next to them, like Alder, others had weird devices they were playing around with.

I was looking around the room when I noticed that one of them had a device in his hands that was exactly like the one Jack had given me. Last night I had hidden it in the far back of my closet, in the pocket of a coat I would probably never wear. As far as I could tell we did not really go out much, most of the training seemed to take place inside of the compound

I choked on my food, causing Alder to finally look up. I had already averted my gaze from the man, but it felt like Alder still knew. He raised one of his eyebrows at me.

"Just went down the wrong pipe." I coughed, trying to ignore the glances I was getting from the other mentors.

I watched Athena last night as much as I could, which wasn't a lot. No apprentice wanted to talk to her and she didn't seem all that interested in talking to the mentors either. She left hours before anyone else did.

When I finally did stop coughing, Alder handed me a bandage.

"Put it over your tattoo, so it won't open up." He said. With the help of his directions, I placed the bandage over the tattoo.

After breakfast, I followed Alder into one of the workout rooms. It seemed like some other mentors didn't like waking up as early, a few of them just started going down to breakfast.

"We all train you in a different way." Alder explained once we entered the deserted room. "We are fully based on teamwork. It wouldn't make sense for us to train you all in the same way, you need to have different strengths."

"What will mine be?" The workout room that we entered was much smaller than the one we had used in the military.

There was one large mat, a few training dummies and something that looked like target practice on the far end of the room.

"Well, that's what we need to find out." He said. One side of the room had a few large windows that looked out over the green forest surrounding the compound, while the other wall was occupied by several closets that held guns, knives and protective gear.

"What's yours?" I asked as Alder grabbed gauze and started wrapping his hands in it.

"Sniping." He said. "I am also often used as a driver when we go beyond. Though that isn't my speciality, it's Gavin's. The guy drives like a maniac." He grabbed one of my hands and started wrapping a new set of gauze around it.

"We won't know what yours is until we go on a mission or at least a simulation." He said.

"What kind of simulations?" I asked.

"The missions test you to see if you are ready for certain things that can happen beyond the fence." He said and moved over to my other hand. "I'm not really allowed to tell you about them yet. It has to be a surprise when they come along." He took a step back. "But first, we need to train you."

What he called 'training' I called a very unfair fight. We spend about three hours each day just on different fighting techniques. Somehow, they all ended with me getting harshly knocked against the mat with Alder hovering over me.

"Again." He kept on repeating every time I fell down. After two weeks I at least had stopped tripping over my own feet, but it seemed like Alder was doing everything at inhumane speeds, while I was stuck on average human mode.

The training was tough and discouraging, especially after I had watched Teryn. Greyson trained him a little before and after dinner. Teryn didn't fall nearly as often as I did, though his mentor made it seem like he was in a far worse state than I was. Teryn wasn't one to complain though, he even tried helping me with my fighting quite a few times.

The afternoon was always reserved for more practical lessons. I, again, got a rundown on military ranks and several terms often used in tactical operations. I also starting learning on how to survive in different types of environment.

I noticed that all the hunters did not refer to the wall as a wall, but called it 'the fence'. When I finally worked up the courage to ask Alder why, he told me that once I'd seen it, I would understand.

Finally, after over a month of training, I got to see Alder's talent in action. We would be starting target practice.

"We'll start with figuring out which one of the stances is the right one for you." Alder said. "We are only going to be focussing on standing today, crouching and lying down will be for another day." Today was a group lesson, but Alder got to take the lead because of his special skill in the subject. We hadn't received any other group lesson so far, so I think everyone still had to get used to not being the centre of the teacher's attention.

"First stance." Alder said, he picked up his gun as though he had done so a million times, like it was not a lethal weapon, and pointed it at the wall. He was slightly crouched down, with his feet planted a little apart from each other. He kept the gun as far away from his face as his arms would allow it. "The gun will recoil after every shot." He warned us. "So, you can either stand like this or with your arms bend and the gun closer to you." He showed us the second way of holding a gun, it now looked more like he was hiding behind the gun, instead of shooting it.

"Everyone get in the first stance and point your gun at the target." He instructed. Soon all guns were in the air. Most of us had chosen for the first way of holding it, it seemed more secure than having that thing so close to my face.

Alder went one by one, commenting on things to change or nothing at all. He stopped at Athena, who was standing next to me, but didn't say anything. She was doing the stand correctly but did a mix of the position of the arms. She didn't keep it nearly as far away from her face as I did, but she didn't keep it as close either. She seemed pretty relaxed about it though.

I had kept a close eye on her, whenever Alder would allow it. I didn't follow her around, mainly because I thought that she could instantly tell. Instead, I chose a different technique. I befriended her.

We weren't quite to the point where we could talk about boys and braid each other's hair, but she did smile and greet me whenever we saw each other, and once we even ate lunch together. She didn't seem too eager to share a lot about herself, so instead we mainly talked about what was going on around the compound, or sometimes I would tell her stories of when I was little.

"I would try the second way, Julia." Alder said to me. "The recoil will be easier to manage." He hadn't said this to anyone else, just to me. But then again, Teryn, myself and one other person were the only people who weren't fully trained by the military yet. The others at least had some strength to them already. He was right, I simply did not have the arm strength yet.

"Fire at will." Alder said after he had finished with the last person.

Firing a gun was like nothing I had ever experienced before. It was such a small thing in my hand, but it contained so much power.

I had never even seen someone fire a gun before, the recoil was far worse than what I had imagined. I almost dropped the thing immediately.

Everybody fired once. I hit the target, but not the person painted on it. Some people didn't hit it at all, while others did manage to hit the person. The people who had previously been in the domestic side of the military hadn't gotten any gun training yet. Only one of the apprentices got a clean headshot.

"Well done, Holden." Alder commented. Holden was the oldest out of all of us. The army was trying to recruit him for command before the hunters stole him away. I hadn't dared watch him train, I don't think my confidence could take it.

Alder showed us another stance, which was with one foot a bit forward. I held one of my arms straight and the other one slightly bent. It was easier to aim like this. So when Alder told us to get in our favourite position I went for that one, even though I was one of the few.

It was hard to get used to the sound of the gun. It was so loud, every time it went off I felt a wave of panic wash over me, like I am supposed to be running away from this sound and not making it. By the end of the training, it felt like the ringing in my ears wasn't going away any time soon.

Shooting and aiming came far easier to me than hand to hand combat. It took some time for me to get the hang of it, but once I did hitting the target became logical almost. Teryn didn't feel the same way, that night at dinner he was quiet. He didn't want to speak to anyone.

"Do you have practice?" I asked him after we got up to put our dirty plates away.

"No, Greyson wanted to leave it to shooting today." He answered.

"Good." I smiled at him. "I need your help."

Though I had enjoyed my day off from regular training, where I was just being constantly thrown on my ass, I realized that I needed to make a smart decision. Teryn was a great fighter already, but more importantly: He remembered what it is like to not be one.

We found an empty work-out room quite easily and jumped on the mat. "I don't know how to train someone," Teryn admitted. "I don't want to accidentally hurt you."

"My mentor does it on purpose." I joked and walked to the other side of the thick, blue mat. "Just fight me and give me pointers on where I messed up."

Teryn seemed more eager to fight Greyson during his lessons than he did with me. He pulled his fists up to his face to protect his body and stood with one of his feet a little bit more to the back. This was obviously the best stance for him, he was big and strong. I was small and needed to be able to dodge. Teryn learned to take the hit and see the new opening.

I stood in my stance, with my weight pressed on the ball of my feet, so I could easily move around. My fists were also near my face, so that my arms could protected my torso.

Teryn stepped forward and swung his fist towards my face. He seemed to be holding back, I could easily dodge it by going a bit to the left. I took a step closer to him and tried punching him against the jaw, but I only grazed him. He easily brought his arm back and elbowed me in the face. The familiar numbness before the pain started to spread around my nose.

"Shit! I'm-" He started but I cut him off by punching against his jaw. Sure, I didn't like being elbowed in the face, but I needed this lesson to become a better fighter.

All of the things Alder had been teaching me about strategy, different terrains and the different, known, cultures beyond the fence had interested me enough to actually want to remember.

The fighting, however, wasn't the same. He would teach me something new, but the moment it came down to me actually having to fight I went into a full panic mode and forgot everything.

Teryn took a step back to recover from the blow but soon retaliated by kicking me against the side of my ribs. I hadn't had my arms in the right position and was way too late to block it. I lost my balance and fell onto the mat.

We fought until the moon was already at its peak before finally settling in for the night. I had a fresh pair of bruises, mainly on my shins because Teryn loved kicking people, but overall I actually felt better than before. I had been able to find his weakness, he didn't keep his arms up enough to protect his face, and I even managed to make him trip once. Sure, it was only once, but it did wonders for my confidence.

IO

Though the mentors weren't allowed to say when our first simulation would be, it was pretty clear that it was coming up soon. We had been training for a few months now, I no longer was the weak little farm girl who was in way over her head. I still couldn't take Alder down, but I had started practising with the other apprentices who were much easier to fight.

I especially started training with Athena. In the beginning, it was just because I wanted to spy on her, I needed to spy on her, but after a while I realized that it was pretty useful too, she fought the way people beyond the wall fought.

I didn't manage to beat her, not even once. She was always faster or she outsmarted me, but I learned a lot from her. And eventually, I found myself feeling guilty. She was slowly actually becoming a friend, not just a fake friend I spy on because the leader wants me to. She never talked about her past or her time beyond the wall, only small notations when we got taught something new that was inaccurate, which was quite often. There wasn't a lot of information available. We did talk about the hunters, about our training and studies but most of all: we gossiped a lot.

Athena wasn't overly fond of Teryn, she thought he was hiding something. I thought that was hilarious, seeing as she doesn't even tell us her last name. But still, it was fun to talk to another girl.

I fell straight into bed after another training session with her. Alder had given me a day off, something that was quite unusual for him. Most of the people had been given some leisure time, except for mentors like Greyson who preferred to drill their apprentices until they die.

Dorian had been right to warn us about the competitiveness of the mentors. Though the apprentices all got along just fine, that wasn't the case for mentors. It ranged from playful comments toward each other to Alder muttering curses about Greyson under his breath every time he walked passed us. The mentors were happy to see us training together on our own, but it also added a new layer to their competition. Antheas did not shut up about Devin beating me for two whole weeks. He only stopped after Devin got put on his ass within a minute by Teryn.

It seemed like I was woken up only minutes after I had gone to sleep. Alder was standing over me, with a grin on his face. He never entered my room when I was asleep, he always just pounded on my door screaming bloody murder to wake me up.

"Rise and shine." He said to me. There was something in his voice that woke me up a lot faster than I usually would. The smile on his face told me that it wasn't a life-threatening situation, but he still seemed very serious. He had woken me up for a simulation.

Alder brought me downstairs. He had put a black bag over my head, I couldn't see anything, the hallways were completely dark. I could only hear some things, our footsteps on the wooden floor, Alder greeting another mentor, it seemed like my breathing was incredibly loud, everything else was all hushed up.

In the welcoming hall, the bag was finally removed from my head. Almost all the other apprentices were already here, looking around sleepily. Teryn was leaning against the wall, he had his eyes closed and looked dead asleep already. Athena was one of the few people who looked alert.

"So this is what is going to go down." A mentor by the name of Stevan said. He was one of the older hunters, easily identified by the large scar that went right across his face through his right eye.

"We are playing our own little version of 'hide and seek'. You will be sent in one by one. Somewhere in this building are four items you have to retrieve. They will be different for every one of you so that the seekers." He pointed at a line of the mentors who were grinning maliciously at us. "Don't know which one exactly you have to find. They will be trying to find you. If you get tapped, you are out."

There were seven of them, one of which was Alder, who send me a playful wink as I went into full panic mode. Sure, we had discussed ways to quietly sneak around but we hadn't practised anything.

Greyson was also one of the seekers, as well as Ferik, who was Athena's mentor. They didn't really get along according to her, but that was solely because Ferik couldn't stand that she was from beyond the wall, he wanted to teach her everything from inside, even though her knowledge was often better than his. There were also some other mentors, like Antheas and Creed who were much younger and seemed to remember what it was like to be in our shoes.

"Take your positions, gentlemen." Stevan sent them off. Alder gave me one last creepy wave before he went after the other mentors. We waited for about five minutes before Stevan stood up again. "First up: Arturo." No one was really surprised at that. Arturo was Stevan's apprentice. Arturo hardly looked like he was awake but went to the front to see the list of things he was supposed to retrieve.

"Good luck." Stevan said to him, hitting Arturo on his shoulder. Arturo was a lanky kid, with not a lot much muscle on him yet, even after months of training. He was incredibly smart though, and great at making strategies.

As always, I was one of the last ones to go. Athena and Teryn had both already gone in. They weren't allowed to say anything to us, but both looked incredibly pale and sweaty to me. Athena had lasted a good while, but Teryn came out only minutes after he went in.

So far not a lot of people had been able to retrieve items. Athena came back with two, which probably raised some respect for her. Most people didn't even get one. Or they found it but got tapped on the way back to the hall.

"Julia." Stevan said after Nero had gotten back seemingly only seconds after going in. There were only two people left to go in after me, both sighing heavily as my name got called out. We were at a disadvantage, the shock of being woken up in the middle of the night had long worn off, so we were all struggling to keep our eyes open. I was hoping that maybe the hunters inside would be getting a little tired as well, but it seemed very unlikely. I was at a huge disadvantage next to them.

"Goodluck, have fun." Stevan grinned and handed me my list. There were only four items on it:

Ball
Painting
Map
Knife

I had no idea where I would find a ball, I hadn't seen one here. I knew where I could find a map, the only problem was that it was on the fourth floor, where all the classrooms are. It's too far away, I have to do the easy one first so I can at least get one item back successfully. I could get my own knife, the one I got tattooed with, but that was in my room. The hallway that led to it was a dead-end.

The painting seemed the safest one, there were only a few on the walls. The hunters didn't really appreciate art, not a lot of people in the kingdom did. It is a waste of money that could have better been spent on food or clothing.

It was incredibly dark in the hallway. They had sporadically placed candles throughout the building, and a few of the lights were on, but no hallway was entirely lit.

I remembered seeing one in the dining hall, it was of the king. It was easy to get there, I only had to cross one hallway, but once I entered I realized that I had been stupid to think they would have just left that one up. A painfully empty spot on the wall stared back at me.

There were two entrances to the cafeteria, I heard the other door slowly open. I quickly I dropped down and hid behind a chair. Please don't come in here, I thought to myself. There was no place to properly hide in the cafeteria, the chair in front of me hid most of my body, but one good look and I would be found.

I held my breath, but the hunter didn't enter. He closed the door again, I heard his boots tapping against the floorboards as he walked away.

An idea popped up in my head. I quickly untied my shoelaces and discarded my shoes into the corner of the room. I could move a lot more silently now, I'd just have to watch out for anything sharp on the floor.

It was the complete silence that freaked me out. Hunters are masters at hiding, and they expected me to be able to face that already? No, they can't expect us to come out of this with four items. This was to get inside our heads.

I quietly made my way up the stairs to the first floor. I knew one hallway had an old painting of the original hunters on its walls, I just didn't remember which one it was.

I think it was one in the west wing, but that place was like a maze, and my memory was failing me.

I forced myself to stop and lean against one of the walls, taking a few deep breaths. I wasn't going to panic. I needed to stay calm. This was nothing more than a game, I was in no real danger. I already outlasted the last guy, so I wasn't the worst. There was no need for me to be the best either, I needed to prove my worth. Which I would by staying calm.

I peeked around the corner and saw an empty hallway, but as I slowly made my way down, I heard soft footsteps approaching. A surge of panic washed through me, I opened the first door I saw and hid inside.

The room was dark, there was no candle in here, the only light came from the moon through the open window. It was someone's bedroom.

I don't know if my mind was playing a trick on me, but I could swear I heard the footsteps inch closer to where I was hiding. I crept further into the room. The closets had too many shelves in them for me to fit in it, like the one in my room. Though this didn't look like a room an apprentice would sleep in. The person even managed to have a double bed with a comfy mattress.

A wave of giggles washed over me. How funny would it be if I just laid down there and slept through it all? Would they be able to find me? I had to cover my mouth to stop me from bursting out in nervous laughter.

The door didn't open, and the footsteps made their way down the hall. I could finally breathe again. As I got up, I realized that the moonlight reflected against something on the table. It was a knife.

I wanted to jump up and down in happiness, but it wasn't the time. This must be one of the knives of a hunter stationed in the darkfort. They usually left their knives back at home base, so they don't lose it. I picked it up and saw how much different it was from my knife.

Each hunter has his own knife, the same knife that we got tattooed with. It was something like a badge that said: 'he's a part of the club'. I had seen Alder's knife, but that one had been almost similar to mine. This one, however, was completely different. It didn't have a leather handle, only a wooden one. The blade also didn't have a curve to it, it was rigged at the bottom part and ended in a sharp point. The handle had the initials 'JA' carved sloppily in it.

I popped my head out into the hallway to found it deserted. Though I knew the hunter must still be close.

Instead of being sneaky and quiet I rushed down. They weren't allowed to follow me into the hall, nor were they allowed to camp me out. Four other apprentices had been tapped on their way back with one item, I couldn't let that happen to me.

I thought I caught movement from the corner of my eye. Through our training, we discovered that I am a good runner. I could easily outrun Alder already, though admittedly he never really worked on his running but more on his sniping skills. I threw all caution to the wind and sprinted to safety.

My eyes had adjusted well to the darkness, so it was almost blinding when I burst into the well-lit hall. I wasn't allowed to stay here for longer than thirty seconds. I calmed my breathing down as I walked to Stevan and handed him the knife. He inspected the knife. When his eyes landed on 'JA' I could tell he was trying not to burst out in laughter. Surely the mentor will be made fun off because an apprentice stole his knife.

As I turned around, I caught Teryn's eye. He finally looked like he was awake and gave me a thumbs up as encouragement. I took a deep breath and walked back into the darkness.

I had only taken a few steps in when I noticed someone walking around the corner, about twenty metres away from me. It was too dark to see who it was, but that wasn't my main concern right now. I had no idea if they were allowed to team up on me.

I sprinted to the stairs and went all the way up. I had no idea how close he was, though I did hear the rapid tapping of feet on the stairs below me. It looked like I had to rush everything. It's probably for the best, I don't think my heart could take all this sneaking around.

The classroom was a little away from the stairs. I couldn't afford to carefully look around. They at least didn't know what was on my list, they wouldn't know my heading.

I hid in a service closet. I had to cash in on the fact that I outran whoever it was. It was hard to keep my breathing under control. I had gotten lucky twice already, was it too much to ask for a third time?

Footsteps were scouting out the area near my closet. I tried hard to remember my training. Alder had put the emphasis on remaining calm. "You have to try to blend in with your surroundings." He had said. "Or you should climb up something. Not a lot of people look up when they are searching for something. Then find something to defend yourself with."

I couldn't really defend myself here. Their goal was to touch me, so by trying to fight them off I would be eliminating myself. There was nothing I could climb up here. I knew I wasn't the prettiest girl alive, but I wasn't so ugly that I would blend in with a mop.

"Have you figured out who it is?" Another pair of footsteps had joined in. I didn't recognize his voice, though I had definitely heard it before.

"Julia." Greyson answered, sounding a bit out of breath. Greyson was the one who had spotted me, I got lucky. He was a good fighter but not the fastest guy around. "She has one item already."

If only they knew that they were having their little chat right next to the room I was hiding in. "What was it that he wrote about her?" The other guy was thinking out loud. This has to be a scare tactic, they would never say these things if they knew someone was around. I may have been able to outrun him, but I couldn't have gone half a building away.

"Smart and fast, but insecure," Greyson answered. I don't know about the smart part right now. I did hear them move around, their voices becoming more distant. "She'll slip up." They were definitely saying it to get in my head, even though I realized it it was still hard to let it all just slide off of me. Alder would never say that about me. He'd be much more detailed about it, the guy can't tell a story without giving all sorts of unnecessary details.

Their footsteps moved away from the room I was hiding in, until I could only faintly hear their voices in the distance. Undoubtingly they were still bad mouthing me, but I ignored it and sneaked away. I stayed as low to the ground as I could, hugging the wall every time I had to make a corner. Luck really was on my side, I encountered no one.

The classroom was empty, but it did have the map I needed on the wall. I quickly took it down and rolled it up. I had to keep it tight or it would just unroll. I didn't want to have to drag an entire map behind me.

There wasn't anyone in the hallway, I made my way down three flights of stairs until I saw someone.

His name was Ulric, he trained Weston, someone who I had not once spoken to. Ulric himself was still quite young, though I doubt he was from the last batch of apprentices. He had dark, black hair and even darker eyes. He was also the only hunter here who was taller than me, though not by a lot.

I turned on my heel and ran back up the stairs. He was faster than anyone I had encountered before, especially while we were still on the stairs. I think I got off on the third floor, but it could have been the second as well.

He didn't allow himself to get shaken off quite as easily as Greyson and the other mentor had. I ran and ran but every time I glanced back, he was still only a few metres away from me. I clutched the map tightly under my arms and sprinted for the other staircase.

The hall. That was my safe haven. He wasn't allowed to follow me in there. As long as I outrun him until then I'll be good.

I could tell he was still close to me as I went for the other staircase. This one was less used because it was outside of the building. Alder told me people used to use it to escape from fire, before the war, but that we didn't really use it now anymore. Why go outside into the cold when there is a perfectly usable staircase inside?

And cold it was. It had rained the entire day, resulting in not only a cold night but also a slippery staircase. My bare feet were absolutely freezing off, but I had no time to spare on being careful, I ran down the steps. I may have not looked so graceful, but luck was on my side, I didn't fall.

The wind outside had made it impossible for me to hear if Ulric had still been following me. I didn't hear the door open after me, he must have fallen on the staircase.

It was the home stretch, I had to run through two more corridors and then I would have successfully brought back two items. I couldn't feel my toes after the cold steel outside, but I ran as fast as I dared to. There was something different about running with someone chasing you. During practice, I had all my headspace to think of ways to make it easier for me, for ways to make me run faster. But while Ulric was hot on my heels I had absolutely no time to think about anything but the quickest way to get away from him.

As a result, I was absolutely winded. I slowed down my step a bit, convinced that I had left him far behind me and went through the last corridor to the hall.

Something heavy knocked me from the side. I fell to the ground, the map rolling away from me.

Ulric had charged down the stairs that were inside the compound and knocked me harshly against the ground. With him this close to me I could make out the fine lines in his face. A small scar underneath his right eye, a clearly broken nose, but most of all: Those pitch-black eyes.

"You are damn fast." He complained. He still had me pinned down, but I was happy to see that I at least had given him a run for his money, he was panting. Maybe not as much as I was but he looked tired almost.

I heard footsteps approaching as he got off me. Alder peeked around the corner before walking in with his arms wide open.

"You caught her!" He laughed. "Of course, you did."

"Why is it obvious that he would catch me?" I asked. Alder held out his hand and pulled me up to my feet.

"Ulric is the fastest runner out of all of us." Alder explained. Ulric also got to his feet, glancing between Alder and me.

"I still managed to stay ahead of you for quite some time." I grinned at him, a sense of pride filling my stomach.

"Old age is getting to you, my friend." Alder said, hitting him roughly over the shoulder. "Happens to the best of us."

"How long have you been using that excuse?" Ulric fired back. I tried to hide my laugh by coughing, but Alder glanced over at me. It was all in a good joking manner, he didn't seem very offended. Alder pushed me towards Ulric.

"Go on. You tapped her." He said to Ulric, before turning to walk back down the black corridor. Every time someone got tapped the mentor who did it had to come into the main hall too. Ulric had tapped quite a few people already.

"How did you manage to cut me off?" I asked before he opened the door.

"I only followed you outside for one flight before heading back in and cutting short through the main staircase." He said. "You did well Julia. The guys will give me so much shit for letting you outrun me for so long."

"I won't tell a soul." I grinned at him. I couldn't really tell in the darkness, but I thought I saw him smiling back at me. He had a nice smile, one of those that you hardly ever get to see. Like his face just isn't used to being in that state.

II

Athena had managed to get the most items back out of all of us. She was finally starting to get accepted into the group. Though breakfast and lunch were the times that everyone sat with their mentor, during dinner we all sat together. That was until almost a week after the simulation, we were missing two people.

Nero and Ethen were absent from our table. No one really pointed it out, maybe their mentors wanted them to study or maybe they wanted to eat in their rooms. But after Arturo pointed out that he hadn't seen them during lunch or in the hallways either, we got worried.

"Alder." It was breakfast time, though we sat together he was always focussed on something else. Whether that was writing something, reading a piece of paper or playing around with an old piece of technology, he ignored me for the most part.

He looked up, it had been an unwritten rule that I let him be in the mornings, especially before he had his breakfast. It was like talking to a toddler before he had eaten.

"What happened to Nero and Ethen?" I asked him. He put down the blue pen he was writing with.

"Factory." He said. "They didn't make the cut."

I had survived the first elimination round. Was it all because of the simulation? Both Nero and Ethen had been running in the middle of the pack. I didn't remember much about Ethen, except for the fact that he was smart and a bit shy. Nero hadn't lasted very long in the simulation, neither of them had brought anything back, but he had beaten me in a fight once.

"Why?" I asked. I had to ask. Was I up for the elimination as well? Had Alder put his neck out for me to stay?

"I'm not allowed to say that." Alder tried to get back to the paper he had been working on, but he sighed again and looked up. "Don't let this get to your head, Julia. You're smart and fast but-" I cut him off.

"Insecure?" I finished. Greyson hadn't been bad mouthing me, he had repeated what Alder was thinking.

"Where did you hear that?" He asked me, putting on his strict mentor face. I used to get intimidated by his clear blue eyes and stern look very easily. However, I had been around him for so long, and the other intimidating hunters, that the effect started to wear off. It was all a façade in the end.

"Greyson and someone else said it during the last simulation." I straight up told him. "I was hiding, I overheard them."

"Do you disagree?" He asked me. I was quiet for a few seconds. I liked it better when we were silent in the morning.

"It doesn't help that you point it out." I just answered. Alder glanced around before leaning closer to me.

"You were brought up in the meeting, I won't say by who, but let's just say that he got shot down quickly. By a lot of people." He reassured me. "You'd have to mess up horribly to be send away."

Alder wasn't an emotional person, he rarely complimented me unless I had made actual progress. I smiled at him, thankful that he shared classified information just for my state of mind. There was one person here who didn't believe in me, I would bet all of the money in the world that it was Greyson.

The group was a bit shaken up by the sudden departure of two other apprentices. It seemed like everyone was now fighting to get noticed.

Most of us thought that staying in the middle of the pack was the way to go, the way to not be a showstopper nor a failure, but we were proven wrong. All of the mentors seemed to have noticed our new drive as well, they only started grilling us harder. It seemed like every bit of humour had left Alder's body, he was now only focussed on training.

"Are you going to continue to make the same mistakes over and over again?" Alder asked me. We had been doing target practice. I was a good shot, far better than Teryn and some of the others, but because it was Alder's speciality, he never thought it was good enough.

"I am trying." I sighed. I am supposed to hit the target in the head standing up, crouching and lying flat on my belly, all under one minute.

The first one was easy, I had been practising standing and shooting since the beginning of my training. The other two didn't come quite as natural. Especially laying down on my stomach and still hitting the target in the head seemed impossible.

"You're moving too slow." He noted, getting his own gun out and showing how it's supposed to be done for the hundredth time. "In a real gunfight, you don't have the time to calmly lay down."

I tried again and again, but each time I was either too late or a little off on my shooting. It seemed like Alder was truly pissed off. Eventually, he just dismissed me for dinner and walked off.

Most apprentices seemed to have gone through a similar day. Everyone around our table looked tired enough to fall asleep into their food. Athena for the first time looked like she had been struggling as well.

"It'll be fine," I reassured her. "You're the best fighter here." I wasn't lying to her, she was unbeaten. Not even the people who had trained with the military for years could take her down.

"I'm good at fighting," she nodded. "But I'm not smart enough." It was odd to see her so insecure. She had tried to look like she wasn't bothered by it all for so long. It was all a mask so the others didn't mess with her too much, but now that she was one of us she finally let that go. "They don't have schools out there."

"Well, where did you learn how to read then?" I asked her. She looked ashamed almost, glancing over at her mentor before returning to me.

"I don't know how to," she answered. "I only started learning it here with the hunters. The military didn't care about it."

"He's teaching you how to read?" I now also glanced over at her mentor, Ferik. He was clearly one of the smart ones, and not super strong. I got her frustration now, she is scared of being sent home just like the rest of us.

On our first day here, a lot of the mentors had reacted a bit surprised to hear about Ferik being Athena's mentor, this was because everyone had expected that role to go to a man named Cephas. As it turned out, Athena was not the first radiate to be allowed to join the hunters. Cephas had done it before her, a good forty years ago.

To make matters worse, there was still one person who did not like Athena. His name was Kyon, and he came from one of the border regions. He sat down next to her with his familiar malicious grin on his face.

"I bet you are excited about this week." He said to her.

"And why is that?" I asked him. I hadn't really spoken to Kyon much, With the exception of the one time we trained together because Teryn and Athena were both busy. He glanced over at me, looking almost annoyed that I intervened.

"United Day of course." He smiled at me. "Are you climbing the wall again Athena? Or are they dead?"

I had completely forgotten about United Day. We would be allowed to leave the base and visit our family. To be honest, my family hardly ever popped up in my head anymore. These people were my family now. If I make it they are the ones I have to depend on, not my parents who never left their stupid bubble.

"They would be dead." Athena answered, putting her unbothered face back on and staring him down. Kyon looked like he wanted to say something back, but several mentors coming over to our table stopped him.

"So," Ferik said, holding a piece of paper that had our names on it. "We allow you to return home for United day, even while you are still training." Alder stood on the right side of Ferik. He didn't seem that angry anymore luckily, but then again, he wasn't training me at the moment.

"A lot of the mentors are gone too for the next three days, so we expect you to keep training yourself, should you decide to stay here." Ferik explained to us. "Who here wants to stay at the base?"

Athena's hand shot up, and so did Ryder's and Arturo's. I had to make a quick decision. Would I stay here and train or go home?

There really was nothing left for me there, I thought as I also put my hand up. My siblings will have long forgotten me already, like they did with my brothers, and my parents will only pester me for money. I'll visit them once I am a full-fledged hunter. I need to focus on my training.

Ferik put little X's next to our names and asked the others what regions they were from. The government always makes sure everyone can go home, so they send out busses even to remote areas.

Teryn left to go visit his parents in Calgary. The base immediately started feeling a lot less homelike.

Ferik had been right, a lot of the mentors left. When everyone was here there were at least thirty people, now there were only ten.

Alder left as well, without so much as a goodbye. I couldn't help but sleep in on my first day of him being gone.

I liked Alder, I was so happy that he was my mentor. But that didn't mean that I agreed with him all of the time. He is great with guns and shooting and therefore wants me to be great with guns and shooting. I wasn't bad at it, I was getting pretty good. But pretty good wasn't enough, he grilled me to become better.

While he was gone, I did not touch a gun. Instead, I trained hand to hand combat with Athena. She still beat me every time, but I was learning loads.

Another thing I wanted to spend more time on was running. I absolutely loved it, and I was getting faster and faster too. Alder despised running, so we didn't train it nearly enough for my liking.

I had not spoken to Ulric since the first simulation, which had been weeks ago. He hadn't left to visit his family, so when I saw him walking down the hallway an idea popped up in my head.

"Ulric!" I called out for him. I had just eaten lunch and in all truth, I wanted to spend my last free afternoon doing absolutely nothing. This was just too good of an opportunity to pass up on. Tomorrow he would be back to only training his apprentice again.

He turned around, allowing me to catch up with him. "I was wondering if you could help me train my running?" I asked him. He was quiet for a few seconds before shrugging and signing me to follow him.

Surrounding the base was a concrete floor until it stopped at a fence. The concrete had been there since before the war, there were many large cracks with weeds growing out of it. So far, I had only trained my running inside. It had been more than half a year since I even last ran outside.

"Sprint from this side of the fence to the other." He instructed me while he stood in the middle so he could observe. I jogged over to one side of the fence and started sprinting.

There was something liberating about running, especially if you go fast enough. The wind takes over all other sounds, the only thing connecting me to the rest of the world is my feet tapping on the concrete.

The concrete did give an extra obstacle. I couldn't just run in a straight line, I had to jump over some of the cracks, and make sure that I landed correctly. Still, I felt that I ran the difference pretty quickly.

"A good start," Ulric said, with a small grin on his face. "There are some improvements you can make. Watch me." He went to one start of the fence and did the same thing I did, only ten times faster. How I outran him in the simulation was beyond me.

"Notice any differences?" He asked me. I tried thinking, but I came up empty. Running looked like running to me. Maybe he was a bit more crouched down than I was? "Come on Julia, I'm not just going to give you the answers."

"You were crouched down more." I said.

"You have long legs," he answered. "Take bigger steps, that and your feet of course."

"My feet?" I asked.

"Make sure that while you're sprinting you only touch the ground with the ball of your feet." He instructed me. "Didn't Alder teach you any of this?"

I tried running that way, and it did help me to go faster. I felt even lighter on my feet, even though dodging the cracks here and there became even more important.

He gave me more tips and helpful insights for the rest of the afternoon. I actually liked Ulric's company. It didn't feel like he was an older hunter I needed to impress, he felt more like a friend.

"I think we're done here." He finally said.

"No." I smiled at him. "You promised me I could race you."

"Fine then." He said, faking annoyance. "On your marks."

We walked to one side of the fence. "When do we start?" I asked him. He glanced around until his eyes fell on a bus that was approaching the gate.

"When the gate opens." He said. It was one of the busses undoubtedly carrying back some of the hunters who went to United Day. The bus rolled up to the gate, one of the military guards who had been watching us sprint all this time got out of his little booth and made a little chat with the driver. Just a few more seconds...

The other guard finally walked over to the gate and started pulling it open. Instantly I started sprinting away. It was different with someone sprinting next to me, it became harder to remember literally everything he had just taught me. He had been slower at the start but gained in on me very fast. Still, I could tap his shoulder if I reached out far enough.

I made a mistake. My concentration slipped for a split second when I noticed a strike of lighting in the distance. I absolutely hated thunder. I misstepped, my foot landed right into a crack, and I fell down.

I had fallen a lot since I came here. The actual impact of the fall didn't hurt that much. It was my ankle that felt odd, as though there was a weird pressure on it.

Ulric was next to me within seconds. "Are you okay?" He asked me, kneeling down beside me. My forearms were a bit scratched from the fall and probably looked worse than my foot. Even though it hurt like all hell, I wasn't going to admit that. I already had being a girl against me, I wasn't going to be the damsel in distress.

"I'm fine," I said. "I just twisted my ankle a bit." Ulric moved closer to my leg and carefully pulled up the bottom part of my pants. He pressed his long fingers against my skin softly. I wanted to pull my leg away, or curse him out, but settled on biting down on my lip, hoping to somehow deflect the pain. He was just trying to help, I had to keep repeating it in my head.

"I don't think it's broken." He told me. He got up and held out his hand to pull me up.

I couldn't stand on it, it hurt a lot. There was no way of walking without flinching every time my foot touched the ground. I cursed myself. Why did I get distracted by something as stupid as thunder?

"I'll carry you." Ulric said as he saw me limping. He moved closer to me and put his arm on my lower back, I pushed him away though.

"Absolutely not," I told him. "I don't need to be carried."

"You can't walk, it will just make it worse." He argued with me. He tried picking me up again, but I hopped away from him.

"You're not carrying me." I insisted.

"Fine, just lean on me okay?" He said. At first, I didn't trust him, I thought he would just try to pick me up again, but he kept true to his word.

He put his arm around my waist while I had mine around his neck. I tried to ignore it, to only stay focussed on my feet and where I would plant them next, but it became very hard. Suddenly I wished he had picked me up...

No, I wasn't a damsel in distress. My foot wasn't dangling off my leg, I could just walk. I had never focused too much on Ulric, because I never really spoke to his apprentice Weston. I suppose he was rather attractive, he had the whole dark eyes and dark hair mystery going on. I hadn't really focused on anyone as attractive, my mind was always busy with either training or studying.

Once we were inside, we quickly ran into Ferik, who immediately left to inform the doctor. I had only seen him a handful of times. He was a bit odd and kept to himself almost all of the time. His eyes were hidden behind a pair of small, circular glasses and he always looked like he drank a bit too much.

"I'm sorry." Ulric said to me as we slowly made our way to the doctor's room, which was luckily and smartly placed on the first floor.

"Unless you put that specific crack in the concrete you have nothing to be sorry for." I answered.

"I shouldn't have raced you." He said, his grip around me tightening as we reached the last few steps.

"Because I would have beaten you if I hadn't fallen?" I grinned at him.

"I believe I was far ahead of you." He said back. "Maybe you only fell because you realized you could never beat me."

"Oh no," I said dramatically. "My evil master plan is revealed."

We started laughing, it was fun to have someone around with the same sense of humour. Athena especially never really gets sarcasm, and always thinks I'm being serious. Teryn, on the other hand, gets the joke, but never laughs or comments back on it.

The doctor informed me that I had sprained my ankle and gave me one of the worst treatments ever: rest. I wasn't allowed to stand on it for longer than an hour a day, for at least a week, preferably longer. Now I just needed to figure out how I would tell Alder that.

Everyone returned the following day from their reunions with their families, which was a pretty special thing. United Day was also the day that people often ran and tried to cross the fence, to avoid having to work for the factory for the rest of their lives.

Though I guess it made sense all the hunters returned, they had one of the highest paying jobs in the kingdom.

Ulric made sure that I was following doctor's orders until Alder returned. He made sure I kept my leg up and even brought up my dinner and breakfast. To make matters worse my ankle had swollen up a lot overnight, making the injury look about as bad as it felt.

Ulric didn't stick around after he had brought me breakfast, he had to go back down to talk to his apprentice. I ate my bread in silence, paging through one of the strategy books Alder had given me.

It wasn't a very interesting book, but it did date from before the war. Many of the strategies used before the war were unusable now. Either the terrain had changed too much because of the bombs or the weapons were simply too advanced or too dated. Especially the part about the use of drones I could just skip, they wouldn't make it twenty metres into enemy territory without being shot down.

A few knocks landed on my door. "Julia, are you awake?" Alder asked.

"Yeah, come in." I said, closing the book and putting my empty plate on top of it. Alder entered my room. It almost looked like he had aged ten years just in those three days. He had dark circles underneath his bright eyes, he looked like he hadn't slept since he left.

"So," he said before I could ask what had happened. He sat down on my bed. "What did you train?"

"Fighting, both hand to hand and with knives, and running." I said, laughing sheepishly and glancing towards my ankle. It was still hidden under the covers. No doubt he would grill me for getting injured later.

"Not shooting?" He asked, raising one of his eyebrows at me.

"Figured I'd wait until the master at it comes back." I said. Though I wished I had settled for shooting instead of running, I would be a lot less injured then. Alder just nodded, quickly glancing around my room. I had kept it tidy, he had warned me on my first day that he hated messy rooms.

"Why didn't you go down to breakfast?" He asked me once he saw my empty plate. A realization quickly dawned on me.

"Oh, they didn't tell you yet." I said.

"Didn't tell me what?" He asked me. "What did you do?"

I let out a nervous laugh. "I messed up my ankle." I pulled the covers away from it, revealing my swollen ankle. Alder inspected it from all sides while mumbling under his breath. It had turned blue and purple overnight. "The doctor said I have to let it rest for at least a week." I informed him sadly. "I'm sorry Alder."

"Don't be." He quickly said. "I thought you were angry at me or something, that you just skipped on breakfast together." He glanced up at me. "How did this happen?"

"I asked Ulric to train running with me. I fell." I told him.

"Ulric?" Alder looked surprised. "Never thought he would train you." He patted me on my knee. "But this is fine. We'll just change out the physical exercises for theory."

I don't know if it was guilt that drove Ulric to my room so often during my resting week, but I didn't really mind. He was good company, and a nice change from Alder constantly bugging me with new books I could read.

I soon realized the second simulation was coming up, it had been a few months since the last one and the same signs as the last time kept coming up. The mentors seemed to become more frantic with their teachings, their behaviour becoming weirder and weirder by the day. But what gave it away most of all was my visit to doctor Groen.

He inspected my ankle about a week and a half after I had fallen. It had healed nicely according to him, and he allowed me to slowly start exercising again.

"We need you up and running by Friday." He had murmured to himself, revealing the exact date of the next simulation. I had been smart about it, I only told all the other apprentices with the message to keep their mouths shut about it to their mentors.

During dinner on Thursday, I sat beside Teryn with Athena right in front of me. We were discussing what we might be doing next.

"Definitely running," I said to them. "That's what the doctor said."

"I also had to train shooting more often." Teryn said while Athena nodded along. They still weren't really overly excited about each other, but I hadn't seen them being excited about anything anyway. I wanted to believe that they were starting to become friends as well.

"Who do you think is next to go?" I asked quietly. The rest of the group was talking and laughing together loudly, they didn't look that worried about tomorrow. Alder had told me that I had to mess up badly to get cut, but would my injury be held into account? I didn't dare put a lot of stress on it yet, so if we would be running in the next simulation my one strength might be my downfall.

"Arlo maybe?" Teryn whispered back. Arlo was very strong and had both his training and his good background as definite plusses for him. His parents were influential people in the king's court. Though he didn't necessarily lay that well in the group, he often came off as entitled and cocky.

"They wouldn't dare." Athena said. "Definitely Weston."

Weston was Ulric's apprentice, though he never really spoke about him. Weston kept to himself, he didn't really like talking to others a lot. I didn't mind him that much, he just skated by in my mind, never really taking the spotlight.

After dinner, the mentors stopped us from just returning to our rooms. We were let outside, to a large bus that was waiting to pick us up. We weren't even allowed to change clothes or shoes. I sat down next to Athena, in the far back of the bus. Teryn sat down next to Jai, someone who he had befriended a little bit

It came to no surprise when they told us we were heading to our second mission.

12

A loud foghorn signaled the start of the simulation.

We were left in a large forest. Each apprentice started at the edge of the circle. In the centre of it was a small mirror. Whoever first touched that mirror first wins.

But that obviously wasn't the whole story. We were given a gun. Not with real bullets of course, but little balls of paint. They probably thought themselves hilarious when they assigned me the vibrant pink colour.

The second way to win was to 'kill' all the others. We had to go face to face with our friends, but only a paintball could take them out.

I was told that there were several more guns hidden in the circle, I wanted to find at least one backup gun, for insurance, but my main goal was to touch that mirror first. I knew I wasn't the strongest nor was I the best shot out of all the other apprentices, so I just needed to be the fastest.

My ankle didn't feel all that bad as I started on a jogging tempo to the centre. I was also provided with a GPS tracker, that showed me exactly where I was in the circle, but sadly not where the others were.

The trees had started shedding their leaves weeks ago, it was like walking in a world made of brown, red and orange. It felt like I was walking through the forest to go to school, like I had done hundreds of times back home.

I used to hate going through there. My brothers would tell me stories of the trees having eyes and watching me, to make sure I would go to school. If I didn't, they would reach out with their branches and grab me, and I would become a tree too.

Splat! A red paintball exploded on the tree next to me. I was immediately pulled out of my memories and took shelter behind a tree.

It was Holden, who was by far the best shot out of all the apprentices. He must have realized this, and instead of going to the centre he had decided to just take us all out. Knowing the hunters, they would probably favour winning that way rather than touching the mirror.

Another paintball exploded against my tree. I needed to make a quick decision. I don't think I could shoot him before he shoots me, I needed to survive longer than five minutes. I could wait him out? I don't know what gun they gave him though, nor how many bullets he has.

I went with the most stupid plan I could think of. I threw a rock to one side of the tree and ran from the other side as he shot the rock. I focussed on sprinting the way Ulric told me to. I stayed on the tip of my toes, I made sure I had an explosive start and this time actually minded where I was going.

"You're running?!" He shouted after me, shooting rapidly at me. I kept going from left to right, so it would be harder for him to hit me.

"Never underestimate the power of the zig-zag!" I shouted back, waving him off. A few paintballs hit near me, but he wasn't able to hit me directly. Most of the trees blocked his bullets, as I had definitely thought outthey would.

That may have not been my most gracious moment, but it worked. I sincerely hoped Alder did not see that, I had no doubt he would make fun of me until the day I die.

Careful not to accidentally start daydreaming again, I slowed down my pace to a jog. Holden wasn't very fast due to his size, and he didn't have the durability to sprint for a long time either, I felt a bit safer.

In the distance, I saw a small, run down shed made of wood. If I was a gun, that's where I would hide, I thought to myself and made my way over to it, making sure that no one was around to snipe me.

I was right, there was a bigger gun in the shed, as well as a water bottle. My throat had gone dry from the tension, I drank it all in big gulps before discarding it.

A branch snapped outside. Through the cracks in the wooden door, I saw a figure approaching. I silently moved over so I could stand right in front of the door. I crouched down, figuring that they would be expecting a tall person to shoot and not someone low to the ground, and quickly put some paintballs in the new gun. My fingers were trembling, I dropped some onto the floor. I rushed to load more into the gun. Not only was it bigger, it was also automated, it could fire several bullets with just one squeeze of the trigger.

The person was doing the same thing I did, scout out the area first. He must think that he was the first to reach this. Eventually, he moved in front of the door, I heard him readying his gun, his arm reached out and slowly turned the doorknob.

The moment the door opened, I started firing. I hit him square in the chest. The sudden impact caused him to fall back into the dirt.

"That hurts." Kyon grunted. He was gasping for breath, the wind had been knocked completely out of him. Two vibrantly pink bullets had hit him on the right side of his rib cage. I couldn't say that I felt too bad about it, he was still the only person who openly hated against Athena, even though she had proven herself to be worthy of her place more often than any of us had.

"Are you okay?" I asked him, holding out my hand to pull him up.

"Yeah. The only thing hurt is my pride." He grinned. "Good shot."

"Thanks." I answered. "Now if you don't mind, I want to loot your dead body."

He handed me his revolver with navy blue bullets and a protein bar. I absolutely hated them, so I handed it right back to him, as well as his bullets.

I took a few minutes to load up all of my new guns with the correct colour bullets. "Do me a favour," I said. "If anyone asks you which way your shooter went, send them the wrong way."

"Why would I do that?" He asked me, pointing at the pink stains on his shirt. "You did just shoot me."

I laughed. "Do you want to lose to the person who died ten minutes in or to the person who won?"

"Fair enough. Good luck." He said, sitting down so he could lean against the walls of the shed. I knew he probably would get some sort of instructions from the GPS device on what to do next, or he'd have to wait until the foghorn sounds again. We really don't get instructions on what to do if you fail.

The closer I moved to the centre the more gunshots I heard. The environment also started to change. More and more old houses popped up, and the forest went away completely.

"Hey, Julia." I was greeted. I quickly pointed my gun to whoever was talking but saw that it was Teryn sitting against a tree, his shirt nearly fully dyed with orange bullets. "Jai wanted to make sure I was dead." He said. "Don't get shot, it hurts like hell."

"How long ago were you shot?" I asked him. By the look of the suns position, the mission had started two hours ago.

"Like twenty minutes ago?" He guessed. "Really I-" He got cut off by a voice coming from his GPS.

"Dead people don't talk." Greyson scolded him. I rolled my eyes and waved Teryn goodbye after he mouthed 'good luck' to me.

I walked for five more minutes. According to my GPS, I was still at least two hours away from the centre, but I hadn't encountered anyone. That was until I saw her.

Athena was just about to enter a house. Would I shoot my own friend? I quickly hopped behind a hedge and decided to play it the smart way.

"Athena!" I called out. "I have a brilliant idea." It was quiet for a few seconds, but I didn't dare pop up and see if she heard me, I couldn't give away my location in case she had no problem shooting me.

"If this is some stupid thing to get me to lose then forget it, Julia." She answered. She had probably taken refuge in the house she was about to enter.

"No, I'm a lot smarter than that." I said. "Imagine this: Working together to kill all the guys. Prove the leaders wrong and show that we belong here." She was quiet, probably weighing her options. Together we could take out a lot of them, even though eventually we'd have to fight as well.

"Is that even allowed?" She finally asked me. I could tell she moved a bit, but she didn't seem to have located me yet.

"They didn't specify." I answered. I stood up from my hiding spot and saw that she had taken refuge behind a half broken down wall. She pointed her gun at me but didn't shoot. It didn't look like she had managed to loot, so I could tempt her with that too. I grabbed my GPS and held it close to my face.

"Athena and I are going to work together. Please tell me if this isn't allowed." I said to it. I knew Alder must be listening in, Greyson had listened to Teryn.

Athena moved closer to me. She lowered her gun a bit but still held it ready to shoot me if I betrayed her, which I definitely wasn't planning on doing.

I had met a lot of the current hunters because they were mentors, but beside Jack, Norton and Dorian, I had not met any of the ones stationed in the Darkfort. They might not be as open to the idea of accepting girls as the hunters who now knew me. If they heard that we were the top two in the mission, we might earn some respect.

My GPS remained silent. I looked up at Athena and held out my hand for her to shake. "Truce?"

"Truce." She smiled back at me, shaking my hand. I gave her the revolver I took off Kyon and in return she told me the number of people she had taken down already.

She had shot Jai, Ryder and Asher. I told her about Teryn and Kyon, leaving out that I didn't actually shot Teryn. She didn't need to know that.

"So that's seven." She said. "Five guys confirmed down and the two of us."

"Six left." I replied, glancing at the GPS. We were slowly going further and further into the middle of the circle. I remembered my lesson with Alder about spacing, so we made sure to always stay at least ten metres apart from each other.

There was no reason to loot, we had more than enough bullets to take out thirty guys. Neither of us felt the particular need to find food or water. Everyone would be close in the centre now, the mission would be over soon.

Both of our GPS's turned on at the same time. "Five remaining, all deceased leave the circle in a straight line." Athena and I smirked at each other. Three guys to take down.

My ankle had started nagging hours ago, but it only just now started to actually hurt again. I didn't want to show Athena this, so I tried to hide my limping. I'm not sure if she could tell, she did slow down her pace a bit so it would be easier for me to keep up.

"What do we do if we kill everyone?" Athena asked me.

"We split up and walk in opposite directions for five minutes," I answered. "Then it's game on."

We heard gunshots, not far away from where we were. We both immediately crouched down and found cover. Athena moved into a garden, while I took refuge in a house.

I walked through the hallway, closing the door behind me. I wanted to move over to the living room. The windows hadn't had glass in them for a long time, I could easily hide next to them and shoot into the street.

I had let down my guard too much, but thankfully, so had he. The moment I entered the house I saw Conall climbing through the window, also seeking refuge from the bullets. For a moment we locked eyes, then the shots started.

The final few minutes were all out war. Athena was taking fire outside, while inside we were painting the walls with yellow and pink. Conall wasn't the best of shots, he prefers to fight hand to hand, so it came to no surprise that he decided to rush me.

I had been firing to where I thought he was hiding when he managed to creep up to the other door that led to the living room. I tried to shoot him, but he knocked me over against the wall, and the gun slid away from me.

I hit my head against the wall, and for a moment I thought back to Djorn and the other guys. Where were they now? Did they move onto another victim to shove into walls and scare? I had not thought back to them once in the last months. I was stronger now, I knew what to do.

Conall tried to grab his gun from his belt to finish me off quickly, but I brought my knee up and hit him where the sun doesn't shine. He doubled over in pain, mumbling some colourful words while I went and grab his gun, before realizing the kill wouldn't register because it was his own bullet.

Conall recovered quicker than I imagined. There was an air of understanding between the other apprentices. This was a simulation, we needed to show that we could apply what they had been teaching us. However, it was only common courtesy to never do that in a way that brings someone else down.

Conall seemed to have forgotten that. He looked furious. He grabbed my hair, which was up in a ponytail, and yanked it away from the wall so I would fall on the ground. I stumbled but thankfully did not fall. Next, he swung his large fist at my face.

It was like Alder was right beside me, guiding me through what to do next. Dodge his fist, prepare for his inevitable next kick, find an opening and attack.

But I knew I would never win this fight. Conall was not only twice my size, he was also a great fighter. Besides, the point was to shoot him and I couldn't do that with, my two guns were laying on the ground.

I ducked underneath his next swing and pushed him aside. I knew it was either a suicide mission or a successful one. I let myself fall to my knees and tried to reach my gun, but he pulled my leg back.

I managed to kick him in the stomach and grabbed my gun, but once I turned around to fire it was too late. He shot me twice in the stomach with his own weapon.

I wanted to apologize to him for kneeing him in the balls, but he just rolled his eyes and stepped over me to the street. He had a clear shot of Athena and hit her in the back. Before he got eliminated by the one person Athena could not hit: Arlo.

13

The ending of the simulation was messy, but eventually I found out that I had come in fourth place. I was sad that my alliance with Athena hadn't worked out better but at least I did not die first.

They took us to the 'control centre'. It was modelled after what real control centres usually look like in areas of war. They had set it up in an old house on top of the hill. There were three rooms, what used to be the living room, the dining room and the kitchen. The rest of the house had too many holes and not enough ceiling to really be used.

The dining room and kitchen were adjoining, the living room was separated by a wooden door. The same bus that had taken us to our positions in the circle brought us to the house. Outside were all of our mentors, waiting patiently to scold us on our faults.

"'Never underestimate the power of the zig-zag'." Alder said once he saw me, failing to hide his grin while attempting to look angry. "Seriously Julia?"

"It worked didn't it?" I smirked. He slammed his hand down on my shoulder.

"You did great kiddo." He said to me, holding his arm around my shoulder, so I could lean on him and not on my ankle. "You have made me both very proud and eternally embarrassed."

"It's my one goal in life." I answered. We were given some food and water, as well as some medical assistance if need be. The nurse scolded Alder and doctor Groen for letting me partake in the simulation.

"She shouldn't have been here." She mumbled under her breath. She looked back up at Alder, who was standing behind the chair I was sitting on.

"You have sent her right back to square one. Two weeks of no walking, nor training." She quickly added when she saw Alder beginning to protest.

"Maybe it will give you some time to focus on shooting." Alder said to me, eyeing the nurse as she walked away. She had given me a cold compress to lay over my foot as well as a small stool to put underneath it.

"From a wheelchair?" I asked him back.

I had not been able to see into the living room, the door was closed, but when it swung open the atmosphere in the room changed from light-hearted to serious in a matter of seconds.

I didn't really need to look who caused it, I already knew. Jack Alvarez came out, flanked by two other hunters. They didn't look like the happiest bunch, but they were the ones in charge.

"We'll call you in one by one to evaluate your mission." One of the other two said. He had black long hair that reached his upper back and a deep scar in his cheek. "Kyon."

Kyon rose up shakily from his chair and followed the leaders into the living room. I saw a small peak of what was inside, there was one wall full of screens playing what had just happened during the mission. The last thing I saw before the door closed was a video of myself zig-zagging away.

"For your sake," Alder said, clearly having just seen what I saw. "I hope they don't underestimate the power of the zigzag."

It seemed like it was my curse that I would always be picked last. I watched my fellow apprentices going in one by one and coming back out looking lot paler. None of them really spoke after they went in. I wanted to go to Teryn, who looked extra pale and sweaty compared to some of the others, but Alder told me I wasn't allowed to stand up, under the approving eye of the nurse.

Even Arlo, who won, seemed a bit out of it when he came back out. He only spoke to his mentor in hushed whispers. The longer the people had survived the longer they were inside, I think Arlo actually took half an hour, though there was no real way to tell the time.

"Any advice?" I asked Alder. He was leaning against the wall behind me, looking around the room.

"Be honest with them, take it seriously." He said. "It might be a simulation now, but they need to see if you are up for the real thing."

"So how do I honestly tell them that I didn't have a plan half of the time?" I whispered. Alder knelt next to my chair and eyed the door, waiting to see if it would open.

"In that case, you spin the story." He whispered. "You sure looked like you had a plan to me. Use that."

Not much later, I got called in. I wasn't even last, that would be Athena this time. I limped over to the door and was let in by none other than Jack himself. He held it open for me so I could wobble my way to the free chair at the head of the table.

The room was dark, the only light came from the screens mounted on the walls, which were now only playing videos of me. The two men were sitting on my right, and Jack took his place at my left.

"Anthony and Elias." Jack pointed to who was who. "This is Julia, Norton's project."

Right, great start.

I shook hand with both of them, feeling incredibly uncomfortable. Not only was I classified as 'Norton's project' I also was only wearing one shoe and limping.

"Where in the simulation did you get injured?" Elias asked me, he was the one who had spoken to the group before.

"I got injured about two weeks ago," I answered. "During training."

Anthony wrote something down on his notebook in front of him and nodded at Jack to start.

"We are going to walk through this simulation. You have to give your reasoning behind your actions." He said. The screens now all acted as one large one. I saw myself standing in the middle of the forest, jumping from one leg to the other, waiting for the foghorn.

The camera cut to a different angle, I saw the first person I had encountered: Holden. I hated how incredibly surprised I looked.

"Your reasoning?" Elias asked me.

"I did not hear Holden approach," I explained. "My first priority was to take cover and find out who the shooter is and his location. When I saw that it was Holden, I knew that shooting back was useless, he's a better shot than me. I wanted to play into my strengths, which is running, so I threw the rock to distract him and sprinted."

And zigzagged, I thought to myself. Undoubtingly they had heard me say it in the simulation but now didn't seem like the time to crack jokes.

I saw myself approach the shed, they even had a camera inside there. My head snapped up when I heard Kyon outside.

"I heard a branch snap and could see a figure approaching through the door. I figured it would be safer to be close to the ground and try to get a good shot." I explained.

The next scene they showed me was when I saw Athena. They even played the audio where I heard my own, much squeakier than I thought it was, voice say: "Prove the leaders wrong and show that we belong here." Anthony openly grinned to Elias, but Jack did not seem to want to participate in the irony of it all.

"What made you want to work together with Athena?" Jack asked me. There was an underlying pressure to answer the question, one only he and I got.

I had not seen one single thing that would indicate that Athena was secretly a rebel. If anything, I had become more and more convinced that she had a horrible life before she entered the Union and was willing to die protecting it. On the other hand, I had not heard Athena talk much about her life before anyway, she could still be hiding something.

"She's a good shot." Was the first thing that popped up into my head. "But more importantly, I meant what I said: I wanted to see the two girls win." Jack held eye contact for a bit longer than the other two, I could tell he wanted to know more about her. But this wasn't the place to tell him.

Up next was my final fight with Conall. I thought something had snapped in him that made him try to beat me up, but when I saw it replayed I realized that there was something odd about me too. The moment my head hit the wall it looked like I was in some sort of trance, like I wasn't me.

"Can you tell us the way now that would have resulted in you winning, should this have been a real mission, not a simulation." Anthony asked me, pulling me out of my thoughts.

"If it was real, I could have easily gotten his gun and shoot him with it." I answered. The fight kept repeating over and over on the screen. It looked like I went into pure attack mode, like I wasn't able to tell that it was all a simulation and not reality.

"Why did you not stand your ground and fight?" Elias asked.

"My opponent was both twice the size of me and had twice the amount of fighting experience. I used the knowledge I had of him and deduced that it was a fight I could not win." I answered. There was something unsettling about seeing me change like that. I couldn't look at the screen anymore, I was psyching myself out.

"Your previous mission," Anthony said, paging back in his notebook. "We don't have any video of it, only the accounts of people there. Please tell us in your own words what happened as well as your reasoning again."

I told them about my hide and seek experience when I reached the part about hiding in the room and finding the knife, I saw Anthony and Elias visibly struggling not to laugh.

"Why does everyone think that is so funny?" I had to ask, more mentors had made comments on it, but I never found out who the knife belonged to, only that Stevan got tasked with returning it to the owner.

Anthony and Elias were full on laughing now. Jack turned to me. "What were the initials carved on it?"

"J…"

Oh. Oh no.

JA, Jack Alvarez.

I had no idea if I should apologize. I broke into his room and stole his knife! Jack had been tattooed with that knife back when he was still an apprentice. Most hunters leave their knives at the base inside the fence. If you lose your knife the rest of the hunters will make fun of you for the rest of your life. And I had stolen Jack's.

"The laughter makes sense now." I just said awkwardly. Alder could have given me a heads up about this! He must have known that it was Jack's. I am going to murder him.

The other two men quickly got their faces back in check, and I went on to tell my story about the first mission all the way until I got tackled by Ulric.

"Knowing what you know now, what would you have done differently?" They asked me again.

"I would have glanced behind me on the staircase and see that he wasn't following. That way I could have deducted his next move and avoid him." I gave my final answer, rounding off the evaluation.

I understood why no one felt like talking afterwards, it's horrible to have to give your reasoning to three seasoned leaders. To admit every mistake and tell them the, sometimes obvious, ways to fix it. I just sat back down in the chair after they had dismissed me.

Alder gave me the cold compress again and asked me how it went. I just mumbled the word 'fine' and watched Athena go in last.

They took a long time with her. It wasn't Athena's style to show us any emotion, especially after a beat down, so when she came out looking as normal as ever, no one was surprised.

We were told to go back to the bus, which would take us back to the base. Alder offered me his shoulder to lean on, which I gladly took.

There were some other apprentices that got pretty banged up too. Weston, Ulric's apprentice, fell wrong after he had been hit by a bullet and hit his head against a stone wall. He had a large wound on his forehead, as well as a concussion according to the nurse.

"Alder." Someone said before we got on the bus.

"Jack." Alder greeted him back, shaking his hand, even though he had the other one still tightly around me, so I could use him as a crutch.

"Might I borrow your apprentice for a second?" Though he asked it, it was obviously a command, not a question. I knew that this had to be about Athena. Still, I had nothing to report to him. She hadn't written or sent any letters, nor did she really seem all that interested in making friendships with the other apprentices.

"Of course." Alder answered, letting go of me and walking a few steps back to the bus. He went to stand beside Ulric, who kept a close eye on Jack and whispered something to Alder.

I had not told Alder about my mission. It was the one secret I had kept from him all these months. He looked confused to say the least, though I couldn't really blame him for that.

"This way." Jack said to me. We walked, more like I wobbled, to the back side of the house, far out of sight from anyone. In the distance I could see storm clouds approaching, the sky was a pitch-black colour, and the birds were flying low to the ground.

"What did you find out about her?" He asked me. I leaned against the wall to rest my ankle and contemplated my answer for as long as I dared to.

"Nothing," I answered truthfully. "I tried following her in the beginning, but it was impossible. Then, I befriended her. She hasn't been in contact with anyone other than hunters or apprentices."

"And you don't think this 'friendship' clouded your judgement of her?" He asked me. I was taken aback. He was the smart leader, I had literally just started my apprenticeship when he gave me this task. How the hell was I supposed to know everything about her if she didn't indulge it to me?

"I think she has told me more things than she told her mentor." I told him, obviously not pointing out that maybe he should have asked someone more experienced to spy on her. "I think her life was horrible before she entered the Union, and that she'd rather die than go back to the way things were before."

"And you base all of this off of what?" He asked me back.

"Her behaviour. The things she says, or sometimes the lack thereof." I answered immediately.

"And you don't think she could fake all of that?"

She could. Athena was smart enough to. She was strong enough. But even then, my mission was to see if she did anything shady. And she hadn't.

"She hasn't done anything that would show she is a rebel." I said to him. "Realistically, if she was, this wouldn't be the time where she would take risks. She'd have to wait until she finds out about classified information so she can send that over the wall. Our personalized training schedules aren't valuable enough to risk her position over."

Jack looked at the storm in the distance too, though he hardly seemed impressed by it. Hell, it would have to be a full-blown natural disaster to impress someone like him.

"Keep an eye out." He said. "Contact me if she contacts rebels."

I wobbled back to the bus thinking about our conversation. Athena was my friend more so than Teryn or any of the people I went to school with. She knew my secrets, all except for one, there was no way she was a rebel. She just couldn't be.

14

Weeks went by. My ankle healed up normally, within no time I went back to training my sprinting with Ulric, while Alder taught Weston how to shoot better. Most of the apprentices were on edge after the stimulation. We were counting down the days since, to see when the next batch of people would be cut. But it seemed like either the hunters were in no hurry, or we all pulled through.

That wasn't the case though. It was late one night when I heard the familiar sound of a bus pull up through the gate. I had left my window open a little to let some fresh air in, so I could even hear people greeting each other.

I got out of my warm bed and looked out of the window. I was right, a bus had pulled up, but with the exception of the driver, it was still empty. I didn't know if I was even allowed to see this, so I put the flame out of the candle that was on my nightstand and peeked out of the window.

People were starting to come pouring out of the building in one straight line. It was too damn dark! I couldn't make out faces. They were all accompanied by what I figured were their mentors. Most of them were comforting each other, while some were so far apart they didn't even look like they knew one another.

I made it, I didn't get cut. But who did?

There were limited streetlights outside, they were only placed at strategic points to save energy. As luck would have it, the bus had stopped underneath one, I could see who went in, one by one.

The first was Kyon. I felt a pang of guilt in my chest, I had been the one who shot him so quickly in the mission, that must have weighed heavily on his evaluation.

Still, I had not really befriended him because of his hatred of Athena. He was one of the few people who still really had it out for her. He hugged his mentor once and got on the bus, not looking back at the building that had been his home for months.

The next to go on was Jai. He didn't seem very eager to say anything to his mentor. I had spoken to him multiple times, mostly because Jai had befriended Teryn early on. I had trained with him, and I had been able to beat him.

Weston climbed on to the bus. He batted no eye towards Ulric, who almost looked like he cared. It wasn't like him, he doesn't really show emotion. Deep down I had expected Weston to be on the next bus home. He simply wasn't the brightest of people, and his fighting left something to be desired. Still, I wanted him to succeed so Ulric could succeed.

Lastly was Conall. I must admit, this one surprised me. He had beaten me on the day of the mission and had proven himself to be an excellent fighter. He hugged his mentor tightly and grinned at him. He hardly seemed heartbroken, unlike the others.

I was ready to get back into bed when I noticed that Conall was not the last person to go on the bus. There were two more people standing just outside the light. They were talking calmly before one of them stepped forward and took one last glance at the building behind him.

Teryn.

My first reaction was to go down the stairs and run after him. There must be some sort of mistake. Teryn is a great fighter, he is smart and he beat me multiple times, fair and square.

He also had one of the most horrible mentors here. One who was so focused on the internal competition between the mentors that he cared little for his apprentice.

I didn't know if he could see me, though his eyes brushed over my window. He then turned around and got on the bus.

The bus left faster than my legs could register that I had to run after it. I had to make them see that they made a horrible, stupid mistake. It wasn't until after the bus left through the gate, and the mentors had long gone back inside, that the feeling in my legs returned.

I had to understand why. I would never be able to go back to sleep anyway. I burst through my door and ran down the hall to the ground floor. Maybe one of the mentors would be able to tell me everything?

I only got to the third floor when I ran into someone. Ulric looked absolutely defeated as he walked back to his room. He didn't even acknowledge me, though I had not tried to conceal my footsteps.

"Ulric." I called out for him. He turned around, quickly getting his face back in check.

"Hey, what are you doing out so late?" He tried to sound light-hearted like he had just come back from training instead of watching his apprentice being sent away.

"I saw what happened outside," I said, walking a bit closer to him. "Why did they send Weston away?" We were going to his room, I had been there a few times before. It was an absolute mess compared to Alder's. Ulric didn't really mind clutter, as long as he could sleep in his bed and drink coffee at his table, he was content.

"He was at his limit." He told me. "No matter what we tried he wouldn't improve anymore." His voice trembled a bit, though I highly doubt if he would cry. All of us had really bonded with our mentors. They were our closest allies in all of this, besides the other apprentices. Alder had definitely pushed me to do my best. They hadn't been lying when we were told that the mentors liked to get competitive.

I was wrong, his room wasn't a mess anymore. It hardly looked like anyone lived here now.

There was only one duffle bag on the desk, but it told me everything I needed to know.

"You're leaving." I said. It was hard to hide my sadness about it in my voice. Though it seemed like neither of us really wanted to admit what we were feeling. He was still trying his best to look like he did not care at all.

"Tomorrow morning." He said. "To the Darkfort."

I didn't know what to tell him. I wanted to tell him to stay, but it was futile. He took orders from Jack, he would be leaving no matter how much I begged him to stay. I was losing two close friends in one night, and it was a little more than my heart could take.

The silence in the room was thick. Ulric just leaned against the table, staring at me and waiting on me to make the first move. Words were completely failing me, I couldn't think of anything to say to him.

There were too many things going on inside my head. I wanted to tell him that I'd miss him but I was afraid that he would never say it back. I wanted to kiss him, but I could not dare to look so weak. I had fought too hard for my place here.

I turned around with the full intention to leave. However, the moment I touched the doorknob I felt his hand on my shoulder.

He hugged me tightly to his chest. It wasn't the kiss I wanted, but somehow it told me more than enough. I did not think of Teryn, Weston or any of the others I had left behind.

15

Ulric left that morning, along with many of the other mentors. I wasn't too upset to see the likes of Greyson leave, and neither were many of the remaining mentors. Greyson had been training the top apprentices for years on end, they were happy to see him 'fail'.

I was in a bad mood for most of the following days. Not only had Teryn, my partner in crime since the military, been cut out. I also had managed to make my relationship with Ulric incredibly confusing.

I never dated anyone. I kissed a boy once, but I hated it. It felt like he was trying to suck my tongue out of my mouth, instead of kissing me. I also got in a lot of trouble with my brothers. So in the end, it wasn't even worth it.

I wonder what my family would think if they saw me now. Had I changed much? I definitely managed to grow some muscle thanks to Alder, but that was about the only change I could tell. My hair was still the same frizzy mess it was when I left, and I hadn't really been able to practise any social skills here.

I was, quite literally, knocked back into reality by Alder. He had hit me square across the face, even though I would have easily been able to dodge it had I not been daydreaming.

"What has gotten into you?" He asked me after I fell down on my ass. "Are we back to week one? Have I time travelled?"

"Get off my case." I snapped at him, standing back up and going for the attack. I tried to punch him back, but he deflected my fist and moved aside. I had to take a few steps to regain my balance, which was, of course, all it takes for Alder to get me back down on my ass again.

"I am serious Julia." He calmly said after I had tried to attack him again. "You're distracted and moody. Tell me why."

"It's nothing." I answered. I purposely had not told a single soul about the Ulric. Who would even understand? Athena wouldn't get the appeal of liking people, she had only just grasped the concept of friendship. Alder would only get weird about it, probably giving me another lecture on how I was bringing my future in jeopardy if I carried on like that.

"Is it because of Teryn?" Alder guessed. It seemed like we had an understanding that I wouldn't talk about the apprentices leaving because he cut me slack last time and told me where I was standing. "Did you like him?"

"As a friend." I immediately told him. "Why did he get cut anyway?"

"He was going to get cut the first time if Greyson hadn't promised improvement." Alder said. "Teryn cracked under pressure. Both during the first and second simulation. He wouldn't be able to carry out a mission beyond the fence."

"Where is he going?" I had to ask.

"Factory." Alder said. "The other workplaces wouldn't take him when we showed the reason we let him go."

He's going to factory, the one place he hated more than anything. Maybe he'd get placed with Elska. They could get married and have wonderfully large babies. I needed to believe that fantasy, that in the end they would both end up happy and not with their dreams crushed.

"Did I get brought up again?" I asked. Greyson must have wanted to retaliate. The old guy never really was fond of my friendship with his apprentice. He thought I distracted him too much.

"No, Ulr-" He started but quickly stopped himself. "The person who called you out the first time seemed to have started liking you."

"Ulric?" I knew what I heard. No other name here started with Ul.

"Yeah." Alder eventually gave in. "He was the one who brought you up the first time. He didn't the second time though."

Ulric almost caused me to get sent away the first time. The same Ulric who I had definitely developed feelings for only a few weeks later. Sure, we hadn't been friends before we started training together, but did he really just sell me out because he wanted to be the only one who was good at running? It was one of the worst specialities to have anyway. Why would anyone want to team up with someone who is a good runner instead of something useful, like a good shot or a good fighter?

I could tell Alder was studying my face. I also know that Alder is not a moron and that he would never 'accidently' spill something important like that. He knew what he was doing. He knew there was something going on.

"You know that thing about trust you told me?" I said, staring at him blankly. "Mentors need to be able to trust their apprentices during their training."

"Yes?" He said, still looking as innocent as ever.

"Trust should go both ways." I dropped the roll of tape I was holding and walked off, making sure to slam the door loudly, so the whole building could hear it.

Ulric betrayed me, and he never even told me about it. I could understand that he did it, we weren't friends then, but how long was he going to wait to tell me? Would he ever? I thought back to all those nights in my room, where he would tell me about missions he went on or give me advice on training. We had become close, I saw him as a friend, and he had betrayed me.

And then there was Alder. I don't know what he was trying to get at, but that wasn't the way to do it. Not if he wanted to stay my favourite person in this building.

I didn't know what to do with myself. I also did not want to talk to anyone just yet. I jogged back up to my room and grabbed the coat I never used. Running cleared my mind, and that way I was still training, so I wouldn't feel so guilty later.

I had to climb the fence to enter the forest. There was no other way out of the compound's ground beside the gate, and I doubt the guards would let me go without at least informing one person.

I started my run off slowly, though my angry mind was tempted to go faster. I had to force myself to listen to the rational part of my brain. If I start too fast I could get into trouble later. I didn't know these woods, so I needed to be extra careful of my surroundings.

The trees were pretty dense, I had to watch out or I'd straight on walk into them, and I don't think my confidence could take that right now.

The air was cold, even though it was heading towards noon already. The leaves covered me from most of the rain that had started slowly coming down. It wasn't enough for me to get soaked by, but it did nothing to lighten my mood.

It's funny how I was literally running away from my problems, yet they always followed me in my mind. I would try to clear it of thoughts completely, but then Ulric's running tips would come up in my head, closely followed by his betrayal and Alder's snooping.

After I ran for far longer than I should have, I leaned against a tree to catch my breath. It was at that moment that something odd happened. I had only touched this jacket once before in my life, which was when I put the small device Jack gave me in it. I had not stopped to think about it as I ran. But now, for the first time ever, it made a sound.

The device had been on standby mode, as it was programmed, because I shoved it in the back of a dark closet. Now that it was outside, it had managed to generate some energy again.

I fished it out of my pocket and saw a weird envelope symbol on the main screen. When I pressed down on the large button it opened revealing a message I was incredibly glad to receive with only a seven-hour delay.

> *'Watch Athena closely, she will make her move now.*
> *JA'*

Jack had been wary of Athena's intention for a long time, I knew that. But never to the point of reaching out to me through this. Something must be happening. Something big enough to involve us.

It took me some time to figure out the typing, but I wrote him back.

> *'What is happening? What do I look out for?''*

It didn't take Jack long to write me back. It looked like he spends far more time sending messages like this.

> *'You will hear it soon. Watch her carefully, only report odd*
> *behaviour to me.'*

I will hear it soon. With that in mind, I started my run back to the compound, hoping that I wasn't too late.

16

When I returned nothing had changed. The rain was still coming down in a light drizzle. Every exercise room I passed had voices coming out of them, alongside with occasional punches or gunshots. Somehow, I had imagined that people would be on red alert, that half the kingdom would be up in flames already. But life still seemed undisturbed.

I returned to my room. I knew Alder must have come here, I was at least ninety percent sure that I had left the door to my closet opened, yet now it was closed.

I locked my door, something I almost never did, and plumped down on my bed. Another thing Alder did, he made my bed. I could tell because I would never be able to get it this neat, but the clean freak could.

"Where did you go?" Alder asked through the door. Was I going to give him the silent treatment? It seemed childish yet entirely fair in this situation. I did not want to speak to him, couldn't he tell by the locked door?

He tried the handle, before knocking against the door. "I know you're in there, I saw you enter."

Silent treatment. I would just ignore him. I closed my eyes and laid on my side, maybe I could take a nap. I haven't done it since I was a toddler. Maybe I could have actually fallen asleep, had it not been for Alder outside my door.

"Fine then." He said. I heard him leaning against the door, then a soft sliding sound told me he sat down. The small digital clock in my room told me it would be at least another hour until lunch started. Maybe I should skip it, I know Alder won't. He would never skip on a meal.

I brushed my finger over my tattoo. I had not really looked at it all that often. It felt like it was fake. Like it was temporary, as it had been for Teryn and all the others. The tattoo had healed up well and looked identical to the ones all the other hunters had.

I heard some movement outside my door and figured Alder had finally given up. I closed my eyes again, trying to go to sleep.

A key slid into the other side of my lock. Alder entered my room, luckily for him he didn't look too smug about it though. I might have thrown something at him if he did.

"You know a locked door means 'please for once in my life give me some privacy' right?" I told him. He closed the door behind him and sat down on the edge of my bed. I turned my back to him and kept my eyes focused on the plain, white wall in front of me.

"I am sorry about Ulric." He said to me. "I just think that you don't realize the consequences."

"And what might those be?" I asked, making sure that my voice sounded as hateful as I could. Did I actually hate him? Of course not, but he definitely wasn't on any of my favourite lists right now.

"You are doing so well. The leaders, Jack, they are really starting to see you as a hunter, and not as a girl." There was an air of tension once he mentioned Jack. I hadn't told him why he wanted to talk to me after the simulation. The day after he had just ignored it and went on with his training as nothing had ever happened. Still, we never mentioned Jack.

"If you start a relationship with someone, they'll see you as a girl again." He said. "As a distraction."

"No one in the hunters is married?" I asked him. I had been wondering about it for some time, but no one here seemed to be dating anyone. They didn't get visits, nor did they seem to write any letters.

"A few." He admitted. "Mason and Bryan are dating, they are both hunters." He said. "Some have wives in the towns nearby the fence. They only see them a few times a year."

"Are you married?" Alder had not really told me anything about his past. I didn't even know where he was from, or what his parents did. He was even more secretive about it than Athena, who occasionally gave me hints.

"No." He laughed.

"Right, who'd be stupid enough to marry you?" The tension faded away as we both laughed. Alder was just worried about me. He wasn't, like most hunters, the most touchy-feely type of guy. He wanted what was best for me and had no idea how to voice that to me.

I sat back up, driven by both guilt and a new-found trust, and reached inside the pocket of my jacket. I grabbed the device, though I didn't give it to him.

"Where did you get that?" He asked me.

"Jack." I told him. "He gave me a mission. That's why he wanted to talk to me after the simulation, so I could give him an update."

Alder studied both me and the small device for a few seconds. "I won't ask what the mission is, you did well with keeping it a secret. I had no idea." He looked almost proud of me. "Why did you tell me now?"

"Guilt." I said. "And... I think something is happening."

"Like what?" He asked me.

"He has never contacted me before," I said. "He just did, he told me to focus solely on my mission, and that I would 'hear what was happening soon'." Alder glanced back at the device. "Please tell me it's just another simulation."

"It's not. We don't have anything planned for another five months." He said. "I didn't hear anything odd either."

"Maybe it's not something big." I tried comforting myself. "I mean why would he tell me before he tells any of you?"

"I don't know," Alder said. He got up from my bed and walked towards the door. "I'll go to the communication room, see if we got anything. You just... Stay here." He glanced towards a few books I had already read on my desk. "Study."

The communication room was located on the roof of the building. It was a small room build later on, it looked incredibly out-of-place. Inside were a bunch of computers, and other devices that could transmit messages to other compounds, both military and hunter.

I had no need to reread any of the books on my desk, they were all about engineering because I hated that and Alder figured I should get better at it. I glanced outside my window. The guards were playing some sort of card game, and no one was around for miles.

I reread Jack's messages. I had been the one who told Jack that if Athena was a rebel, she would only strike once properly important information arose. Which means that he would only risk me being seen with this mission if it did. He had no idea if I kept the device on me at all times, or if I stuffed it into the back of my closet.

The grey sky seemed more ominous. My bad mood had gotten replaced by a worried one, what the hell was going on?

Alder did not return to my room. I did not know if that was bad. It meant that he had found something in the communication room, though it could also mean that he was waiting there for something to happen.

I am guessing it did. Before lunch even started, a loud alarm went off inside the compound.

It sounded somewhere similar to the foghorn used in the mission, but it got repeated over and over again. I remember being told by Alder that the alarm could mean two things: An inbound attack on either us or somewhere else in the kingdom. Both those things meant that we had to come together in the dining hall.

There was no way of knowing how inbound the inbound attack was. I grabbed my knife and put it in the sheath of my belt, just for some extra security, and headed out.

The halls reminded me of the first simulation. The bright lights had cut out and instead the emergency lights were on. They were dark green, so our black clothes could blend in easily.

My heart was beating in my throat. The alarm covered all other sounds. I could not hear if anyone was approaching, or if I was as alone as I felt. My hand constantly hovered over my knife, ready to grab it if I saw someone.

My knife throwing had at least been better than my shooting. The problem with it was that I only had one knife and that it would never be enough if this was a real attack.

"Julia," someone called out. Athena was standing there. Her room was on the fourth floor too, yet she was without her mentor. "What is going on?"

"I don't know," I answered. "Maybe a simulation?"

If Athena was a rebel, she would know exactly what was going on. Jack's messages kept on popping up in my mind. Though in my heart I still believed that Athena just had a rough go of it out there and was as dead set on becoming a hunter as I was. I had already long forgiven her on taking one of the places in the apprenticeship. She deserved it just as much as we did.

"Where is Ferik?" I asked her as we walked down the stairs. She had also gotten her knife, though it did not look used.

"Early lunch." She said to me. "I didn't feel like joining him."

Ferik and Athena had a rocky relationship. She did not respect him because she could easily beat him in a fight, and he did not respect her because inside the fence no one is illiterate. He thought she was a moron for struggling with it.

Athena was now able to read, though not any long words yet. Her accent had also slowly started to fade out more and more, though that could also be because I stopped noticing it.

We made our way to the dining hall without encountering anyone. When we entered, we were greeted by most of the apprentices already, and a few confused mentors. I noted how Alder wasn't there yet, and that most of the older mentors weren't here either.

It was an unwritten rule of the hunters that the older ones receive more respect. Experience is everything out there, newbies can't be expected to make well-informed decisions without having gone through it first. Alder wasn't as old as some of the other ones, but he was incredibly smart. Ulric told me a rumour that Jack wanted to train him for command. I hoped it was true, he would make an amazing leader.

I did what Jack asked and kept close to Athena. Of course, that wasn't as hard as it was before. When we started here there were fifteen apprentices with fifteen mentors, now there were only eight apprentices left. We had all become a close-knit group.

"This isn't a simulation." Athena whispered in my ear. It was clear that it wasn't. Our mentors were smiling when we went on simulations, they were whispering advice in our ears, they acted weird days beforehand. Now, they were all grouped together, speaking in hushed whispers, each of them looking worried.

Alder entered, followed by the remaining few mentors who were missing. Alder looked confident in his step, while the others weren't too sure.

They looked mortified. They were probably looking pale too if it hadn't been for the green light. I counted seven mentors, which meant one was still missing.

It was Antheas that was not here, one of the younger mentors. Devin, his apprentice, seemed to notice too and was looking around worriedly. Alder met my eye for a second and tried to smile reassuringly, though he didn't really pull it off.

"We have been training you the past year to become hunters." Alder started, the room instantly became silent. "You are supposed to be training for four more years before going on any solo missions. However, something came up."

"We received intel from one of our spies beyond the fence that a rebel organisation is planning an attack on the royal family. Tomorrow night. Let me put the emphasis on this, had the Darkfort been closer, we would not be doing this. This is not a test to show your worth, this is not a simulation. If you mess this up, someone in the royal family may die. Which is a huge win for the radiates, and something we can't afford."

The doors to the dining hall opened, and Antheas came out carrying three duffel bags. He put them down on the table and unzipped them, they were filled with guns and knives.

"In six minutes, we will be entering vehicles outside. Return to your rooms and put on fresh clothes and get ready for a long journey." He finished. Everyone immediately ran back out. It would take me at least two minutes to reach the top floor if I walked. Instead, I sprinted up closely followed by Athena.

Athena. I could not let her go to her room alone. She could have the same sort of device in her room like the one I have.

"I just put my laundry in." I lied to her. "I have about the same sizes as you, can I borrow?"

"Yeah sure, this way." She did not hesitate, her voice did not falter. I felt a pang of guilt about lying to her. But then Jack's mean face resurfaced in my head, and I didn't feel as bad anymore. Maybe it's not a bad thing that I am lying to her. Maybe everything I find out can be used to build a case for her, not against her.

Her room was about the same as mine. Neither of us received any tokens from home, like Teryn and some of the others had. It was just a plain room with no decorations, with the exception of the words all the hunters had painted on their walls. She handed me a pair of fresh clothes and immediately undressed.

"Three minutes left." She said as we quickly undressed. Her clothes were a bit tighter than mine, but I could still move around easily because of the stretchy fabric. It was all I had been wearing since I joined the military, workout clothes. We haven't received any uniforms or anything, we weren't in the hunters just yet. We didn't have time to do anything about our hair. So instead we just put the things we needed in our pockets and ran back down.

We were the only two with rooms on the top floor, so we were the last ones down. We did not travel by bus this time, instead there were five black, government-issued cars waiting outside the doorstep. Alder ushered us into the last one and closed the door behind us.

We immediately took off, driving faster than I had ever seen a vehicle go. The trees flew by our windows in a blur an it seemed like the rain didn't even hit us anymore.

Alder was in the front seat, next to the driver. One seat behind him was Ferik and another behind that were Athena and I. Ferik turned around, handing us both a handgun and an assault rifle. Ferik wasn't as good as hiding his emotions as Alder was, though they were about the same age.

"Why do we need these?" I asked. Ferik pretended like he didn't hear me. Alder adjusted the sniper rifle on his lap and turned around for a brief moment.

"Reassurance." He just said. His voice sounded tense, though he tried to play it off with a kind smile.

We did not need to talk about a strategy of watching our surroundings, it came logically. Alder kept his eyes straight forward. Ferik was looking out of the left side. Athena was sitting on my right, so she checked that while I turned around in my chair and watched our backs.

I understood why Alder had the need to tell us to get ready for a long journey. We didn't just sit back and watch the scenery fly by. We were constantly looking for threats. So much so that the entire minute I spend putting my hair up in a high ponytail I felt wave after wave of panic wash over me, even though I could still look outside.

"There!" Athena said. Everyone immediately looked to the right, though she was pointing at a car ahead of us. About two cars further to the front someone had rolled down their window and a gun barrel was sticking out.

"What is happening Creed?" Alder said into a small radio, that had been silent the entire time.

The barrel was obviously following something, it moved as the car moved, though no immediate response came. "Julia, keep watching our backs. Ferik, take the left, Athena look for a possible target." I don't think I ever heard Alder talk so rapidly

It was hard to keep my focus, knowing that an attack might come from our right at any time. I found myself bracing for it already, though nothing was happening. The car remained eerily silent.

I shouldn't have, but I peeked. Both Alder and Athena were looking out the car window, though Alder was doing it through his scope. The driver was also tense, he kept on glancing towards Alder.

The driver was a factory worker, his block tattoo told us so. It was one of the better jobs to have and required loads of training on how to handle the car, and the people in it, properly. The man must have been in his sixties already, his wrinkly hands were gripping the steering wheel tightly.

"False alarm." The radio eventually croaked.

"What was it?" Alder asked. The radio was quiet for a few seconds.

"A deer most likely." It answered. Alder cursed loudly and relaxed a bit in his chair. We rolled our windows back up and continued our journey.

<h1 style="text-align:center">17</h1>

We arrived early the next morning after a mostly sleepless night. The sun had just started to rise into the sky when we entered a dark tunnel, dipping us into darkness once again.

If I would remember anything from this trip, it would be when we drove past the shore. Alder told me that it wasn't even the full ocean we saw, there was still land in the way for that. But it did not matter to me, I had never seen that big of a lake, nor had I seen people fishing. They used wooden sticks and strings to catch the fish. I thought they would do that with nets, but apparently this way was better. I had never gotten to eat fish, it was too expensive to get shipped so far inland. Besides, our teachers warned us that the oceans are filled with radiation.

It was unclear if the tunnels underneath Vancouver had been there before the war or not. I heard a rumour that they were once used for something as simple as the transportation of mail. Now they were solely used by the military and the hunters.

Vancouver wasn't just the capital and the home of the royal family, it was also used as the political centre of the kingdom. The city housed the hundreds of politicians when they weren't dispatched into their designated towns and cities. A successful attack here could leave the kingdom defenceless.

I had kept an eye on Athena, whenever I could spare one. She didn't look like she knew this was happening. She hadn't washed her white hair the day before, leaving it almost greasy looking. Halfway into the night, she fell asleep, only to wake up a few minutes later and focus on scanning the lands that were rapidly passing us by. I would judge her for falling asleep if I hadn't done the same thing only moments later.

It was clearly important that we got into the city unseen. Otherwise, we would have been able to take a more direct route. Eventually, after a good twenty minutes of driving down the tight tunnels, the cars stopped, and we got out.

The tunnels had gotten too small for the cars to continue. We were clearly in the old parts of the city. The tunnels didn't look as sturdy anymore either, some of them had deep cracks in them.

We were given clothes from one of the trunks. They were the clothes of the wealthy. We were all given pants made of the finest material as well as a shirt. Though the boys received different ones than the one Athena and I got. Ours was much longer and resembled something more of a dress. We were told to leave our weapons behind, all except for our knives, which I hid underneath the dress.

I wasn't claustrophobic, at least I had never shown any signs of it, but I couldn't help like feeling that there was absolutely no air in here. I tried to take a deep breath, I tried to take several, but it was like my lungs refused to take in any oxygen.

The feeling only got worse and worse as we went further down the tunnels. They got even smaller, to the point where we had to walk in one straight line, we couldn't fit shoulder to shoulder anymore.

I started to feel like the small apple I ate about halfway through the night was gonna come back up. The walls were twisting and turning around me, and only getting closer and closer. I didn't know if the tunnel was actually becoming smaller again. No one spoke, we just focussed on not falling into the little stream of water that was underneath us and followed Alder.

My breathing became more rapid. I felt it happening, I knew that if I continued I would start hyperventilating, but I couldn't stop myself. I needed to get more air and breathing fast felt like the way to do it.

Eventually, the tunnel came to a round end. Three large military men guarded one single ladder. Each armed to the teeth with assault rifles and submachine guns. They all aimed them at us, before noticing our tattoos.

"Lovely weather isn't it." Alder said to them. To which one of the men nodded and mumbled some words into the radio on his shoulder. Above, the lid that covered the hole the ladder led to was removed. The room was bathed with light, but it didn't make me feel any better.

"The palace is above us." Alder informed us, finally giving us some information. His eyes scanned the crowd before they landed on me. I couldn't tell if I had started the official hyperventilating yet, but it felt like I was getting close to it.

"Julia, you go first." He said. People around me had obviously noticed my poor reaction to the tunnels and happily parted away for me. I couldn't help but feel that the military men were judging me. I was supposed to be a badass hunter, not someone who gets scared of tight spaces.

Alder wrapped his arm around my shoulder as I took the last few steps to the ladder. "After you get up, hold your breath for fifteen seconds." He whispered to me. "Breathe for twenty. Do it until you feel better."

I climbed the ladder as quickly as my trembling legs could. The room above it wasn't much better. It was dark, tiny and windowless. But anything felt better than those tunnels.

I did what Alder told me to, combining it with a few breathing tricks Ulric had told me. I still felt so panicky. My hands were shaking uncontrollably and I was sweating more than I would do in a workout. Athena was trying to comfort me, but she couldn't really figure out how to, so she just settled on staring at me until I would stop.

Before the last person was up, the door to the room opened. Antheas was the only mentor who was up yet and immediately jumped to the front of the group.

It was Dorian who had shown up. Though he was in charge of the apprenticeships he barely spends any time at home base. When he was present all he did was talk to our mentors, and not to us. He was the one who eventually decided who got cut and who didn't. The only person he'd have to answer to was Jack. He shook hands with Antheas, asking about our journey here. Obviously, Antheas did not mention the deer scare and told him that it went smoothly.

Dorian glanced around the group. Most of us already looked horrible. Some mentors had allowed more sleep in the cars than others. Especially Devin and Ryder looked like they could fall asleep any second. Dorian's eyes hanged around me for a good while. I can't imagine I looked anywhere near the 'strong apprentice' standard he had for us. I felt clammy, and his hawk eyes could probably see my shaking.

The thing I did have going for me was Athena. She had decided that people hug each other when they are comforting someone. So she had placed her hand on my back. I at least looked like I was listening to Jack's mission and keeping a watchful eye on her, though I wasn't sure if Dorian was even aware of that mission. I figured Jack would have told him. After all, we were both apprentices.

Alder came up last. He spoke in quiet whispers to Dorian, who then took over the lead. Alder hung back, waiting for me to catch up to him.

"You never told me you were claustrophobic." He whispered to me.

"I didn't know. It never happened before." I answered him. More mentors had started to check up on their apprentices. Not all of them got to be in the same car as each other.

"It's fine. We'll work on it." He said. Dorian kept walking at a steady pace. Clearly, he knew where he was going. We had come up in the basement of the palace, and by the looks of it somewhere in a forgotten corner too.

"You'd make a good leader." I said to Alder, smiling at his surprised face. "I'm serious. I'd listen to you and I actually know you're a moron, the others might not even know that."

"I have no aspirations to lead." He answered me. There was something gleaming in his eyes. Normally he'd laugh and retaliate when I called him a moron. Now he seemed lost in thoughts. Before resurfacing as his serious self.

"This mission, all of this here, it is going to uncover some things." He said to me, speaking even more on a hushed tone, so no one around could hear. "Some things not a lot of people know yet. Please just... just remember who I am okay?"

I wanted to comment on it, but Dorian stopped the group in front of two large doors. I looked back at Alder. Maybe it wasn't worry about the mission ahead he had sketched on his face, but more self-preservation. There was something here he wanted to keep hidden from me or the hunters in general.

"We will now enter the main palace building." Dorian warned us. "The radiates will have spies, they can't know that we are here. That's why you will be wearing this over your tattoo." He held up a tube. Inside was something slightly pink-tinted. I had read about it before. People used to call it 'foundation' before the war. This one, however, had been enhanced. It changed to the skin colour of the person wearing it and was thick enough to cover our deep, black tattoos.

In groups of two and three people went out of the room, after they had applied the mixture to their skin. It didn't burn, it just smelled kind of odd. But it was nothing compared to the nerves I felt.

This was my first ever real mission. I had to at least redeem myself from my poor reaction in the tunnels, I wanted to look like I fit in. I made sure I got paired with Alder, and together we walked into the busy halls of the castle.

The door itself did not stand out at all, I'm sure dozens of people pass by it every day without noticing it. The trick was to look like I belonged here. Which was far from true. I was from the countryside, I had never even seen a city this big, let alone a palace. It was hard not to just stare at all the old paintings that were hung on the walls like they were worthless children's drawings, nor at the golden details in the ceiling and floor.

The people built the palace long after the war as a gift to the family of James Alexander. The family was still heavily involved in politics, until eventually one of them got crowned king. I could see why they did that, this place was only fit for royalty.

It was the easiest for Alder and me to act like a couple. We did not look related. It also helped in the way that he could lead me. It would look like he was just whispering something sweet into my ear, when he really told me to stop staring around like a fish in a bowl and blend in more.

I had taken my hair out of the ponytail. I did not know any rich people. I had only seen paintings of the royal family. They always just let their hair flow lose, so that's what I would do too.

The bottom floor of the palace was easily accessible for the people of the city to visit. It gets used as a city hall, however, only the rich have the money to live in the capital. I noticed how not a whole lot of people had tattoos in their necks.

The rich never took the interview. Especially the ones born into royalty or high up on the social ladder. Their official job titles were politician, but I don't think they ever worked a day in their lives.

We went up one floor. The guards did not bat an eye towards us, though they did grip their guns tightly, which I doubt they do every day. The palace guard uniform was simple and easy to recognize. They had on the standard military blazer, realistically they won't have to do a lot of fighting, with long fitted pants. They were all dressed in a vibrant red colour, so if something happens they are easy to locate if you need help.

The staircase was nothing like the one back at the home base. That one was made out of stone with most of the steps being worn out by all the commotion that happened around the base. The one in the palace did not look like it got used all that often. It was made of marble, and like everything else here, it had golden details.

There was a major difference between the ground floor and the first floor. We did not encounter nearly as many people here. The ones who we did pass by looked at us with distaste like they were far superior. I even caught several of them speaking different languages, something I had never heard before. There was only one language in the entire Union, with maybe a variation in some accents.

We went up to another floor. Again, the red guards did not ask any questions. I noticed how Alder gave them a small nod, yet they seemed to have their eyes focused on me. It would make sense, Alder looked like he belonged here, while I looked like I was the freeloader.

We weren't on the top floor yet, but this part of the castle was only reserved for guests. At the end of the hallway, we took a sharp right and entered a ballroom.

The people who had exited the room before us were mostly all in here. A few took a major detour and were coming in after us. If anyone would enter, it would just look like a meet-up point for the guests of the king.

It took a good thirty minutes for everyone to arrive. We were very much secluded, no one even passed our room with the exception of the hunters who knew where to go. Athena was one of the last to enter and immediately broke away from her mentor to stand near me.

"You okay?" She asked me, eyeing Alder. Athena had quite a few problems with her mentor and therefore did not understand why I got along with Alder so well. As far as I knew she was one of the few who didn't really get along with her mentor, the rest of us all had formed tight friendships.

"Yeah, I just hated it down there." I played it off. I doubt the fearless Athena would understand. I don't even fully get it yet. I had never been forced into such a small space before, I didn't realize the effect it had on me.

Dorian entered as the last one. He didn't have his tattoo covered, nor did he change out of his black uniform. It wouldn't really matter for him anyway, Dorian was stationed in the palace most of the time. People would recognize him either way. He locked the door behind him and returned to a fully silent group.

"As you may realize, tomorrow is Kingsday." Dorian said to us. "Which means tonight the king will throw his annual feast. As always, he has invited plenty of lords and ladies as well as a few new guests. Royals from overseas."

I never celebrated Kingsday, no one in my area did. It was the day of James Alexander's birthday, and it celebrated the royal family.

It wasn't something you'd celebrate when the royals were hundreds of miles away, as well as them never caring about the poor. I didn't even know they held a feast here, though it hardly surprised me. It also meant that next week my brother Arthur would be taking his interview.

"We will be posing as guests, as well as palace guards. Now, the king," Dorian clearly looked annoyed. "Insisted that we treat everyone the same, and not solely focus our attention on our royal family. He emphasized the importance of overseas relationships for the growth of the kingdom."

"Now, we are all going to act as though we care about them too. But if you find yourself in a situation where you must either protect the prince or a foreign guest. I trust you all to choose the prince." He added with a gloomy grin. He had been holding a notebook in his hands. I recognized it from when I had my evaluation. It contained all of our personal strengths and weaknesses. Undoubtingly he would use it to find our ideal positions.

"Athena, Nero and Holden," he said, skipping through the pages. "You three will pose as guards. Report to the royal guard on the fifth floor for your correct placement."

Athena gave me one last look before she left. She must have realized that the leaders did not trust her. It wasn't surprising of course, but I almost thought she looked annoyed by his decision. Before I really had time to figure it out, she was gone.

"The rest of the apprentices will be posing as guests." Dorian said to us. "You will either be their distant relatives or their date for the night. Might I remind you all to not mess this up. Act like professionals and always stay alert."

He went one by one to tell us who will get paired off with whom. As always, I was the last on his list, and only the rest of the mentors remained in the hall.

"Alder puts a lot of trust in you." Dorian said to me. Most of the mentors had started talking to one another and didn't really need to know where the apprentices would be placed. We were all supposed to not know each other.

"For once, you being a girl comes in handy for us." He continued, handing me the room number I was supposed to go looking for. "You'll be with Prince Roderick for the night."

Prince Roderick. The crown prince might I add. I had seen him on paintings numerous times, I thought I would meet him once or twice in my life should I make it as a hunter. But I never dared to think that I would be his date.

"Don't mess it up." Dorian told me. I had not messed up with Athena just yet, so I am guessing the leaders really did trust me. Or at least they were forced to. He couldn't exactly place one of the mentors with the crown prince, everyone knew he liked girls.

I left the hall after sending one last pleading look towards Alder. He had obviously heard who my date for the night was. He immediately broke away from the group of mentors and went to talk to Dorian. He trusted me, but not to the point where the royal family were at stake. I wouldn't trust me with that either.

I walked to my destination very slowly. For one, it was because I couldn't find it. But I also was hoping that someone would come chase after me and tell me it was all a mistake.

I took a deep sigh and tried to appear more professional. I wasn't here as his date, I was here as his bodyguard.

18

I knocked twice on the big doors. With some help of the guards in the castle, I found the room I was looking for. Most of them stared at me oddly, the room was obviously located in the royal living quarters, and I sure didn't look the part just yet.

The sun was now fully up, the streets surrounding the castle were crawling with people, who were getting ready for another day of work. Maybe they got some time off here to celebrate Kingsday. Factory workers definitely didn't, but I wouldn't put it past the politicians to take time off whenever they could.

The door opened and a servant boy, who could be no older than ten, looked at me with big eyes. Behind him, was the prince.

Prince Roderick was somewhere in his twenties, I knew that, though he looked like he was much older already. He had brown hair that just brushed over his shoulders and a thick, brown beard that covered up most of his face.

"Let her in." The prince said to his servant, to which the boy politely stepped aside.

"Your grace." I greeted, bowing for him. I had gotten a brief rundown from Alder on how to treat royals. Though that was months ago already and he had told me I wouldn't be meeting them for years to come.

"What is your name?" He asked me. He stood upright, the proper stance for a king.

"Julia Thorne, sir." I answered him quickly.

"How long have you been a hunter?" He asked me, folding his hands behind his back. If I didn't know better, I would think I was talking to the king right now. He definitely had trained enough to take over when his father dies.

"I have been training for about a year." I answered him truthfully. "The situation here isn't ideal, but we have to play the cards we have been dealt." The prince moved over to the table underneath his window and poured two glasses of what I could only hope was water.

"I thought the hunters did not accept women." He said, handing one of the glasses to me. It was quite possibly the fanciest glass I had ever held, it looked like it was made out of pure crystal.

"They made an exception this year," I told him. "A project of some sort. Two girls were allowed in, neither of us has been told to leave yet." I could see his eyes sizing me up. I figured someone must have told him that women were also accepted this year, but I guess it just happened to slip Dorian's mind.

"And out of the two of you, you were the better pick." He didn't ask me, he just stated it. It was a good thing that he didn't question me about it too, because I don't think I could have answered truthfully. Out of Athena and I, she was better. She was stronger, she was more fit to be a bodyguard. Sure, I had my strengths too, but especially for this role she would have been great. If Dorian had trusted her.

"Have you been to many balls, Julia?" He asked me. I took a sip of what thankfully was water and shook my head.

"This will be a first." I told him. He smiled against his glass.

"A good first time too." He smiled. "Countless foreign royals and politicians, as well as our own. Who will, of course, keep an extra close eye on you if you are my date."

I smiled as well. "Any tips then?"

"Where are you from?" He asked.

"Countryside, near the wall." I answered him. There was a small table with two chairs in the corner of the room where we sat down.

The seats were odd, instead of just wood they had some sort of pillow on it, making it softer to sit down on. It made me never want to leave this chair again, especially after the night I had.

"You should play into that." He said. "I visited the wall last month, it would make sense for me to have met someone there."

"Fair enough." I said, thinking back to the girl I was, the girls I knew, back when I lived there. Francesca, the girl who I always sat next to in class, had told me that she wanted to marry Roderick numerous times, but that she'd also settle for either of his two younger brothers. Most of the girls in my class dreamed of that, and I'd be lying if I said it hadn't crossed my mind before. I would be in a life of wealth and prosperity, with no worries about food or money like I had back then.

"Obviously we need to get you cleaned up." He said. "I'll have some madams come by."

"Madams?" I asked him.

"Right." A small smile gracing his face, making him appear younger almost instantly. "A madam is an older woman of nobility who helps with making sure the youngsters find their proper ways. This includes clothing as well." He told me. "It might be best to play your role already, they like to gossip."

He was right, the moment the three madams arrived, they did nothing but criticize me and all the other girls they had once helped. They asked me many times how the prince could be interested in a girl like me, and never really stopped the hear the answer.

I got washed under their watchful eyes, which made me feel even worse than when I had to shower with a bunch of boys watching me in the military.

The women looked me over with their hawk eyes. Especially commenting on all the little bruises and scars I had collected over my months of training. The worst thing about it was that they didn't even say it to me, they whispered it into each other's ears, thinking I couldn't hear it.

The worst out of the three was a woman named Gizelda. She told me her husband used to be lord of blablabla, and that her son had now taken over that 'influential' spot after her husband's death. She had the biggest mouth out of all of them and used it whenever she could.

My dull brown hair got combed out by a servant girl, the women still refused to touch me, who was surprisingly delicate. I usually just pull the comb through, hoping that my hair doesn't accidentally break it in half.

I would have enjoyed the pampering experience if the three women weren't there. They commented on the servant who painted my nails a vibrant red colour like she wasn't there. The girl went nearly as red as the nail polish but kept on painting them in silence. After she was done, I made sure to thank her for the great job she did on them, hoping that she could forget about the madams.

The picking of the dress was apparently incredibly important and took over two hours. Gizelda wanted me to wear a navy-blue dress, which fit tightly around my chest and only flared out around my ankles. Almarida preferred a black dress but was quickly dismissed by the other two saying that I wasn't going to a funeral. Danhia was torn between an orange dress that I could barely move around in, or a dress full of small gemstones. They couldn't know it of course, but I was looking at the best dress to conceal weapons in. I definitely needed my knife, I wouldn't leave that anywhere, and also a handgun, if not something bigger.

One of the benefits of being a prince is that you can walk in anywhere unannounced and people will still like you. If Alder had walked in on me dressing, I would probably punch him in the face. But when the prince arrived, the madams immediately were much nicer to me.

"What a lovely date you have, your grace." Danhia said to him after she had bowed. I, of course, wasn't just standing there naked, they at least had given me a bathrobe to cover up.

"I am glad to hear it." Roderick told them, kindly smiling at them. "Would you give us a moment of privacy please?"

The ladies looked like he had said something scandalous, and left almost immediately, exchanging looks amongst themselves. The servants who had helped us also left shortly after, leaving me with the prince.

"I have something for you." He said, handing me the box. Inside was a long red dress with a tight top but a long flowing skirt. The dress concealed a range of handguns and knives, as well as a note with my name on it.

"It's from Mr. Felthove." The prince said. "Instructions I believe."

Stay with Prince Roderick, go wherever he goes. The rest of the royal family is not your concern. Should an attack happen, escape with him to the tunnels and exit the city as quick as you can.

Remember to act the part.

"Well, that should be easy enough." I lied to myself. I was only tasked with ensuring the future of the royal family. He was the next in line after all. Roderick didn't look concerned in the slightest.

"This is not the first time rebels try to kill my family," he told me. "It will not be the last time either. They have never been successful. The royal guard ensures it."

I decided not to tell him the small amount of training they receive and just smiled. "I'm pretty sure that I am the one who is supposed to keep you calm."

"I will be king one day." He said, puffing his chest out proudly. "I always need to keep my calm."

"Thank you, for this." I said, gesturing towards the dress and weapons. "I was beginning to wonder how I am supposed to be walking in the dresses they laid out for me."

"What did you tell the madams about yourself?" He asked me.

"My name, where I was from, that we met when you visited us and invited me here." I told him. "I tried to look pretty naïve about everything."

"That's good." He said. I noticed him glancing at my bathrobe before straightening up again. "See you tonight, Julia."

I was forced to spend the entire day with the three madams, getting ready for the feast tonight. I got the quick rundown on how to dance properly, eat properly and act like a lady. The three women were not convinced that I could do it in the end, but they were forced to leave and get ready themselves.

I wore the red dress and even received a diamond necklace to go with it. My unmanageable hair was somehow working with me today and looked slightly okay, though not nearly as good as most of the women who actually lived in the capital. I applied more foundation over the tattoo, and soon enough there was a knock on my door.

The prince wore a suit that looked like it was made just to fit him and no one else. His hair had been cut a bit shorter than when I last saw him, and his beard seemed to be trimmed too.

"Everyone is ready downstairs." He told me and handed me a small box.

"Another gift?" I asked.

"From Mr. Felthove again." He said, looking to the box with as much anticipation as I had. Inside was a small bracelet that fit the necklace, design wise. It didn't make sense for Dorian to care this much about fashion choices. It fit around my wrist perfectly. The moment the little clasp clicked together, it showed that Dorian indeed had other intentions.

Inside a few of the, fake, diamonds were small projectors. They put little blue letters on my wrist, almost looking like another tattoo. It now read 'this will be your contact with the control centre' before flashing off again.

"I see the funding to the hunter-engineering lab paid off." Roderick said, reading the message with me. "Ready to go?"

I was absolutely not. Alder was a great mentor who could teach me the entire history of the world in one afternoon and I'd remember it all. The madams were different. They all cackled through each other and gave me contradicting advice.

We walked through the halls in silence. He had linked his arm with me and nodded towards several of the guards we passed. "Nervous?" Roderick guessed.

"I'd rather be in a gunfight right now." I said to him.

"Well, how about a deal?" We slowly walked down one flight of stairs. I hadn't worn heels before and found them to be incredibly inconvenient. They would be the first thing I take off if the radiates come in. "You keep me safe from the rebels, and I'll keep you safe from the guests."

"Sounds about fair." I laughed.

The feast was held in a giant ballroom. A proper logistical nightmare, there were at least six entrances, not even counting the massive row of windows.

There was a small group of harpists playing on one of two stages. The other one was occupied with one long table, seating the royal family.

The portrait that had haunted me my entire life was incredibly inaccurate. The king was much older than they had painted him, and clearly not as strong anymore. One of his sons was not a warrior either but seemed more interested in eating food. The queen was also much older, her hair had turned grey even though the portrait always had it painted as gold.

People parted away for Roderick like he was the plague himself. They looked at him with admiration, while they looked at me like I was a nobody. Which I, of course, was compared to the crown prince.

"Mother, father, this is Julia." He introduced me. They obviously knew exactly who I was. Dorian must have reported everything about me in detail to them. Otherwise, I would have never been allowed to pose as his date.

"Welcome to Vancouver." The king shook my hand, he had the same kind of smile Roderick had. A careless one, with the ability to un-age him.

Roderick had two brothers. Prince Elijah and Prince Cludius. Cludius was no warrior at all, but Elijah had taken up a spot in the military. I don't think he had to do any of the training I had to in my short-lived military career, because he was not much older than me but was already called 'commander'.

The king and queen sat in the middle of the table, on tall, throne-like chairs. On their left was Prince Cludius with his wife, while Prince Roderick and I got seated directly to their right, with Prince Elijah sitting next to me.

During dinner, loads of people came up to the king and queen to either greet them, give them gifts or to talk about current affairs.

It seemed exhausting, every time I wanted to dig in on the delicious food a new person showed up, and I had to be introduced all over again.

I eventually located nearly everyone I knew in the room. I couldn't find Alder though, or he at least hadn't shown up to greet the king yet.

Prince Roderick was nice to me, occasionally grabbing my hand and telling me that I was doing great. To outsiders, it might have looked endearing, but for me it was one of the few things keeping me calm.

Really, I preferred a gunfight over this.

After we had eaten, everyone made their way over to a second ballroom, this one only had a few tables with foods and drinks over to the side, the main floor was reserved for dancing.

The madams had told me that the first dance was always reserved for the king and queen. So when they suddenly moved away from us to the open space I wasn't entirely surprised. What was surprising was when the song was about halfway through, Roderick guided me to the centre of the room, and joined in on the dance.

He put one of his hands on my back and with the other one held my hand tightly. There was a small orchestra producing entrancing tunes like I had never heard before.

Prince Roderick was incredibly close to me now. Too close, it felt like I was breaking some sort of rule just by touching him. I had put my hand on his shoulder and let him guide me through it. All the knowledge about dancing the madams had told me seemed to be seeping away from my brain.

"You might want to consider a career switch." Roderick smiled kindly at me. The music was loud enough so that no one could hear us, as long as we didn't get too close to the edges of the circle.

"This isn't the life for me." I told him. "Besides, I already took the interview, I have to finish my training."

"And you don't think I can overrule that?" He said.

"I'm sure you could." I said. I finally spotted Alder in the crowd. He didn't look all that happy, though I doubted it had anything to do with me. He was standing next to an old man with the exact same expression on his face. And the exact same eyes, nose and jawline.

"Who is that man?" I asked Roderick. He glanced over, though he didn't try and be discreet about it.

"Shane Madin." He said at once. "My father's advisor."

I had heard of him countless of times before. The Madin family had been helping the Alexander's rule since the first days of the Union. 'Some things not a lot of people know yet. Please just... just remember who I am okay?' Alder's voice sounded through my head. Every time I had complained about the royal family to him, every time I had criticized the way things are happening in the kingdom, he had been a part of it all.

Why the hell was he a hunter? If he was really the son of Shane Madin then he could have just not taken the interview and live off of their fortune for his entire life. He wouldn't have had to go through training and countless dangerous missions. Why had he been so selfish and take up that spot over someone who needed it to survive? How did he dare judge Athena while he did the same damn thing?

"Are you alright?" Prince Roderick asked me, pulling me back into reality. I focused my attention on him again, his bright eyes, the wrinkles caused by worrying that circled his face and his hand that had slid down from my upper back down to my hip.

"My apologies," I said to him, faking a smile. "I thought I saw something, but I was mistaken."

"I think we would hear the gunshots." He cracked a small smile as well. "Truly Julia, Mr. Felthove overreacted. Enjoy your evening here before you go back to training."

Coming to think of it, I had only heard bits and pieces of the intel they received. How would they even tell if it was true at all? Roderick was right, there had been previous plans to kill the king and all of them were stopped before they were even put in motion.

The song came to an end, though it did not take long for a new one to start. Everyone was now allowed to dance and did not hesitate to do so. Roderick and I stayed for a little while, before going to the side and join his brother, Elijah.

Elijah had been drinking quite a bit already, so it came to no surprise that he greeted his brother with much enthusiasm. He even went to hug me, had Roderick not stopped him.

"Act like a prince or leave." He said on a low tone to him, keeping up his friendly appearance to everyone else. He took the cup from his brother's hands and finished it himself.

"It's boring here." Elijah complained.

I never thought I would find myself in the company of the royal family, especially because I wasn't their number one fan. I understood that the stories published about them doing good things helped the moral throughout the kingdom. To me, that was all they were good for. Roderick was a good person and would make a great king one day, but I couldn't help but think back to every time I had to walk through my old town, where everything was falling apart because they spend all their money on Vancouver and their stupid palace.

Elijah complained about being bored, while his belly was filled and he received a title he did not deserve. I kept my face blank from any emotion, but I really wanted to slap some sense into him, or at least tell him what it was like growing up with twelve siblings and only having enough food for six of them.

"Keep an eye on him." Roderick told Elijah's personal servant before leading me away from him. "My apologies, he always does this."

"You have these kinds of parties often?" I asked him as we passed by Arlo, who was the date of a beautiful girl. We made eye contact for a few seconds before he turned to laugh at the girl's joke.

"Whenever there is something to celebrate." He said. "So, yes. Too often."

"Is that something you will change when you are king?" I laughed. "Fewer parties?"

"Maybe I'll make sure they take up less time." He answered and leaned against the wall next to an open door. "Don't the hunters throw parties?"

I laughed. "No, we don't." I said to him. "Every few months Gavin takes out his guitar, but that is about all the music we enjoy."

The party went on and on, making me understand his comment about how long they take. I was dancing with Roderick for the fourth time when I noticed my wrist lighting up with blue letters. I moved my hand closer to his neck, so I could see the letters clearly written out on my skin.

'Gunfire ground floor'

I glanced over Roderick's shoulder, just in time to see Dorian exit the ballroom. I didn't receive any instructions on what to do in this situation, but from all around the room I saw people reading their wrist, and a whole new kind of dance began.

Alder and his father went to talk to the king as well as Antheas who was the date of none other than Gizelda. Prince Elijah and Prince Cludius were being covered by Arturo, Ryder and Creed while the queen was kept occupied by Gavin and Ferik. Everyone else moved out of the ballroom and followed Dorian.

Did they really just entrust the crown prince to me?

"Is something happening?" Prince Roderick asked me after he saw me glancing around. I smiled and moved closer to him, a seemingly innocent thing to do for anyone on a date.

"There is reported gunfire downstairs." I whispered in his ear. I felt his muscles tensing up, this was the closest radiates had ever gotten to him and his family.

"What do we do?" He asked me.

"We wait." I answered, feeling the barrel of my gun pressed reassuringly against my thigh. "We let the guard handle it and don't cause a panic. Your entire family is covered, they'll be safe."

"And the guests?" He immediately asked, sounding very much like his father.

"They have their own guards." I answered. It was true, several of them refused to enter without their bodyguards. That was only the foreign ones though, the people of the Union trusted the king blindly.

I kept a close eye on everyone else, as well as my wrist. Suddenly, making sure that I was being proper in front of everyone else seemed the least of my concern.

"I guess you were hoping for that gunfight a bit too much." Prince Roderick smiled, breaking the tension only a little bit. I laughed out my nervous giggles and stepped a bit closer to him to allow a very swinging couple to dance by us.

"They'll be fine," I said, comforting the both of us. "Especially with the backup they just received."

I made eye contact with Alder from across the room. He didn't look worried, he knew better, but I could feel him checking up on me. Trying to see if I had figured out his little secret.

"I do have to say, you settle in quite easily." Prince Roderick said. I raised my brows at him, ignoring Alder's stares.

"What do you mean?" I asked.

"You looked like a lost duckling this morning. Now you look like you have been doing this for years." He said. I could tell he was just trying to forget about the message we just received, so I played along.

"Well, I never really thought this would be my job description." I said to him.

My wrist lit up again. I saw his eyes flicker over to it too, but he couldn't see it from the angle it was positioned.

'Three R dead.'

"They killed three radiates." I said to him. Roderick's face lit up with a smile, he didn't seem half as worried anymore. His grip on my waist tightened, and we continued dancing.

"What is Shane Madin like?" I asked him.

"He's a genius." Roderick immediately told me. "Great military expertise, besides knowing what problems surface in the kingdom. My father repeats every day that he couldn't work without him."

I wanted to believe that he was actually an asshole, that Alder didn't leave to chase glory of his own. But sadly, all the evidence seemed to be pointing to it.

"Have you met his son?" I asked Roderick, trying to make my voice sound as casual as it could be.

"I grew up around Alder." He said, seeing right through my clever questions. "His younger brother is now next in line to become my advisor."

"He never mentioned anything like this to me." I admitted to him. "I was just curious."

My wrist lit up one last time.

'All radiates killed, Keep character.'

"They killed them all." I informed Roderick, letting my hand drop down to his shoulder again.

"It feels wrong to smile about that." Roderick admitted.

"Well, they did come here to kill you." I cracked a small smile. He smiled too, though he seemed lost in thoughts for a few moments.

"They'll receive a burial." He decided. I kept my opinion to myself and finished the dance.

Two hours later, the party finally died down, and many guests were starting to go back to their rooms. Dorian had not returned to the ballroom but let us know through the bracelet that the mission was completed.

I found the rest of the hunters in a deserted lounge room after making sure that Roderick got back to his room safely. All still dressed in their party outfits, everyone was ecstatic about the mission, especially the apprentices. They had somehow gotten their hands on the remaining alcohol that was left from the party and were passing around bottles.

"What happened downstairs?" I asked Athena, who was in a red, palace guard uniform.

"Five guys entered." She said to me. "We picked them out even before they opened fire." Athena had covered up all of her tattoos, not just the one on her neck. She looked different without them, innocent almost. Maybe that's why she got them, to look more like a badass.

"Did anyone get hurt?" I asked.

"One palace guard died, two other ones are still in surgery." She shrugged it off. "No one on our side."

I hope Dorian saw Athena firing at the radiates, maybe he would believe her innocence then and tell the other leaders. He wasn't in the room with us now, he had gone to inform the king about the shooting.

"A toast to all of you worthy apprentices!" Gavin said, raising his glass high up into the sky before gulping it all down. There had been alcohol at the base before, but we never celebrated anything, so no one really drank from it all that much, especially the apprentices. The mentors seemed to be eager to change that tonight.

They were all fighting about which kind of alcohol they should serve us first. Eventually, the bottle was just passed down the line. Most of the guys were taking big swigs and drank it down easily.

Athena was next. She took a big sip and swallowed it down harshly. "Oh, are you kidding me." She said while the mentors laughed. "Do you guys piss in a bottle and try to sell it on this side of the fence?"

"What the alcohol outside is better?" Ferik challenged her.

"The alcohol outside actually contains alcohol." She laughed.

"What about drinking games?" Alder asked, handing her the green bottle he had been drinking from.

"We'll need five glasses and a spider." She answered.

"What is the spider for?" I was almost too afraid to ask her. Spiders weren't exactly my favourite animals.

"All the participants get blindfolded, one of the drinks has the spider in it. If you are the one who swallowed the spider and you guess it correctly you won't have to compete for next round." She explained like it was the greatest game in the world. Everyone loudly complained and threw pillows at her

"So that is what we are not going to do." Alder laughed, stealing his own bottle back from her.

Eventually, we played a more hunter like game. They pinned a pillow to the wall and whoever got their knife to go through it and stick into the wall would be excused from drinking.

I was happy to see Alder fail time and time again, getting more drunk with every fail. I myself wasn't doing too good either, but none of the other apprentices were. It didn't really matter all that much. The booze may have tasted like piss, but it made me feel free and giddy. Something I had never felt before.

I wouldn't say everyone planned to get hammered that night, but the festive mood definitely contributed to everyone pushing boundaries. Even Dorian returned and happily joined in on drinking, praising us apprentices on our 'splendid' performance.

We fell asleep in the lounge. Either on the soft carpet floor, the couches or one of the many chairs. I was one of the last ones to go down and looked around at the people who looked like absolute fools sleeping on the ground like that. My true family.

19

I woke to the sound of small pops. For a moment I thought I was back home in the shabby house near the wall and one of my siblings got a hold of a bouncing ball again. I ignored it, hoping that my parents would tell them off this time and I wouldn't have to. I tried to lay a bit more comfortable and felt the red velvet couch shift underneath me. I realized that it wasn't the sound of a bouncing ball, it was the sound of a gun silencer.

Gunfire erupted shortly after that. While my brain was still trying to comprehend what was going on several others had gotten up and reached for their weapons, which they had discarded throughout the room in a drunken haze last night.

A bullet hit a little above my ear, just hitting the top of it. I felt the pain, but I didn't progress it. I just saw the room.

Dorian was positioned behind a blue velvet chair, taking heavy fire from the five men with the silenced guns. They looked even more like radiates than Athena had when I first saw her. They were all covered in a layer of dust and started to slowly one by one collapse onto the floor.

Athena and Alder were behind the same couch, they had woken up too, and were returning fire using measly handguns.

Another bullet hit near me. It would have hit my head had I not moved to lay on the ground. It felt like this was all a weird dream, as if it wasn't happening. It couldn't be, there was too much blood pooling onto the floor. I didn't even know we had that much blood in our bodies.

The firing stopped as quickly as it had begun. It took a few seconds for the room to start to move, and for us to notice the ones who weren't moving at all.

Ferik, Creed, Arlo, Asher, Devin, David, Horyn. They all laid lifeless on the ground. Most of them I wouldn't have even recognized if it wasn't for their clothes. Half of their heads were either just gone or covered in blood.

I felt some blood dripping down from my ear onto my neck, though I hardly registered it. Athena looked at Ferik with absolute horror written all over her face. She kneeled down beside him and checked for a pulse. It was a logical thing to do, though it was clear to everyone that he was dead, the gaping hole on the side of his skull attested to that.

"Gavin, Ryder." It was Dorian who first spoke after a few seconds of absolute silence, he assessed the scene and like a true leader told us what to do next. "Go to prince Elijah, protect him."

They quickly ran out the door, carrying two handguns and nothing else. I reached under my skirt and got my own gun and knife. "Julia and Alder, you two take Prince Roderick."

We followed Gavin and Ryder out, having no idea what state the castle was in. "Are you alright?" Alder asked me, glancing over to the blood that was now staining the dress. It bled a lot, but I could not feel any of the pain. All I felt was the adrenaline.

"Just the ear." I answered.

I had not spoken to Alder the night before, I did not want to bring down the party atmosphere. I knew that one day I would get to be angry at him for not telling me about his family, but that day seemed like ages away compared to what was happening now.

We heard gunshots, several of them, ring through the halls. It was clearly not directed at us, but it told us all we needed to know: the castle was under attack, it wasn't just us.

We had been so stupid. We should have realized that something could still have happened during the night.

We should have placed a guard, or at least stay with the royal family.

They were probably already dead if they also had the time to come finish us off.

As we rounded the corner Alder peeked first. He quickly ushered me to run past him. There were people shooting, radiates versus the red palace guards, but they paid us no mind. We just looked like lost guests, not anyone worth shooting.

We sprinted up the staircase, taking three steps at a time. Like it had been before, the higher we got up in the castle the less crowded it seemed. There were no bloodstained carpets here, no one was firing guns, It was eerily quiet.

I did not like the silence. It allowed thoughts to come back up into my head, thoughts I did not want to have. I remembered their faces, or what was left of them. I just felt like going into foetus position on the ground and cry.

But we pushed on until we eventually reached the door to Prince Roderick's room. The sun had started to rise up, but I doubt anyone but the farmers were awake already. There was no formal knocking or anything, Alder just threw his shoulder against the door and broke the lock.

Why Prince Roderick did not have a personal guard was beyond me, a simple lock is supposed to keep any attackers out. But he got lucky, he was lying in his bed unharmed.

"Wake up." Alder said, going to the side of his bed and poking him roughly in the arm.

"Al?" Roderick asked sleepily. He looked around the room, shocked to see his door just busted open. Then his eyes landed on me, and he looked a little more aware of what was going on.

"Close the door, Julia." Alder ordered me. I closed it to the best of my capabilities, but the lock had given out, so it kept trying to open on its own. I put a chair in front of it, but there was still a small hole where the pin went into the lock.

"The palace is under attack." Alder quickly informed the prince. "We do not know the magnitude."

"My family?" Roderick shot up from his bed and walked over to his closet. I averted my eyes and looked through the hole the lock had created. We were lucky that his room was at the end of a hallway, no one could sneak up on us.

"The other hunters are checking them." Alder said, not informing him of the deaths we suffered. Roderick quickly got changed, while I heard Alder mumble curses behind me.

He was pressing odd spots on his wrist, pushing harder and harder before finally sighing deeply and looking over to me.

"Do you still have your bracelet?" He asked me. I took it off and threw it to him.

"Are you sure you are okay Julia?" He asked me again, his eyes only focused on the bracelet. He started twisting and turning the small diamonds. Creating faint letters that shone into the air.

"I'm fine." I brushed my fingers against the tip of my ear and felt that maybe there was a bit more damage than I had initially thought. It felt like the entire top of my ear was just missing, and bleeding frantically. The bullet had also grazed my head, the wound was bleeding, but not deep.

My fingers were covered in blood, my blood, but I couldn't bring myself to feel anything. It was like my emotions had turned itself off and only focussed on the mission: Protect Roderick.

The dress had a modification to it, I could take off the skirt and keep the top. They had added it in case Roderick and I needed to run away from the ball. Underneath it were my regular workout pants alongside a gun holster and a knife sheath. I tore the skirt away and discarded it to the side.

"King and queen are secure." Alder read out from the bracelet.

I let out a sigh I didn't realize I was holding in and resumed my position as the lookout. There was absolutely no one in the hallway, all the other doors were also still closed.

"Who lives in the rooms next to yours?" I asked Roderick.

"Personal servants." He answered, leaving his walk-in closet wearing what could be described as a rich person's version of comfortable clothes. His shirt was made out of an expensive fabric that fit him tightly, much like the suit he had worn just hours ago.

I clutched my hands together to stop them from shaking and kept on looking. It was really all we could do at this point. Look and wait.

"Elijah is secure." Alder said, followed up only seconds later by. "Cludius is safe too."

"Good." Roderick said, and sat down on his bed only to stand back up seconds later. He disappeared for a few moments and returned with a first aid kit, which he handed to Alder.

"Let's patch you up." He said to me. I moved my hair to the side of the face and made sure I could still see into the hallway.

He started with disinfecting the wound, which stung a lot. I gripped my hand tightly, so tight that it started to hurt, and waited it out.

"After this is done, you need to go to a doctor." Alder told me and put gauze over my ear. He worked carefully, trying not to hurt me, though it seemed almost impossible.

I saw something move in the hallway. I pushed Alder's hands away and quietly pointed it out to him. Alder took over my position and peeked through.

"It's Dorian." He finally said, quickly getting up and removing the chair.

Dorian's fancy military uniform was practically drenched in blood. "Where are you hit?" Alder asked, closing the door behind him and putting the chair back.

"Just a little nick on my arm, the rest of it is not mine." Dorian answered and turned to Roderick. "Your family is safe, we are going floor by floor to clear out the radiates."

"Leave two hunters with each member of my family. Take the rest and help the guard." Roderick commanded, seemingly confident of his case. Dorian glanced over angrily at Alder. We had not told him about the casualties yet.

"We had some losses." Alder said to Roderick. Roderick had told me that he and Alder grew up together, and I could definitely see some similarities between them. They had the same dark brown hair, the same built and height and even the same smile that could take them from commanding to nice in seconds. Though no one was smiling now.

"How many?" Roderick asked, looking between Dorian and Alder. I felt like my legs were going to give out, and I wasn't really contributing to the conversation much anyway, I sat down on a chair near the door and tried to calm my nerves.

"We have eight left." Dorian answered. "And one injured."

"Who?" Alder immediately asked.

"Antheas." Dorian said. "He got shot on his way to Cludius. Athena is taking care of him now."

At the mention of Athena's name, Dorian looked over to me. He trusted her now, he had no other option. Our numbers were too far down and he must have seen her reaction to her mentor's death. She was not faking any of that.

"What's the plan?" Alder asked Dorian. It wasn't that weird to ask someone a who is a rank above you what to do, but it felt awkward because of Roderick. There seemed to be something unresolved between the two of them. Roderick just glanced over to Dorian as well, accepting that he might know how to deal with the situation.

"The military has been alerted for back up, they'll work their way up while we work our way down." Dorian said. "The palace guard has been told to start protecting civilians. A dozen have been called up here to guard the Prince."

We had to wait for them to show up. I felt the adrenaline slowly wearing off, and realization settle in. The realization of never hearing Athena complain about Ferik again or seeing Creed and Antheas chase after each other throughout the compound. It would all be different now.

I heard the door open and I saw Alder talk to the palace guards, though what they were saying didn't register in my brain all that much. It felt like I was in a daze, like the pain that had started to pound in my head combined with sleep deprivation had pulled up a screen in front of my eyes. It wasn't until Dorian kneeled down in front of me that I understood what was going on, or at least could register words again

He clicked the bracelet around my wrist again. It just read 'unsafe' onto my wrist in red letters this time.

"Are you in fighting condition?" He asked me. It wasn't like Dorian to look concerned or worried, but even he must have a breaking point. He seemed to be in dire need of a break himself but would of course never give in to it. No one expected this to happen, no one was prepared.

"Yes." I answered. He moved my head to the side and peeked under the now blood-soaked gauze. Alder was still instructing the guards. They at least looked like they weren't fresh out of their training.

Dorian went through the first aid kit until he found a small bottle with some grey liquid in it. He removed the gauze again and carefully applied it with a piece of fabric. "Numbing cream." He said to me, making sure he did not get it on his fingers.

It worked, though the numbing was also an odd feeling. It felt like there was a black hole where my ear should be, and it became more and more tempting to reach out and touch it.

We left Roderick in the safe hands of the palace guard and went out into the hall. I held my gun tightly in my hand, ready to fire at any time.

20

We spend most of the morning going room by room to make sure that there weren't any radiates lurking about. At noon the palace was declared safe, and the military proceeded to go block by block to check the streets of Vancouver.

Our friend's bodies were loaded into a truck, alongside other casualties. Most of the truck was the colour red, many palace guards had given their lives protecting the guests.

As more and more dead bodies were identified it became clear that the royal family was never the target. It was us, both the hunters and the military top. Alongside with a few politicians who worked closely with the military and the builders of the fence.

I sat in a deserted room with Alder, Arturo, Holden and Dorian. We had been given permission to rest for a few hours, while the king decided what would happen next. Though I was tired, I knew I could not sleep. I could not look Athena in the eye, or anyone else for that matter.

We were all silent. Holden had lost his mentor David. A few tears streaked his cheeks, all he did was stare ahead of himself into nothingness. I grabbed Alder's hand, who was sitting next to me on the couch. He gently squeezed in it. Out of all the mentors and apprentices, we and one other duo were the only ones who were still complete. Just thinking about Alder being shot made me feel sick to my stomach. It almost made me happy for the people who got cut. They didn't have to feel this pain.

I thought of Ulric. I wanted to see him again, to finally have the bravery to kiss him maybe. He maybe wasn't a guy of many words, but I knew he could comfort me without saying a thing.

There were no words of solace to be found anywhere in the castle. I had only seen prince Roderick briefly, right after it got announced that two military leaders had been executed during the night by the radiates. He had given a small speech about how the radiates were fools to believe that our country was led by us. He said that the everyday people, the teachers who teach the school children and the doctors who ease our pain, are the reason why the union is stronger than ever. After that, he made some vague threats to whoever orchestrated the attack, though I doubt we'd ever get send after them.

The door opened and a distraught palace guard walked in. He wasn't much older than I was and almost looked scared to be talking to us.

"Mr. Felthove?" He asked, to which Dorian stood up and paced over to him. "We caught one of them."

"Where is he?" Dorian immediately asked as the rest of us also shot up from our seats.

"The throne room sir." The boy said, his voice shaking. We all went passed him as quickly as we could, making our way to the throne room.

Arturo broke off somewhere halfway, to get the others while we ran down the hallways. The throne room was located in the heart of the palace: On the third floor. It was a large room, with at the very end a steel throne for the king to sit on and a wooden one for the queen to be seated beside him.

In the middle of the room was a small uncomfortable looking chair, with a radiate tied to it. He looked to be somewhere in his late thirties, which was relatively old for a radiate already. Life beyond the fence was unforgiving, many people wouldn't make it through their twenties.

Four palace guards stood surrounding him but scattered off once we entered. Dorian paced to the man and grabbed his chin roughly, squeezing so hard I thought he might break his jaw.

"Your name." Dorian said to him. Dorian may have not been intimidating when I first met him, but I could see why he was one of the leaders. When he was angry, he looked absolutely terrifying. Like there was no other emotion but absolute rage in him. The man was practically shaking in his seat but did not answer.

"Make it easy on yourself." Alder chimed in, standing beside me with his arms crossed over his chest. "Tell us your name or face the consequences like a man."

"You are not a man." The man said once Dorian released his jaw. He spoke with a heavy accent, one that was similar to Athena's. "You are a dog. You are worth noth-"

Dorian punched the guy across the face so hard that the sound echoed off the walls. The chair tipped over and the man fell onto his side, gasping for breath as his nose started to bleed and blend in with the blood he already had on his shirt.

Alder stepped forward and grabbed the guy's shirt to pull him back up. I don't know what he whispered to him, but the guy looked even angrier when he was back up.

"Your name." Dorian demanded.

"Kohlyn." He answered.

"Kohlyn." Dorian repeated him slowly. "Are you the leader of this attack?"

"He sure doesn't look like it." Holden spat. It was easy to manipulate radiates according to the books Alder had me read. Their culture was much more instinct based, and not logical like ours. Kohlyn did seem to react to the insult, but he said nothing.

"Very well." Dorian said, grabbing his knife from the sheath and kneeled down in front of Kohlyn.

"You are quite normal looking for a radiate." Dorian traced the knife over Kohlyn's face. "Born without any deformities. That's rare." Kohlyn was shaking in his seat, trying to get as far away from the knife as he possibly could.

The doors to the throne room opened and the rest of the hunters came in. I thought they would just quietly watch, like we had been doing too. But Athena seemed to have other plans.

"*Taw swal ej nalp ihre?*" She said to him. Kohlyn seemed to be caught totally off guard by her. She hardly looked like a radiate, seeing as her tattoos were all still covered up. The only thing that could show it was her pure white hair, but half of it got stained with blood throughout the morning when we helped with cleaning out the bodies.

"*Ej ebt ne olbde revedar.*" He responded. "*Ne fradla.*"

Athena moved closer to hit him, but Dorian got hold of her arm and held her backwards. When she shot him an angry glare he just said "Either speak our language or don't talk at all."

Athena gave him possibly the most venomous look I have ever seen in my life, but Dorian stood his ground. She ripped her arm out of his grip and took a step backwards, all the while Kohlyn was shouting at her in the unknown language.

Dorian tried talking to him again, but something in Athena seemed to have set Kohlyn off. He was no longer scared of the knife that was now threatening to go into his throat. All he did was, what I was guessing, curse out Athena.

"*Ranmo eneb ej ihre?*" She finally snapped at him, ignoring all of our warnings.

"*Jehi rutsed nos.*" He answered, a smile playing on his bloodied lips.

"*Iwe sin jehi?*" She asked him, while Dorian cursed at her again.

"*Edgo.*" He laughed. Athena looked positively horrified, something I had never seen her look. She was brave and fearless. Nothing ever scared her as it did with me. She did not look like herself anymore.

"What did he say?" Dorian asked her, turning his back to Kohlyn who was now straight up laughing at our faces. Athena just looked at him with big, bright blue eyes. She opened her mouth to speak but shut it almost instantly.

The king and his sons entered the throne room and scolded us for starting without them. But it was too late, Kohlyn was not saying another word, and the king refused to turn to violence, even after Alder recited the death counts.

We were forced to spend another night in the palace, due to the city being on total lockdown. The military was patrolling the streets day and night, and were still combing through the buildings to find any strays.

Obviously, we set up a guard system. There were only seven of us seeing as Antheas was in the hospital wing and Ryder had volunteered to watch over him there.

Two people would stay awake while everyone else slept. One would sit by the door and the other one would be lying with the sleeping people, so if anyone came in they would think there was just one guard. It was a classic hunter tactic that according to Alder worked every time.

I slept for a peaceful four hours before being woken up by Gavin to take over his watch. I sat by the door while Holden laid in his sleeping bag.

It was hard to stay awake, but just thinking back to this morning was all the motivation I needed. I made sure to not keep a rhythm in checking the hallways and the room, I needed to be able to catch anyone off guard.

After one boring hour, Athena got up. "Gotta pee." She just said to me and exited the room. I heard her footsteps go down the left hallway and almost just disregarded the whole thing until I noticed that she brought her gun and her knife with her, followed up by the sound of her feet accelerating.

"You're the guard now." I quickly whispered to Holden and shot up from my spot against the wall and ran after her.

I knew Kohlyn had said something to Athena that spooked her, but I never thought she would leave us. She had to work harder than anyone to get here, why would she just throw that all away? Her cold demeanour was just a shield, she cared underneath it all.

I finally caught up to her outside, on the front steps of the palace. A military convoy was just driving by us, but they quickly identified us by our tattoos and the colour of our clothes and continued on. A lucky thing too, because they had been instructed to shoot anyone suspicious, especially near the palace.

"Athena, wait!" I shouted after her.

"Go back inside, Julia." She ordered me. "Keep watch over them."

"You're leaving." I said. She turned around, her hand clenching around a satchel that she must have picked up along the way.

"I have to." She just said, her emotionless self coming back up. I was fed up with it, with it all. It was not fair that half of our people got shot yesterday, taken away from the lives they were supposed to have, and now she was just disregarding it so easily.

"How could you do that?" I asked her. "How could you do that to Ferik? His body isn't even buried yet and you are throwing away everything he taught you!"

"I am trying to stay alive." She snapped at me. "You weren't born beyond the fence, you don't know what it is like."

I needed to take a deep breath and calm down before answering her. I knew what it is like to feel like staying alive is the only thing that matters, but now was not the time to discuss it with her.

"I am also angry and sad," I said to her, trying to keep my calm. "I also want to cry and scream and hide away in a corner, but it just doesn't work like that. Those people inside the castle need our help."

Athena laughed an unhappy laugh. "The likes of Jack and Alder survived long enough without you in their lives. They don't need us. You're a fool to believe that they do."

"Well, I need you." I told her. "I need to stay. They are the only people who have ever acted anything like a family to me."

"I can't stay just for you." She said, her voice breaking off as she struggled to keep her façade on.

"Why do you need to leave?" I asked her back. "Are you afraid of dying?"

"I was never going to stay." She angrily revealed. "I was always just going to learn what I can and leave."

She was going to leave us, fully aware that other people had to leave or weren't even tried because of her. I wanted her to stay, I wanted her to be the friend I thought I had, but I couldn't even recognize her at the moment.

"Why?" It was all I could ask, all I could think. I always thought she was fighting to be able to stay, to prove that she belonged here.

"They'll catch up with me. They always do." She spat.

"You're safe inside the fence." I answered her, trying to keep my calm and not burst out in frustrated tears.

"Tell that to Ferik." She said, stepping closer to me. "Or Devin, or Asher or Arlo."

"What? You think they got killed because of you?" I asked her, trying to ignore the fact that she was up in my face, and looked like she was ready to punch me. "They were killed because radiates despise the hunters and wanted payback. It has got nothing to do with you."

"I am afraid," she started but couldn't finish her sentence. She watched the palace guards that guarded the front doors. They weren't in hearing range but were obviously distracted by the two hunters suddenly having a screaming match outside. "I am afraid because I finally have something to lose, but I know we will lose in the end."

"What is it?" I grabbed her hand. I saw the tears well up in her blue eyes, the absolute terror was etched in her face. I have never seen someone look so utterly terrified before.

"Eryk." She whispered.

21

Holden was a real trooper and did not say a word about our sudden departure when Dorian and Athena had to take over the watch. I tried to stay awake and listen to hear if they would talk, but they didn't, and I couldn't keep my sleepy eyes open anymore.

She was still here the next morning, though she looked like she had not slept in days, which was probably true. None of us could say that they had a good night's rest, but in the morning we finally received some good news.

Antheas was on his way to making a full recovery. The bullet had hit him in his chest but missed his heart by mere inches. It would take time to heal, but he would live.

While Dorian went to speak to the king on what to do with Kohlyn. Alder and I went to the palace's communication room, which was about three times as big as ours was back at the home base.

They had messages coming in from all the military bases, as well as outposts and of course the two hunter bases. Alder was an absolute geek for anything machine related and seemed to feel right at home among all the screens and computers.

We went into a bit more of a secluded area, so we could contact the two bases. An engineer went with us, trying to explain to us how everything worked. Alder quickly showed however that he knew what he was doing and we were left alone.

"We have to tell home base." Alder explained. It wasn't so simple to just click on something and talk to them. It required several codes and actions to be completed, so it couldn't be hacked or interfered with.

Alder typed out his personal code and apparently clicked the right things at the right time, a small pop up opened. Alder went to type a message, though it would be unclear when they would respond.

>>Operation successful. Royal family unharmed. Personal losses: Devin Smis, Asher Miller, Arlo Anderson, Ferik Howers, Creed Deyou, David Brouns, Horyn Nethell. Injured: Antheas Harnisch.

"And now we wait." Alder leaned back in his chair and folded his hands on top of his head.

"For how long?" I asked him, staring at the boring black and white screen in front of me.

"The base leader will get a notification. Which right now is doctor Groen." He answered. "Though if he is in training or asleep, it could take some time for him to respond. Someone else might check the communication room first."

"What kind of notification?" I settled back in my chair, something was telling me we would be here for a long time.

Alder rolled up his sleeve and tapped the letters that now said 'safe, unclear' Referencing to the Vancouver streets which were so far not cleared yet. "Dorian and a few of the other top dogs have them permanently in their wrists. Ours were just temporary."

We sat there in silence for a while, both of us staring at the screen. I hated to admit it, but this was the perfect time to talk about his family. I had barely even thought about it. I hardly felt any anger about it anymore seeing as I had so many other things to be pissed off about. But we were alone, it would have to come up eventually.

"So," I said, breaking the silence. "Alder Madin."

"Yup." He sighed. "Madin."

I peeked over to him. His eyes were glued to the screen and looked like he had been positively dreading this moment.

"Why didn't you just tell me?" I asked him. "You pretty much know everything there is to know about me." Alder laughed.

"Really?" He said. "You didn't tell me about Ulric, nor do you really talk about your own family for that matter."

"Well, that is because I see you as my family. Not them." I answered back without thinking about it first. I wanted to punch myself in the face for just blurting something like that out. Alder looked over to me, a faint smile on his lips.

"Blood makes you related, loyalty makes you family." He said to me. "The hunters are my family."

"You had a proper life here," I answered. "You didn't have to take the interview. You could have been Roderick's advisor for god's sake, that's the highest paying job in the kingdom."

"And I would be miserable. Money isn't everything." He said.

"Spoken like a true rich boy." I instantly responded. We were quiet for a few moments. I kept my eyes on the screen, hoping the message would pop up now and distract us.

"My father tried to stop me from leaving." He broke the silence. "Family pride and all that. The king had to go against him and allowed me to take the interview."

"Did you want to become a hunter?" I asked. I asked.

"I wanted to be anywhere but here." He answered. "My original plan was to take what I can get. If they had put me in factory I would have been just as happy. Maybe marry a pretty girl and settle down."

"Like a pretty girl would want to marry you." I huffed. The tension broke as we both laughed. It felt good to be laughing again. It felt like it had been years since I last did it. "I need you, idiot. Don't keep secrets from me."

A message finally popped up about half an hour later. "Finally." Alder muttered and leaned in to read it.

<<Message received. What was the cause of death? No news has arrived here yet.

>> We got ambushed at night. It appears to be an attack on military/hunters. Any news from the Darkfort?

<< They have not made contact since you left.

"That's not normal is it?" I asked Alder. He had told me that the Darkfort had to send in messages every five hours. If they miss more than two we have to assume that they are under attack, and reinforcements would be sent.

"It's not." He said, worry etched on his face.

I used to be unable to read any of the emotions the hunters had, but after getting to know them I thought it became easier and easier. They weren't as expressive as most people were, but there were small things that told me all I needed to know. For instance, when Alder gets worried or stressed he starts picking at his eyebrows.

He clicked open a new window and retyped all of the codes until a new one popped up that said 'Darkfort' at the top.

>> Royal palace to Darkfort. Status report.

It was a simple message, but it would have to do. I settled back in my chair, getting ready for another long sit.

Ulric was at the Darkfort. If they really were under attack he could be dying right now. I don't know how much more death my heart can take at the moment.

I knew people would die when I joined the hunters, it was a dangerous job with many risks. It was just the way the others were murdered that bothered me.

They didn't get to go out fighting, showing that they had learned and could be full-blown hunters. They went out in their sleep, peaceful, but not fulfilling.

A message popped up a lot sooner than we expected, we both leaned closer to the screen.

<< 82553366

"Julia, run and get Dorian." Alder said to me.

"Why? What does it mean?" I asked.

"Go!" He shouted, making all the engineers near us jump up in their seats and look at us rather annoyed. I ran out of the room and down the stairs to try to find Dorian. I had no idea where he was, or what he had gone to do after meeting the king.

The first place I checked was the room where we stayed last night. There were only two hunters in there: Athena and Gavin. Athena was dead asleep with Gavin sitting beside her, calmly reading a book.

"Have you seen Dorian?" I asked him, my voice sounding frantic.

"No." He answered. "What's going on?"

"Nothing just yet." I said. I had no idea what was going on myself. I wanted to tell him to wake Athena up in case we needed to leave quickly, but I had no idea what the message said. Just that Alder seemed freaked out about it.

I left the room behind me and ran through the castle, I checked the throne room, the king's private chambers and the dining hall. Each turning up empty.

Should I go back to Alder and say that I could not find him? That everything I just did was a complete waste of time?

I was running over the sky bridge to the adjoining building, which housed several politicians, when I finally did spot him. He was sitting in the courtyard garden, staring straight ahead of him, seemingly lost in thought.

It took me two minutes to find my way down. The courtyard was filled with the beautiful ladies of the court walking around, pondering over flowers and art and all that bullshit. I stood out, and they dodged away from me.

"Dorian." I called out, as a few ladies refused to go to the side for me. The courtyard was beautiful, I'll give them that. There were hundreds of different flowers, alongside with herbs and remedies used in the hospital wing. Though I had no mind to look over them now.

"What is it?" Dorian rose slowly from the wooden bench. He looked tired and held his arm that had been hit during the gunfight at a weird angle.

"Come with me, I'll explain along the way." I said, breaking off into a run back to the communication room. When we reached a few more quiet halls I finally felt safe enough to explain.

"They answered within five minutes with some code, Alder told me to get you instantly." I concluded as we got closer to the room.

"What code?" Dorian asked.

"I don't know. It started with 825, but I don't remember the rest of it." A light bulb seemed to have come up in his head, he had the same distraught look on his face that Alder had when he saw it.

The communication room was still crawling with engineers, who looked at Dorian with big eyes. I knew their jobs sucked, they had to spend their entire life staring at computer screens waiting for messages to roll in. Hardly a well-paying job either.

Dorian sat down in what used to be my chair and looked at our brief communication with them. Alder had sent a response, but no one had written back.

>>Confirm with a personal code.

"How long ago was this?" Dorian asked Alder.

"Less than ten minutes since the code came in." He answered. "But... enough time."

The two exchanged worried glances. Dorian stared at the screen for a few quiet seconds, debating on what to do, before turning to me.

"Get everyone ready to leave within the hour. Cars will be out front, tell them to pack weapons." He said.

"I kind of need to know what is going on then." I answered, seeing as neither of them have said anything that could tell me what we are dealing with.

"The Darkfort has been compromised," Dorian told me, shushing up Alder who just wanted to say something. "We were just a decoy."

I found myself running through the hallways of the palace yet again looking frantically for familiar faces and black clothes. I found Gavin and Athena right where I left them.

"We are leaving within the hour." I said to him. "Take weapons, we're going to the Darkfort."

Gavin didn't require any further instructions and woke up a grouchy Athena. Who at first just hit his hand away and turned back around. I did not wait to see the rest of the battle and made my way further into the castle.

I found people just roaming the hallways, I found them in the library, on the training grounds with a few military soldiers and finally there was no other place to go than to the hospital wing.

I had been dreading this part. I knew at least one person was watching over Antheas. I felt bad that he could not join us there, that he was stuck in the palace with a bunch of strangers.

The hospital wing was one large hall, divided into little cubicles by mint green curtains. There were nurses and doctors rushing around me, but no one paid me any mind, even after I asked them about Antheas.

I was thankful the doctors had not chosen me, I don't think I could take this job very long. In every new cubicle there was a new patient. Some looked close to death, others looked like they were lying about their injuries. I saw more bullet wounds than I ever wanted to see.

He was in one of the very last ones, back where it was a bit quieter. I had hoped that he was asleep, but when I peeked in I saw him wide awake and talking to Arturo.

Arturo still was pretty lanky, though he definitely had more muscle on him now. He wasn't Antheas' apprentice, he is Gavin's. But Gavin and Antheas were close friends, which by extend made Arturo his friend.

"Hey." I greeted him with a smile.

"Oh hey." Antheas was tightly bandaged up. He also had several wires going in his arms and a few to his chest, it almost looked like they were trying to turn him into a robot.

"Arturo, you have to get your weapons and go to the front of the palace." I said to him. He looked at me a bit oddly but said goodbye to Antheas nonetheless and took off. I instead took his seat, having already grabbed my weapons when I went to find the others. I had twenty more minutes before we were leaving. I wasn't going to leave him until the very last second.

"You guys are leaving." Antheas stated, laying his head back in the pillow.

"Sorry." I don't know why I was apologising, it wasn't my fault that we were leaving. It felt like something normal to say in this situation.

"Where are you off to?" He asked.

"Darkfort," I said. "We received an odd message, we have to check it out."

I purposely let out the part where we were told that the Darkfort had been compromised. I didn't think his heart was up for it yet. I did not want him to worry, he must know everyone there.

"First time beyond the fence." He grinned at me. Antheas was young, probably only five years older than me. He still had a worry-free vibe to him, something Alder and Dorian could definitely use.

"Any tips?" I smiled back at him.

"Don't get shot in the chest, hurts like all hell." He said. "Or just don't get shot period."

"Sounds about right." I laughed. "What will happen to you?"

He sighed. "I'll stay here until I am fit for transport. Then I'll go to home base to recover further and get back in shape. Only then will I get back out for missions."

"Maybe you'll be good in time to join me on my official first one." I joked.

I kept true to my word and stayed with him until I no longer could. When I left he had started to slowly doze off, there at least weren't any painful goodbyes.

Just outside of the palace were two cars. I was the last to leave the palace and entered the car driven by Gavin. Inside was Alder, who again took the front seat, and Athena. It eerily reminded me of when we came here the first time, and of the person who was with us then.

Ferik's death had hit Athena hard. She told me didn't like him, but she apparently got closer to him than I thought. We all got close to our mentors, whether or not they were actually a nice person. Training with someone day in day out for months on end tends to get people closer together.

The other car was driven by Dorian, and had a nervous looking Ryder, Holden and Arturo with him. There were two radios connecting the two cars, so when we received the all clear from the military, we took off.

22

Gavin's speciality was driving, which definitely showed. Not a lot of people know how to drive in the Union, most roads are either reserved for the military or too broken to drive on anymore.

Dorian's car took the lead because Gavin didn't know which exact route we would take. Dorian was an experienced driver, though his car often hit potholes or swerved just in time. Whereas Gavin, most of the time, just smoothly avoided them. I knew Dorian had gotten injured during the fight, he seemed pretty out of it when he got in the car, to the point where Alder offered up to drive, but Dorian refused.

Athena fell asleep before we even left Vancouver. There was no need for us to constantly be looking out of the windows, the military has been combing through the streets looking for any strays ever since the attack happened. Though in the back of my mind I heard a tiny voice say 'they got to the capital, what makes you think they won't be here?'.

"How's your ear, Julia?" Gavin asked me, making eye contact through the rear-view mirror.

"Gone mostly." I said. "Doesn't hurt though." That may have been a lie, but I wasn't going to complain about a little bit of pain.

I had gone to the hospital wing on Alder's supervision before we went to the communication room. The tip of my left ear was just gone, and the wound a little behind it where the bullet had grazed my head would have turned into a scar.

Luckily for me, the doctors were equipped to deal with it and applied a cream that would make sure there would be no scar, though I doubt anyone could see passed what was left of my ear.

206

They had put a fresh gauze over it, and little butterfly bandages over the graze and sent me on my way, dealing with much more lethal injuries on other patients.

"Well, you only really become a hunter once you have a scar from a mission." Gavin told me, to which Alder laughed in agreement. "I guess this is an early acceptance."

"I want to thank my mentor for always being a pain in my ass." I started my fake acceptance speech. "Gavin for not having killed us just yet." I said as he nearly avoided hitting two potholes in the road. "And Athena for representing my current state of mind." Athena was snoring softly beside me, her head laying on my shoulder.

"Go to sleep then," Alder laughed. "We'll keep an eye out."

Between the roads getting increasingly bumpier, and Athena constantly moving around in her sleep, I couldn't say that I slept soundly. But I slept a little, which was all I could hope for.

I had always wondered what the fence looked like. My teacher had drawn it on the board once, but I doubt he ever saw it in real life. All we received were grainy, dark photos. They had been copied so many times that it had become almost unreadable. And we were all left wondering what was really supposed to keep the scary radiates away.

In real life, the fence looked big and strong, and went metres up into the air. The bottom part was pure steel and blocked the view of the outside. The steel went about three metres into the air, followed up by several stories on which soldiers were patrolling, looking both to the inside territory of the fence and out. Even though I had lived much closer to it than the other apprentices I had never been able to see it. I was almost disappointed that it didn't touch the clouds like my brothers had told me.

All and all the fence was about twenty metres into the air and went on as long as I could see. Every kilometre there was a new watchtower. Especially near the gate.

The gate was made out of two steel slabs, that could be pushed up with a thick chain. After going through a tunnel, we would encounter the same kind of doors again. I finally understood why the royals wanted everyone to refer to it as a wall. It sounded far sturdier than 'fence', though that description did seem a lot closer to it.

We weren't allowed to just go through, no one ever was. Dorian left the car and signed something to Holden, who then followed him. "They'll talk for at least an hour." Alder complained. "Fucking military, thinking they're important."

Gavin and Alder had all the right reasons to be tense. They knew the rest of the hunters. They knew that they could be dying as the military wants to talk it through.

We had been driving for ages already. It took about a day to get from home base to Vancouver, and now we had added half a day to that to get to the fence. All and all we felt like we were wasting time.

"Go outside and stretch your legs," Alder said to me and Athena. "No point in staying in this bloody car."

Athena went to find something to eat, while I just wanted to get on the fence and see what was beyond it. The guards took one look at me before stepping aside and allowing me to climb the many stairs that let up to the top floor of the construction.

The fence was built in a way that it was ever-expanding. Every little section could be dismantled, and a new part could be added as it grew. However, it was often under radiate attack, or there were simply old buildings in the way.

When I finally reached the top, I could feel the wind tugging at my clothes. I went into one of the small cubicles they had built for protection in case of an attack and luckily found it to be empty.

The land beyond the fence was not what I expected. It wasn't filled with savages and deformed animals, it wasn't totally bombed to the ground. It looked normal, like the land we had passed by all day today. The only thing different was that there was not one single soul who dared to go near the fence, and the ones who did got shot by the snipers. The ground was littered with dead, rotting bodies.

"Holy shit." I heard someone say behind me. I peeked over my shoulder to find someone I had not thought about in months: Djorn.

"What are you doing here?" He asked me. He had not changed one bit. He still had the same bulging fish-like eyes, and he was still set like a mountain. The only difference I could tell was that he looked like he had lost the last bit of baby fat in his face.

"Enjoying my view." I snapped back. "At least I was before you came in." I wasn't the same girl I was back when I met him. I did not want to blend in and not cause any waves. I wasn't scared of him anymore.

"I meant on the wall." He said, taking a few steps closer to me and looking out of the same window.

"We're crossing it." I just answered, instinctively stepping away from him.

"Is Teryn here too? I liked him, he was a great soldier." Djorn said, grabbing a pair of binoculars and peering through them to the lands beyond.

"He didn't make the cut." I told him.

"Really?" Djorn looked properly surprised. "And you did?"

"And I did." I confirmed. So far. But he did not need to know that. Even after everything that happened at the palace, I was starting to feel more secure at the hunters. Sure, I wasn't perfect at everything yet, but I did not think they would kick me out anymore.

"Liking it so far?" He casually asked me, slowly checking the horizon for any radiates.

"Why do you want to make small talk?" I asked back.

"Well, the hunters obviously saw something in you that I didn't." He finally responded, after taking his bloody time. His voice, his voice had changed a bit too. It sounded deeper now. "Figured maybe I was wrong before."

"Nope," I said. "I am who I am, and you are... you." I mimicked his familiar look of disdain. "That doesn't change."

"You're louder now." He commented, putting the binoculars away and looking me over with his blue eyes.

"I should throw you off the fucking fence for what you did to me." I just answered, leaning against the wall so I could keep an eye on him, in case he wanted to try something. "You could have gotten us both kicked out you know."

"And instead I am training for command and you are with the hunters." He said. "I'd say it worked out just fine."

This wasn't some stupid children's book where enemies make up in the end. This was real life, and I would never forgive him for threatening me with the knife or kicking the hell out of me. I wanted to give him a proper beating. I knew I could, he was way too slow to be able to respond in time. One properly aimed blow and he would be knocked to the ground.

No. I wouldn't do that. Alder will give me an earful if I do. I didn't even want to think about what Dorian would do, he might tell Jack. I couldn't risk it. I went over to the door to leave, but he grabbed my arm.

"If it makes you feel any better, half of the guys who were there that night didn't make it through the first three months of training." He said. I got my arm out of his grip quite easily.

"You shouldn't be here either." I just said and walked off.

It was a bit of a climb back down, which was even harder to do when you try to storm off angrily. If there was someone I never needed to see again in my life, it was Djorn. I wish I had Teryn to talk to, I never even told Athena about what happened before I came to the hunters. I think her respect for me would take a serious hit if she found out I had not even tried to fight back.

I was off in my imagination, in which I tossed Djorn over the fence, and I was so angry that I didn't even notice someone walking up the stars. I only needed to go down three more flights to get back to the car, but I roughly bumped into someone.

"I hear you almost got your head blown off." Jack said. He looked like he had not slept in days, the colour of his eyes almost matched the dark circles underneath them. He was wearing the standard black combat uniform, with two guns clipped to his belt as well as the knife I had once stolen from his room.

"I got lucky." I answered, surprised to see him here. "Are you going over the fence with us?" He leaned against the wall, his arms folded over his chest.

"I am." He confirmed. "Are you in fighting condition?"

There was that damned question again. No, I was not in fighting condition. I wanted to cry and mourn the ones we lost back at the palace, I wanted to be able to take a second and think before rushing into the next fight. I also knew that if I did any of that I would lose my place with the hunters, not to even mention that I would abandon all my friends.

"I am." I lied. We started to walk back down to the cars together.

"Your mission of watching Athena has ended." He confirmed for me. "Dorian has vouched for her."

"I figured." I answered. "But do you trust her?"

"I trust Dorian." He answered without answering my question

We were stuck at the fence for over two hours. None of us liked to be sitting on our asses, but in the end it was worth it. The military provided us with vehicles and weapons, as well as some food.

"We have four cars." Jack said, rolling out a map onto the hood of one of the cars while the guards started the process of opening the gate, which gave us at least five minutes. "Team leaders: Gavin, Alder, myself and Athena." He looked over to her. "I take it you know how to drive a car."

"I do." She answered him. Pretty much every radiate knew how to drive one, it was essential for survival beyond the fence.

"Good." He said. "Team leaders will be driving, seconds will be shooting to hostiles. Only shoot if they fire at you. We don't want to waste any bullets before reaching the compound." Behind us sergeants shouted orders at the soldiers manning he gates.

"The first car: Alder and Arturo." Jack said. "Second: Athena and Ryder, third: Julia and myself, last: Gavin and Holden."

I would be in the car with Jack. I had no idea why he chose that. So far, I proved that I worked the best with Alder and Athena. The thought of having to work together with the leader, while it was my first time beyond the fence, was beyond terrifying.

"What about me Jack?" Dorian asked a bit confused. Jack sighed, clearly not wanting the conversation to happen this way.

"You'll stay here old friend, go back to home base." He said to him. "I was told you were shot back at the palace."

"Just the arm." Dorian answered, rolling up his sleeve to show a bandaged forearm. The bullet had gone straight through, tearing away some muscle but luckily avoiding his bones.

"You know the policy." Jack said. "Can't have a wounded hunter on a mission."

So that's why he talked to me, to see if the bullet did any actual damage. The only difference it made was that there was a bandage over my ear, which influenced my hearing a bit.

Dorian clearly was not happy about the role assignment but knew better than to go against it. In the end, it was all for the best anyway, he could not use his arm properly.

I sat on the passenger seat of the third car and waited patiently. This car had a different kind of radio installed. It wasn't like it had been before, a straightforward radio that could connect with people on the same signal. We couldn't use that because of the radiates possibly listening in. This one only connected directly to the other cars, and nothing else.

My heart was thumping loudly in my chest. This was it. I would be going outside of the safe fence and into unknown territory. I had been training for it for the past year, but I hardly felt ready.

Jack spoke to the commander of this quarter until the gates started to slowly open, he then shook his hand and quickly made his way over to the car. It felt strangely unnecessary to put on my seatbelt, but I did it nonetheless.

When the gates were finally fully open, we drove out. Djorn was standing on one of the stories, looking down at the line of black cars that were moving out. When he caught my eye, he waved. If Jack hadn't been sitting beside me I would have flipped him off.

The tunnel was dark, with annoying flickering lights every few metres. They kept the lights like that to distract any enemy troops if they came through the tunnel. A technique that had been proven to work, though I doubt idiots like Djorn wouldn't be distracted by them either.

The other set of doors opened, and we drove out into the open, quickly gathering speed. There were no roads here, they ended at the fence. Luckily for us, the military weren't all idiots, they provided us with cars that were capable of going off-roading.

"Do you understand why I put you with me?" Jack broke the silence. The cars had started to get separated a bit, so we weren't such an easy target. There were at least fifteen metres between every car and the distance was only increasing.

"Not really." I admitted. Jack looked relaxed behind the wheel. He had one hand on top of it, while his other one rested on his leg.

"Think about it. What makes everyone different?" He asked.

"There are only four people who know how to drive, so putting them as leaders makes sense." I was thinking out loud. "Holden is a good shot. You put him with Gavin, who is the best driver."

"So if something happens to the front cars they will be there quickly, and shoot accurately." He elaborated.

"Alder is a good shot too, and you put him with Arturo who is really smart." I said. "So that they..."

"So when things go south, Arturo doesn't need a ten-minute break down on how to drive a car while Alder shoots." He said. "Why did I put them at the front?"

"So you have a good shot in the last car and in the first one?" I guessed.

"That, and Arturo excels in geography." He said. When he noticed I looked a bit confused he added. "Alder has no sense of direction. Arturo can read maps."

I managed to hold back my laughter. I didn't know Alder was that bad at reading maps that the leader noticed. Before all of this we spend most of our time at home base where he obviously already knew where to find everything.

"Athena and Ryder." I continued. "Athena can drive and shoot at the same time." I had no idea if it was true, but she once told me it was basically a requirement beyond the wall after I asked her how she could run and shoot so accurately during training. "Ryder... is good at hand to hand combat."

"Athena is an all-rounder. Ryder will be able to provide assistance." He explained. "Not everyone's talents are always useful."

"Which is why you put me with you." I said.

"I couldn't put you with Athena, your friendship will cloud your judgement." He said. "And if something goes wrong, the radiates will be out for my blood. If Alder hasn't infected you with his ineptness to read a map you can reach the Darkfort faster than anyone."

"So I should leave you for dead?" I asked. "I'm sure that will make me very popular."

"If they're rebels, they won't kill me." He sounded sure of himself. "They want to know our secrets. They'll torture me for it first."

Comforting thoughts.

Normally in missions like this, we would switch drivers every few hours, so one can rest up while the other one drives. Now, however, we did not have that luxury and were forced to stop after eight straight hours of driving.

"One-hour break," Jack announced. "We'll sleep on the next one."

Everyone went to stretch their legs. I talked with Athena for a bit, mainly about how she felt going back here, until I noticed Alder sitting away from the group, trying to balance a small, broken piece of mirror against a box so he could give himself a haircut.

"Need a hand?" I offered, grabbing the scissors from the ground.

"Have you cut hair before?" He asked me back.

"I had twelve siblings and no money." I answered. I stood behind him and let his hair out of the bun he was wearing it in. It had grown quite a bit and now flowed over his shoulders. "How short do you want it?"

"Short." He said. "No more buns or anything. It needs to stay out of the way."

I started with cutting his hair to the best of my capabilities. It was much easier to cut his hair than my siblings, they were always squirming around on the chair. However, they always had their hair short. My mother cut the girls' longer hairs. It took me some time to figure out how to cut his.

"So, first impressions." He said, referring to our surroundings. "What do you think?"

"If I didn't know any better I'd think we were still inside the fence." I answered truthfully. In the distance, Gavin had started passing around food and water to the others.

"The landscape only really changes after the Darkfort." He said. I carefully cut around his ear. I don't think he'd want to have matching half-ears with me.

"Do you think they're okay?" I asked quietly. We never really had the time to discuss what could be going on over there. We just knew it was compromised, but we had no idea to which extent. They could have killed everyone already, or they were totally fine and this entire trip was useless.

"Of course." Alder tried to sound sure of himself. "They are all properly trained for situations like these. They know what to do."

Ulric would know or he would just sprint away. I had to believe that, even if it was just to calm my nerves down. After we were done with the scissors Athena asked to use them.

"Do you need help?" I asked her as Alder got up to stretch his legs.

"No, I have a pretty straight forward plan." She started cutting away at her long locks of hair. It didn't look like she had a plan, she made uneven cuts and grabbed locks too big for the scissors to cut through.

"What are you doing?" I asked once her hair was starting to look as short as Alders.

"I didn't exactly leave this place because I had so many friends here Julia." She answered me. "White hair is kind of recognizable in case you haven't noticed."

I helped her with the back of her head and before long Athena was completely bald. She had a millimetre of hair left that we couldn't get rid of, but because it was white it didn't really stand out anyway. She still looked pretty, her high cheekbones came out even more, along with her blue eyes. The others eyed her a bit weirdly, but everyone knew better than to question Athena.

We slept on the next break, with obviously a watch in place, and continued our drive a few hours later. I hoped the Darkfort was just fine and dandy, I really could use a good bed right about now.

As we approached the building and the small town surrounding it, we split up. Two cars drove around it and lined up over there so that we surrounded it like a circle.

The building was much bigger than home base, and sure looked like a Darkfort as dusk was setting in. It was at least ten stories high and looked like it was the only thing that had gotten renovated in the small town. I thought I saw people passing by the windows every now and then, but it could have just been my nerves playing with me.

Jack and I had gotten out of the car. He was peering through a pair of binoculars, while I kept the assault rifle tightly in my hand. A column of four cars driving this way wasn't very stealthy, they must know we were coming.

Inside the car, the radio started croaking. Jack had altered it during our last stop, it could now be used as a radio instead of just a direct line to the other cars.

"Identify.... West 1-4" It croaked. Jack grabbed the small microphone and listened closely to what was being said, while I made sure we weren't snuck up upon. We had driven up a small hill, with behind us a line of trees. It made sure we weren't easily visible, but it was also easy cover for the enemy.

"Jack Alvarez. Alpha, Beta, Juliette, One four." Jack said.

"Jack?" Someone else spoke back on a light and airy tone on the other side. "What are you doing here? I thought you were back at the palace?"

"We received the code." Jack said. The other side was silent for a few moments.

"The message was erased on this end." The man answered. "It's safe up here."

"Do you recognize him?" I asked Jack. It seemed like false information had been getting through a bit too easily lately, and I did not feel like dying because of it.

"Yes. Kel." He said, though he didn't talk back to him on the radio.

"Can you be sure he wasn't the one who sent the wrong information in the first place?" I asked.

"Kel has been with us a lot longer than you have." He answered back, his tone venomous. Still, he wasn't picking up the radio to talk further.

"Dorian said we received information that detailed an attack on the royal family on Kingsday." I defended my argument. "That was false, and we lost people because of it. Then we received a message that turned out to be false with a secret code that only top hunters know, making us come here." I was quiet for a few seconds as we both stared at the radio. "Someone is playing with us, and we walked right into their trap."

There was no way to describe what happened next. Jack grabbed the microphone to talk to Kel, but as his fingers brushed against it, the entire building blew up.

The explosions started at the top and made their way down. The windows spewed out fire as though they were dragons. The ground shook all the way to where we were standing, and finally, the old brick walls started to give out.

The building fell down surprisingly slow. I thought it would just plumb to the ground, but it looked like it landed softly, almost like a feather.

We watched in horror as it happened. The building housed over thirty hunters, who were now all dead. We had lost over forty hunters in a span of one week.

I don't know if it was the entire world that went quiet, if my ears just didn't hear anything after that blast or if I didn't want to hear anything anymore but there was complete silence after that. I could feel my heart beating in my chest, I could feel my lungs filling up with air, but I felt nothing.

"Wha-" I started, but it seemed like this nightmare wasn't even over. In the far distance, I heard the familiar sound of a foghorn. For a brief moment, I thought it had all been a test.

We had to walk around the tree line to see it. There was a line of cars in the distance, they just peeked over the horizon. The foghorn stopped. The cars stopped with it. They just stood there, for a little while, until a loud voice took over the speakers.

"Let the hunt begin!"

Ice filled my veins as the cars started picking up speed. I faintly felt Jack's hand wrap around my arm and roughly pulling me back to our car. I managed to sit down in the chair, though it felt like my soul was no longer in my body.

We were all going to die.

We took off, speeding down the hill and driving further into unknown territory.

23

The town was completely covered in a cloud of smoke and debris. No one could survive that, I thought as we sped by it. I wanted to give in to the sadness, to let it wash over me and just curl up and sob.

"Orders." It was Gavin's voice who spoke through the radio first, pulling me out of my sad daze and back into reality.

Jack moved over to change the radio back to direct frequency, but I hit his hands away. "Keep your eyes on the bloody road, give me the instructions on how to fix this thing."

Suddenly I was thankful for Alder's constant nagging about my engineering 'handicap'. He had made me read tons of books about it and more often than not also gave me practical lessons when we weren't training. The radio was fixed in no time.

"We have to lose them." I repeated Jack. We made it passed the town and now drove into the clearing that laid beyond it. Two of the other cars were already way ahead, while the other one also had just only made it by the town.

I looked behind us and felt my heart drop. They had already gotten much closer. Their vehicles were made for this terrain, for this life. Ours were only supposed to get us here and back to the fence again.

"They are closing in on us, Jack." I said, my voice sounding frantic. Jack laid the binoculars on my lap.

"Climb in the back and tell me what you see." He instructed, sounding as calm as ever. We had used the back as storage for our guns and provisions. I climbed over our seats as quickly as I could, but I fell down anyway because he had to swerve to miss a rock.

Putting the binoculars to my eyes, I saw an image that would never leave my mind. There must have been thousands of them, all of their cars packed to the very last seat. They swung their guns around like they were toys. They were laughing and screaming, some even making rude gestures towards us.

I noticed a slight difference between some of them. Each time there were three or more cars that had the same kind of vehicles, with the men and women wearing the same kinds of clothes.

"What do you see?" He asked me.

"There are hundreds of them," I said. "They all have guns."

Right as I said it, I spotted one man. He was lying down relaxed on the top of a vehicle like they weren't going hundreds of miles per hour. Half of his face was hidden behind a bandana, in his hand he held a battered sniper rifle.

"They have snipers!" I warned him. He quickly repeated it into the radio, but it seemed like we were too late. Gunfire hit right next to our car, and he had to swerve yet again.

"Return fire." He ordered me and the others through the radio. "Focus on the snipers." I dug into the gun filled duffel bag as more bullets hit near us. At least they weren't great snipers.

The bag had loads of guns, it was just about picking the right one. Handguns were useless and so were the submachine guns. At the bottom, I found what I was looking for: A brand new sniper rifle.

I shot out the back window and positioned the gun on the back seat as well as it allowed me to. I spotted one of the snipers when I peered through the scope. I knew I could never make the shot, he was too far away and our car was far from stationary. Instead, I focused my shots on the car.

My first bullet hit the bumper, and my second one hit the driver. I don't know if it killed him, but the car made a sharp turn to the right and bumped into the one next to him.

"One down." I informed him. The other hunters had also started to return fire, more cars bumped into each other and slowed the entire thing down. A sparkle of hope lifted up inside my chest. Maybe we wouldn't die today.

Every time a car went down, a new one just took its place. It was like they had a never-ending supply of people willing to die for them.

The large group of cars caused a giant cloud of smoke and dust to follow us, almost like a storm waiting to catch up. I was peering through the scope for my next target when I spotted one. A large man on a car that was riding out ahead of the herd. He had his gun pointed towards one of the other cars and did not notice me just yet.

I shot. The bullet hit the tire and slowed the radiate packed vehicle down and back into the group. I thought I did well until I noticed how dumb I had been.

The car had been a distraction. To our right was a large truck, with a machine gun mounted on top of it. I frantically returned fire to them, but once the spray of bullets started, I knew we were done for.

The bullets started flying all around us. Jack did not need to tell me to get down, there was nothing else to do. The sound of the bullets hitting everything around us was deafening.

The car hit something, and we came to a crashing halt. I got thrown off the backseat and onto the floor, with the provisions and guns falling on top of me. For a moment I thought the worst: Jack had been hit.

"You okay?" I heard him ask. I let out a sigh and threw the stupid water bottles that had hit me in the face aside.

"I'm fine. Are you hit?" I asked him. He shook his head and fiddled with the radio, trying to see if it still worked.

We had crashed into a tree. There was smoke coming out of the engine, but at least the gunfire had stopped. I grabbed the duffel bag and shoved the guns back inside, as much as it could carry.

"Car three down. Keep heading east. Alder, you are in command." Jack said, before taking his handgun and shooting the radio, so the radiates couldn't use it.

There was a strange sense of serenity at that moment. We knew death was coming, we knew there was no way to fight it. Though I doubt either of us would go quietly. I doubt they would kill Jack anyway, he was valuable. I was not.

When we exited the car, Jack grabbed the duffel bag from my hands and went through it. He slung an AK lazily over his shoulder, grabbed a shotgun and put two revolvers on his belt. I kept the sniper rifle, we had become close friends, and took two submachine guns.

"What's the strategy?" I asked him. The radiates had gotten much closer. It would still take them at least two minutes to reach us though. I threw the duffel bag with the remaining guns into a bush, so it was at least hidden from sight.

"We run." He said, breaking off into a sprint. "Over there!"

There were two houses, right next to what used to be a road. They would act as perfect cover. I started sprinting, the houses seemed too far away. I doubt we would make it in time.

Jack was behind me, every few seconds I looked back. I had to slow down my step too much for my liking. But he had undoubtedly been in these situations before. I needed his knowledge to survive myself.

We were in an open field. One properly aimed shot and they could get us. A bullet hit me near my feet, followed by one that almost hit me. I ripped off the stupid bandage I had over my ear and threw it aside. It only clouded my hearing.

We weren't going to make it. The serenity passed. Instead, the panic kicked in. I wanted my legs to move faster. I wanted to live.

"We're not going to make it." I shouted at Jack. I saw in his face that he agreed with me. I knew that when he said Alder was the new commander, he was certain we'd die.

I could see the dust clouds come closer to us, as well as smoke rising in the distance. A fire had started behind them, probably coming from the remains of the Darkfort. It seemed like that was all I would remember from my last day on earth: Smoke and debris. I was really wondering what was going through my head when I was happy to be a hunter, instead of a 'boring' factory worker.

All of the sudden, a car came from our right. It was built like a battering ram and came thundering towards us. "Down." Jack ordered. We both laid down on our bellies in the grass, but the car had spotted us.

It stopped a few metres to my right. I pointed the sniper rifle at the door, and almost shot Alder through the head when he opened it.

"In." He just said. We both quickly jumped up and got in the black car. Jack sat down on the passenger side, while I threw my guns next to me on the backseat.

"I thought I told you to keep moving." Jack said while Alder urged the car forwards as fast as it would go.

"Yeah, well then you put me in charge." Alder responded. "Arturo and I drove passed an unused vehicle of theirs."

"Is that why the backseat is covered in blood?" I asked, wiping my hands on my trousers.

"It was unused after." Alder said, a smile gracing his face. It was weird how easily that smile broke the tension I felt in my stomach. How easy everything felt. Even if I'd die, I'd die among family.

They were right behind us. Probably with only a hundred metres left between us. This time we had one of their vehicles, however, and we were able to go a lot faster.

"Do we return fire?" I asked. Jack responded by climbing into the backseat as well and shot out the back window.

"Fire at anyone who comes too close." He instructed me. Alder managed to keep the car relatively steady, and because they were so much closer, shooting became much easier.

Jack was a great shot, of course he was, he took out most of the cars on our right side, while I took care of the left. I made sure that the truck with the machine gun mounted on top of it got the first few bullets.

It felt odd. I knew I was killing people. I knew I was ending lives. But nothing registered. If I didn't do this, I would die myself. Suddenly it became about more than just protecting the Union, it was to selfishly protect myself.

There was no radio here to contact the others. Though Alder warned us that we were finally catching up to them. We had to cross a small hill and we would be in another opening.

The radiates returned fire only on our car, the other ones had made it over the hill already. We had to duck down, the bullets were hitting all around us.

They shot out one of our tires, followed by another one. Any hope we had of getting over that hill was absolutely lost. We weren't able to go fast enough anymore.

We rolled back down the hill, right into our pursuers. They caught up to us before we could properly realize it. There were no houses nearby, there was nothing to do but die.

A shot rang out, followed by a loud groan. I lifted my head to see blood gushing out of Jack's right shoulder.

I thought back to those many nights with Alder in the small home base library. He taught me what to do in case of a bullet wound and told me it would be inevitable when you go beyond.

I put my hand on the wound and with the other one grabbed his wrist. "Jack's been shot." I warned Alder. It would only be a matter of seconds before they would be upon us. Jack was in pain, that much was clear, but he did not seem out of it just yet. His pulse was still strong, though my hand was already covered in his blood.

The bullet wound was too high up to have hit his heart or lungs, but it could have hit his bones. I pulled him forward and found a good exit wound. At least the bullet had gone through him and wasn't still inside.

Alder had exited the car and opened the door next to Jack. He checked his pulse, looking as calm as ever. Like this was just your average Tuesday.

"Piss off, you morons." Jack groaned. "Grab the guns, take out as many as you can."

"Sorry, but I think Alder is still in charge." I answered and looked at him. "Your call."

It was too late to make any sort of call. The cars came thundering around us, engulfing us in a cloud of dust. Alder pulled Jack out of the car and laid him on his back. The cars circled around us, while some went and continued the pursuit of our friends.

A gunshot fired near me and the glass of the window behind me shattered into a million pieces. An arm came through the window and grabbed me, trying to pull me out. I reached for the gun Jack had dropped, but it was too far away. Another arm wrapped around me and I got pulled out through the broken window.

There were no words that could properly describe what was happening outside of the car. The loud cars boxed us in from all sides, some stopped while others were thundering by us in pursuit of our friends. I felt like I was back in the tunnels underneath Vancouver. There was absolutely no air here, just dust.

Alder was still trying to save Jack, while the large man pulled me backwards, to his car. It didn't make sense, why didn't they just shoot me? He had his arm wrapped around my waist. I tried kicking him, elbowing him, reaching for his gun. But it was all in vain. I could hear them laughing in my ear.

"Alder!" I shouted. The sound of the vehicles thundering by us was deafening. I had no idea how he even managed to hear me. He looked up, his dark eyes finally revealing how scared he was. He went to grab his gun, but it got shot out of his hand by someone behind me.

Alder was bleeding, Jack was dying. I had trained for months, but I had no idea what I should do to stop any of it.

Finally, I felt metal hit my temple. Everything went black.

24

I thought I was dead. A part of me hoped that I died. I didn't know what horrors the radiates had in mind for me. I didn't know if I should be scared.

I woke up in the trunk of someone's car, the images of Alder and Jack lying in the dirt still imprinted freshly into my brain.

We went over a bump, and I hit my sore head against the ceiling. They had knocked me out, that much was clear, but everything else was still coming back to me.

My hands and feet were tied with rope. They had taken my knife, and by the looks of it also my jacket. It's not like I needed it, I was practically melting from the heat.

I could hear muffled voices. I counted at least three people in the car, but I also heard other vehicles driving near us. It sounded like they had broken off from the party though.

"We'll stop in five." I heard one of the muffled voices say. Beyond the fence, people spoke both English and a dialect. According to Athena, the rebels who hated the Union had also made a new language, so that they could communicate without interference. I thought the men would only be speaking the new language, but I guess I was wrong.

Five minutes felt like hours in the back of the car. I was sweating like crazy, but not enough for the ropes to just slide off. They were digging painfully into my skin, but I still tried to get them off.

Sunlight poured into the trunk when they opened it. For a moment I was totally blinded by it.

I must have been out throughout the night, though the sun wasn't very high up into the sky yet.

Someone picked me up from the trunk and placed me on the ground. The sunlight burned my eyes, but my vision started coming back to me. There were two other cars, that they had parked in a circle.

At first, they just let me sit with my back against one of the cars, while they talked to each other. I counted eight men and four women. Each of them looked like they had not washed once in their lives. One of the women was wearing my bloodstained jacket as though it had always belonged to her.

A man broke off from the group and knelt down in front of me. He was the one who had grabbed me. He was bald, but half of his head was covered in tattoos. He also had a thick beard, though I doubt that was a fashion choice for him here.

"Drink." He put the water bottle to my dry lips, but I kept them firmly shut, turning my head away from him. It could be poison, it could have been tainted with sleeping drugs. Yes, I was thirsty, but I could go a lot longer without water.

He grabbed my jaw harshly and forced my mouth open. I tried kicking him, but he easily placed one of his hands on my legs and kept them pushed down. The water was great, it didn't taste like it had been meddled with. That did not stop me from distrusting them.

He handed the water bottle to the woman behind him and slowly lifted his hand off my legs, trying to see if I would attack again. I didn't, there was no point to it. Even if I did some damage to him, the others would kill me for it. I needed to stay alive, I needed to get back to the fence.

"What's your name sweetheart?" He asked me. He had a slight accent, but he seemed to be able to speak English well.

"Julia." I answered. My hands were still covered in Jack's blood, not to mention the amount of blood on my clothes. Aside from a throbbing headache from when they knocked me out, I seemed to have gotten away with minimal injuries.

"You from inside the fence?" Another man asked me, stepping forward. He was tall with a very crooked nose and had dark skin. The woman behind him sighed and crossed her arms.

"Of course she's from inside you dipshit! Are you blind?" She complained. She had fiercely red long hair that looked about as unmanageable as mine. Her arms were covered in black tattoos as well, only adding to her textbook radiate look.

"Sometimes they take people from the outside and force them in." He answered her. "Besides, hunters are no females. She has to be one of their girls."

The hunter's sexist policy might just have saved my life. They think I was someone's girlfriend or wife, and not a fully trained hunter myself. I could play into that until I get an opportunity to escape.

"She has the tattoo." The redheaded woman pointed out.

"Maybe they mark their women." He said and grinned at her. "Maybe I should too."

The woman kicked the man softly, though the smile on her face revealed she wasn't too upset about it. "Damn job didn't pay us nearly what got promised." He turned to the woman and held her face softly in his hands. "She'll be worth it."

The bald man looked at me almost like he was sympathetic to my situation. Though he still stood up and joined the other ones for lunch.

We paused there for an hour. They had set up some sort of tent under which they relaxed in the shade, while the sun was beating down on my skin.

I guessed it was around noon now, the sun seemed right above me. All I could do was watch them laugh and drink.

The bald man's name was Ivar. He and the other eight men were what they called 'blood brothers'. I had learned from Alder that it meant they were in some sort of clan or group together. They were the strongest men and got sent out on jobs to bring back the money.

The women were their wives. They had the simple jobs of cooking and keeping their husbands happy. They didn't seem as serious about their marriage vows as we did back home. The men who were now without wives, because they died under our bullets, weren't that bothered by it. They were even already discussing which women they would marry next.

A fight nearly broke out when Don said he wanted to marry Ivar's sister. Ivar didn't take too kindly to it and threatened him with his knife. My knife.

I knew what would happen if I lost my knife forever. Frederick, Lucian, Samiel. I only knew their names because they had lost their knives too. Everyone made fun of them. It would not matter if I came back a hero, they would still roast me until the day I die, and probably after that as well.

If I came back a hero, to what? The Darkfort got blown up. Jack and Alder were either dead or being tortured for secrets they would never give. The others would never get away in time. I was most likely the only hunter left alive.

When we continued our travels I was thankfully not put in the trunk this time. I was on the backseat, with my hands and feet still tied up. They had circled the rope around my forearms too, so I could never really relax them.

The front seat was occupied by Ivar and Theodric, a boy not much older than me. The two were clearly related in some way, though I doubt they are brothers.

Every few minutes Ivar would check the rear-view window to see that if I was up to something, while the boy happily chatted away.

"I think Ania will be the one," Theodric said. "She seems ready to get married. I'll ask her once we return."

"Ania will take one look at you and turn you down." Ivar responded, after keeping silent throughout most of the story. He kind of reminded me of Ulric, with his heavy voice and general 'I know things better than you' vibe. "You need to experience more before even thinking about starting a family."

"Weren't you married for like one year before she took off though?" Theodric replied, clearly insulted by what Ivar had said to him. Ivar did not respond to him and instead focussed on driving.

The landscape still had not changed much, excluding the fact that it was much hotter here. It was easy for me to imagine that I was safe at home, inside the secure fence. Until I noticed the people surrounding me of course.

"You're married, aren't you?" Theodric had turned around and was talking to me. I thought Ivar would tell him to shut up, but instead he checked the mirror again, waiting to hear my reply.

"Y-yes." I answered. I figured that if I was someone who is married to a hunter, and not one herself, this should all seem terrifying to me. It was of course scary, even with all my training, but I decided to play into the innocent factor.

"How long?" He asked me, showing me a kind smile. He was missing half of his teeth, as well as his front one being chipped.

"A year." I answered.

"Any kids?" He asked. Having kids at a young age beyond the fence was only normal when your life span is about thirty years less than inside. At least that is what I was taught, Theodric according to the textbooks should have two kids by now.

"No," I answered him. "This was my first time going beyond the fence."

Theodric laughed. "Rough out here huh? Is it true you guys have machines that make food?"

"You mean like factories?" I asked.

"What's that?" He immediately answered back.

"Shut up." Ivar finally said, pulling young Theodric back in his seat by the collar of his jacket. "Keep a watch out, we're first now."

Ivar had pulled up and was now driving ahead of the other two cars. They were driving in a V shape. Occasionally a rock or a few trees would cause the shape to be broken up, but they always came back.

We drove for hours on end. We only stopped because the sun had gone down. Two of the three cars had busted headlights, it had become too dangerous to continue on. They again parked the vehicles in a closed off circle. In the middle of it, they started working on a small fire, gathering sticks from the trees nearby as well as some dried grass.

The ropes had been cutting into me for hours now, leaving my skin red and bloody. I stuck it out however, I knew they would not loosen them for me. They did not trust me yet.

I got to eat dinner with them. They had cooked some kind of animal and gave me a piece of the meat as well as some sort of bread. At least I thought it must be near bread. It was much smaller, and harder to bite into. Though it filled me up quickly.

"Kev, you're on guard duty." Ivar ordered. I had figured out that Kev was the younger brother of the dark-skinned guy quite easily. They were always bantering on together, calling each other 'deorre' though that was neither of their names.

Kev was smart and did not stand guard near us, but a little away from the cars with his back covered against a large rock.

Clearly, not all radiates were dumb savages like I had been taught.

I wonder how much the hunters actually knew about radiates. Just the few hours I got to spend with them countered a lot of things I had been told. They weren't complete savages. They worked for their pay, they protected the ones they loved, they were trying to survive. Just like us.

No, I would not sympathize with them. If it wasn't for them, I could still be surrounded by Alder, Athena and Ulric. I could be with the ones I love, instead of being here, hundreds of miles away from the place where they were killed.

It felt like there was this black void inside my chest where there once was a beating heart. I didn't know if they died. I didn't know if they lived. Logic told me that everyone was dead. But my head could not seem to grasp that fact.

Ivar sat down in front of me once again and held up the water bottle. "Drink." He said. This time when he put the bottle to my lips I did not turn away. The fact that I hardly drank anything last time combined with the heat here had made me parched. Besides, they had no reason to harm me if they were just going to sell me.

Ivar kept his eyes on me as I emptied the bottle. When I was done, he threw it aside and sat down in front of me. His eyes looked me up and down.

"What happened to your ear?" He asked me.

"There was an attack at the royal palace." I scrambled to get my lies in order. "I was there with my husband for his mission. They tried to shoot me through the head but missed and nicked my ear instead." Ivar just nodded twirling my knife around in his hand.

"Your husband." He repeated. "Where is he now?"

"Dead most likely." I answered. Ivar raised his eyebrow at me.

"You don't seem too broken up about it." He stated. Damn, I messed up. There was no point in trying to seem sad about it now, it would just break character.

"It was either get married or work in the factory. I don't regret my choice." I said, though after I looked around I added. "Okay, maybe I regret it a little now."

Ivar laughed. Not a quiet smile I had gotten so used to back home, not a little twinkle in his eyes, but a full-on laugh that caused others to look at us. I couldn't help but laugh with him. The situation was horrible, the people and lands were unknown, but I was laughing.

<h1 style="text-align:center">25</h1>

I dreamed about Athena that night. She was tied up beside me in the car and kept calling Ivar Eryk. Jack was there too, but he didn't say all that much, he just kept trying to kill me.

We drove and stopped, and drove and stopped. My body seemed to be covered in a permanent layer of dust. I very much tried to ignore all the radiation warnings that kept popping up in my head, but it was hard not to get worried as we passed yet another radiation warning sign that the Union had put up.

I don't know why, but the group kept putting me with Ivar. With the exception of Theodric, the rest of them did not seem all that interested in me. Ivar asked me more things about myself and my life before I crossed the fence. Eventually, I just told him that I married Ulric, it seemed the easiest excuse because he was there for him being blown up.

"Sorry, lia." He said, not really being able to pronounce my name correctly. "It was just a job."

I did not respond to him. I didn't know what to say. 'It's fine that you killed all of my friends as long as you don't kill me' that was the situation I was currently looking at. I just wanted to go home.

It took us days, but we finally arrived at their town. It was much smaller than I had expected. There were about fifteen houses all built into one circle. The houses were nothing like the ones back home. They were either made of wood or a clay like material, not the bricks I had gotten so used to. They had torn down everything from the old world, while we had been so focused on rebuilding it.

The ropes were tightened around my wrists again, but the ones around my ankles were removed. Theodric apologised while he tied the rope around my neck and was now holding the end of it like a leash.

The people who they had left in their village were the elders, the kids and the unmarried women. At least that was something the world agreed on, women weren't made for fighting.

They all stared at me out of their windows as we walked through the tiny streets in between the houses. Most of them exited right after and gathered in the town square.

There was a man standing there. Normally in the centre we would have rebuilt the fountain or planted some symbolic tree, but here they had erected a stage. On top of it was the man. He was old, even for Union standards.

Maybe they taught us that the radiates died young because the old ones were hidden away in villages like these. The man was clearly the leader here. Maybe he had been a blood brother in his younger days, his scars sure made it look like it.

Ivar went on the stage and hugged the man tightly. They smiled and smacked each other harshly on the back. "I am glad to see you safe, son." The man said. "How did it go?" Theodric pulled me closer to the stage by the leash. I shot him a dirty glare, which he responded to with an apologetic smile.

"Rough," Ivar responded. "We lost four women because of the damned raiders. First and last job also gave us barely any pay." The man glanced over to the returning blood brothers, and his grey eyes fell on me.

"And where did this little bird come from?" He asked. Ivar looked over to me as well. He looked like his father, they had the exact same eye colour, as well as a bald head. Ivar was taller and padded with muscles and still had some protective gear on, making his father seem even older.

"We found her during our last job. Figured that we at least should get some pay out of it." He answered, looking me straight in the eye.

"Where will you sell her?" The old man turned his eyes on his son again, ignoring me fully.

"I'm not sure yet." He answered. "Maybe we should keep her. She seems strong enough. Good workers are hard to come by."

The man glanced over at me and then back at his son. There was something unspoken between them. I knew Ivar had taken a liking to me, as much as he could without feeling too sorry for me, but he was not the leader here. His father was.

"Very well then." He said. "She can stay of course, if that is your wish."

The other people in the town watch the conversation go down. A few glanced over to me, clearly sizing me up. It seemed like the women here were just as strong and mouthy as the men. They were all shorter than me, and none of them seemed that aware of their appearance. Most of them had hair so tangled up it became little braid like strings.

"What loot do you bring back to us today, Ivar?" An older woman asked. Ivar signed Kev and Don to bring a chest forward. I had not seen it on the way over here, but then again all I saw was the backseat and whatever place we were taking a lunch break or staying the night at.

Rings filled up the chest. Not the wedding kind, but just dozens of thick silver rings. "What is that?" A young boy wondered out loud.

"Edgo has decided it is time for a currency in our lands." Ivar answered. "I must admit, I am not sure of it myself. But we can use these trinkets to buy grain and cattle in Fe San, or any of his cities for that matter."

He picked a few up in his hands and weighed them, before letting them fall back in. "Should his reign fall we'll just melt them and make some bullets."

The word bullets made the bystanders happy. They cheered and chanted his name, as well as 'Sigmund' which I guessed was his father's name. The two quickly exchanged some whispers, while the crowd broke up, getting back to their everyday life.

Theodric handed my leash over to Ivar and went to talk to Sigmund. The two seemed happy to see each other, but I only caught Sigmund celebrating Theodric's first successful run before I got yanked away by Ivar.

Ivar lived more on the edge of town, which doesn't say much seeing as it only takes about a minute to completely walk through it. His house was one of the newer ones, which was made out of hardened clay with a wooden roof. It was pretty small and only consisted of one room, where there was both a bed, a fireplace and a small weapon storage area.

"Sit." He said, pointing to a small pillow that was laying near the fire. The fire was in the very centre of the house, with a lot of cooking equipment laying near it.

"I just saved your life." He said after I sat down. He removed some of his armour, which was an old rundown bulletproof vest and some knee and arm pads.

"Am I supposed to thank you?" I asked back. In all fairness, he was also the guy who pulled me out of the window and took me from my friends in the first place. I hardly felt like I owed him a thank you.

"You could have been sold as a slave on the market." He sat down across from me, with the fire separating us. "You would have given us a lot of money too. A pretty girl from inside the walls."

He twirled my knife in his hands again, the sharp point digging into his index finger. "We'd have to lie about your virginity being intact. You'd give us more than-"

"So why didn't you sell me?" I cut him off.

"I'm not sure yet." He answered, his piercing grey eyes looking me over once again. "You don't seem like most people from inside the fence."

"Well if it makes you feel any better, none of you come near the description we got about radiates." I told him. I knew the value of flattery and friendship. I needed to build a foundation of trust before I could slit his throat with *my* knife and take off. "You don't look like savages." Ivar laughed.

"One tip," he said, sticking the knife in the ground next to him. "Don't call us radiates."

"What do I call you?" I asked back.

"How about humans?"

26

It was hard to keep track of time beyond the fence. They didn't count days or months here, they had no need for it. All they did was follow seasons, so they knew what kind of clothes to wear and weather to expect.

The weather was very different here. It was constantly scalding hot, and I found myself getting used to the sunburns quicker than to the new lifestyle I was thrown into. The townsfolk didn't believe me when I told them about rain so cold it turned into snow. They thought I had heatstroke, which turned out to be great for me because they allowed me to rest for a few days.

In their terms, I was a slave. But this wasn't the life I imagined slaves to have. Things were weird beyond the fence. Every town, every city, had a different set of rules. Sigholm was led by Sigmund, who came here after being a slave himself. He and his son therefore always made sure that I wasn't overworked nor that I went hungry.

In a way, this place was better than where I grew up. There was a sense of belonging, of family. If two people were fighting, their kids could just go to the next house over and be welcomed and distracted. No one hoarded food, even during the cold months when the food supply stopped in the big cities.

I found out about a lot of things the teachers never taught us. For instance, how the Union gave some of the food they grew away to the radiates. I knew that they were just trying to please the anti-rebel movement, but it seemed pretty stupid seeing as they can't even manage to feed all their factory workers.

I had stopped counting the days since I arrived in Sigholm, they all started clumping together into one very long day, but I knew at least two seasons had come and gone. The winter was coming to an end, though I hardly thought it felt like winter here. Back home there would be snow, accompanied by plenty of rain. It rained occasionally here, but the villagers welcomed it with open arms.

"Ready?" Ivar asked me, handing me a bag filled with weapons and ammunition.

"Yes." I answered. Today was the first day since I got here that I would be leaving the village. They were making a trip to Fe San, a large city to the south of the village. I was told that when it would reach peak summer the sun would be too hot to be outside for too long, they wanted to make sure they had enough provisions to last well through the spring and summer.

Fe San was a rebel claimed city, which is why Ivar had tied a scarf around my neck, to cover up my tattoo. Fe San was under the rule of someone named Edgo, though most of the villagers doubted he would manage to keep it

"Every few years there is a new guy who says he will be the one to unite us against the fence." An old woman by the name of Katlien had told me when I scrubbed her floor for her. "Sure, they have never been this bold, but he will never last."

Edgo had surprised most of the villagers by making it through the winter months, which was usually when the Union and the rebels fought the most. Still, no one really cared. He would take the big cities and move against the Union, he wasn't interested in some distant place as small as Sigholm.

We loaded up the cars and took off in the early hours of the day. If we drove fast and without breaks, we would make it by nightfall. According to Katlien, Fe San was built under the sun's wrath and is scalding hot throughout the entire year.

Because of that, it had become a night city. People slept during the day, but at night the city became alive.

To make sure everyone saw that I was a slave, my forehead was marked with one diagonal red line that reached from my hairline to the space in between my eyebrows. Ivar told me that all the slaves had them and that they were usually tattooed on, I guess I got lucky when they only used dye.

I got upgraded from the backseat to the passenger seat of Ivar's car. I had gained his trust over any of the other villagers, it was the easiest to do as well. I slept just outside his house for the first few weeks, before he allowed me to sleep next to the fireplace when he thought it had become too cold outside. Thought it was never really cold here, winter here is like a warm summer back home with my family.

I saw the way he looked at me. He saw me as something more than just a slave. Being one made it easy to overhear the town's gossip, which was all about the leader's son falling in love with the slave.

Maybe if I was born here, I could fall in love with him too. I wasn't though, and in my mind he would always be the asshole who stole me away from the life I am supposed to have. He was the one who was in my way of going back home.

I still wanted to return, even if there was nothing to return to. I would probably have to tell what happened to me. If the hunters really were all dead the military might take me in, but I wasn't betting on that. I wanted my HSC.

The Honorary Services Crescent was a medal bestowed on certain members of the public by the king himself. It meant that the receiver helped the endurance of the Union or improved it in a significant way. More often than not commanders from the military get the medal. Afterwards, they'd never have to work again.

I don't think I did something improving the Union, and I doubt my newly found knowledge about the radiate lifestyle would be enough. My only hope was Roderick, maybe he would take pity on me and allow me to live out the rest of my days in peace.

"Keep your eyes open when we get there." Ivar said, pulling me out of my daze. "Loads of thieves and murderers over there. No one really controls them."

"Not even the Edgo guy?" I asked. Ivar laughed, resting one of his hands on the steering wheel and the other one out of the open window.

"He's off somewhere a little more comfortable than Fe San." He answered. "I'm pretty sure he called it 'the strongest get to live'."

"You met him?" I asked.

"He went village by village to recruit men for his little hunter hunt." It was the first time in months that I had even heard the word 'hunter' being said out loud. It hurt more than I was willing to admit. I felt the black void in my heart expanding over my chest.

I had gone through a bit of a transformation since I came here. The women all did not care about their appearance. For every four guys there was one woman in the village, so they had no need to dress up for them. I did still care, even if it was to preserve a little bit of my old life, so I taught a few kids how to braid. Afterwards, my hair was constantly being braided, so it never got in the way.

That, combined with the constant layer of dust that was to be found everywhere and the clothes they wore, made me look like a radiate myself. They did not have any mirrors around though, the first time I saw myself in months was in the rear-view mirror.

My face looked slimmer. I had lost both weight and muscle due to my new life here. I still had the same boring green eyes with barely any lashes over them though. Not everything had changed.

We reached Fe San a little after the sun went down. The city was just waking up from its slumber during the day. There was one large area where they parked the cars. There was no need to lock them, the stealing of a vehicle had the punishment of death here. According to Ivar, Edgo rather had car thieves being prosecuted than murderers.

The streets of the city were small and packed with people. I saw how it was easy to pickpocket someone here. It was just really impossible to walk by someone, they always brushed against me due to the lack of space.

Everyone visibly had guns on them. Ivar told me that it was something from the days before Edgo, where the city was prone to shootouts and robberies. Now there were guards dressed in grey patrolling the streets, with guns much bigger than ours.

I kept my eyes to the ground. Though slavery was different everywhere beyond the fence, they could all agree on one thing: I wasn't allowed to make eye contact. Ivar had only told me that rule when we were in the car over here.

"So all this time I wasn't allowed to look you in the eyes?" I asked him.

"I don't mind it." He had responded.

Slaves were common in the city. It seemed like every group we passed had at least one with them. They were often young like me but looked like they had never eaten something in their lives.

I hated how it made me feel lucky that I was Sigholms's slave, instead of one of theirs. I was lucky to be alive compared to my dead friends. Though I had not felt like I was on luck's side since Jack had sent me that damned message.

Our first stop was the official Union shop, or at least what had been left of it.

Theodric enthusiastically told me that this used to be manned by people from the Union, but that Edgo had executed them in the streets when he took the city. The Union workers had sold grain and other things the Unions grew 'plenty' of. Edgo refused their help and send their charity grain back tainted with blood.

The shop was busy with people. For a city under the sun's wrath, it sure was cramped here. There were many displays, but they all only held weird drawing and prices. For the actual trade, you'd have to talk with one of the men in grey.

"*Deog gadne, twa mokte u pokne?*" The man behind the counter said. He was small, with a bald head and a constant scowl on his face, though he tried to make his voice sound nice and friendly.

A lot of people here had small deformities. The man's nose was pretty much gone on one side, the girl behind him had a weird lump on her shoulder and the man keeping guard missed an eye. I already knew that it was either because of radiation or simple battle wounds that caused the radiates to look so different, that didn't stop me from getting a little side-tracked every time I saw it though.

" *Wrae, argna ne palep obmo dazne.*" Ivar answered with difficulty. He had not spent a lot of time yet trying to learn the new language. Though he was still the best one out of his village.

Ivar and the man haggled over the price. We had to walk out twice and come back in when the man called after us. Eventually, Ivar handed him half the money we had brought with us, and the two shook hands on it.

"Don't they give it to us now?" I asked after we walked out empty-handed.

"No." Ivar laughed. That's what he did the most, laugh. He laughed about my ignorance about his culture. He laughed about pretty much anything that came his way. "We'll pick it up in the morning, when we leave."

Next up was the cattle master. The town's cow had finally died after twenty long years of service. We needed to buy another one, as well as sheep so the women can start preparing next year's winter clothes.

Ivar was good at haggling the prices down. Maybe it was the fact that he looked like he could crush the guy's skull, but he gave in quite easily to the lowest possible price. All and all the day went by quickly and without much trouble. We even got a chance to stop at a bar before taking off.

It felt weird to do the day backwards. As the morning hours started, we found ourselves in the 'roaches bar' ran by possibly the uglicst woman I had ever seen in my life. She was tiny and so fat that she looked like she was just a ball. She also constantly yelled at her staff.

"Take a sip every time she says 'cunt'." Ivar challenged the group. Within the hour all of them were drunker than I had ever seen a human being be. I wasn't allowed to drink as a slave, so I got to watch the train wreck go down.

I felt my heart beating in my throat as I started to form an escape plan. The urge to leave washed over me suddenly. The longing to be back home only increased as I brushed my fingers under the scarf and over my tattoo.

They were drunk, that much was clear. But Ivar only looked slightly buzzed and was too close to me for me just to run out. He leaned back in his chair and swung his arm over the back of mine. I felt his fingertips brush against my shoulder, and once again I realized that today wasn't the day I would leave.

"Stupid cunt! Watch where you are going!" The old hag shouted, to which the group all drank deeply from their glasses again.

"Here," Ivar said, giving me his glass. "Drink with us."

"Isn't that illegal?" I asked back.

"Not anymore." Ivar responded. He rubbed his thumb over my forehead, blurring the red line until it was completely gone. "There, you're free. Now drink little bird."

The nickname little bird had stuck around. It was mainly because half of the town's folk couldn't pronounce my name correctly. I know they called me little not because of my height but because of my weight. Most of the women looked like they could eat me alive. But where they got the bird part from was beyond me. Perhaps it was the konsi still haunting me.

Athena had been right though, the alcohol here tasted much better. Back home it tasted like pure gasoline or cleaning supplies, whereas here they had different flavours. In some you could hardly taste the alcohol at all.

Being drunk again felt good. Last time I was surrounded by my friends in the royal palace, right before most of them were murdered. Here I was surrounded by people who in any other situation I would have also counted as friends.

Apparently, it was normal to sleep in the bar here. Where inside the fence people would get kicked out, here they were left alone. Eventually, when the sun was already high up into the sky, everyone fell asleep.

I did too sadly. Right in between Theodric and Ivar. If I hadn't maybe I would have been able to escape. Though it still probably wouldn't matter that much, I thought to myself. I had not seen a map since before crossing the fence, I had no idea where home was.

Many members of our group complained about having headaches the next day, though I must say I was just happy to wake up from a drunken haze without dodging bullets. The old hag was screaming our heads off though, so we left the bar in a hurry.

The sky was dark again, and the streets slowly flooded with people getting kicked out of bars. Theodric and Don went to pick up our supplies, while the rest of us made our way back to the cars.

"What are the cities like inside the fence?" Ivar asked me.

"Bigger." I answered. "Cleaner. Also far less crowded than over here." I had to walk closer to Ivar to stop bumping into people. Though I doubt he minded it all that much.

"But you have more people?" He asked back.

"Well yes, but the only people who are able to afford living in a city are the rich." I told him.

"Where did you learn all of this?" He asked me.

"School?" I answered, a bit confused.

"What's that?" He asked. Now it was my turn to laugh about his ignorance about my culture.

"You don't have schools?" I asked. "They teach kids everything. From reading and writing to maths and more boring stuff."

"That is a parent's job." He answered. "It all comes back to you lot being lazy."

He had presented his lazy theory before to me, which I found hilarious. In his village, everyone did a little bit of everything. Whereas inside the fence all the jobs are separated. People specialized in one certain thing. Ivar was convinced that this was because we were all too lazy to learn everything.

I was roughly knocked aside by a group of grey soldiers. They had apparently decided that I was in the way and that I needed to move.

I fell against Ivar, who easily caught me by my arms and stopped me from falling to the ground.

One of the soldiers caught my eye. I thought I had seen him before. He had vibrant blue eyes and white hair. I just shrugged it off, he looked like Athena little bit. But people look all kinds of crazy on this side of the wall.

The soldier stared at me for a long time, until the point that Ivar apologised for me and ushered me to the side. "Are you okay?" He asked me.

"I'm fine." I said, shaking the feeling of the familiar blue eyes off. "Are you?"

Ivar smiled. "What you think that you hurt me?"

I laughed lightly. "Of course not."

"Come on, let's catch up with the others." He grabbed my hand and we continued our walk. I hated the feeling of his hand covering mine. It felt wrong, it felt like I was betraying the Union.

I lightly squeezed his hand and smiled at him. He had a tiny smirk on his lips as well. I wasn't betraying the hunters, I was going to make them proud. I was leaving this place. Soon rather than later.

27

The drive back was greatly uneventful. We had loaded the cars up with several boxes of wheat, grain and some kind of seeds. The cattle would come in later and get delivered straight to our town.

The radiates trusted each other a lot more than I thought. They even had systems in place for deliveries, something I am a hundred percent sure the hunters never knew.

Every little town was different and with every new Edgo type of man taking over most of the rules changed again. As far as I could tell most of the Union's information was incredibly dated already.

Ever since Ivar had blurred the red line on my forehead back in Fe San, which was now already a few months ago I think, my job description had also become a bit blurred too. I wasn't scrubbing floors and digging out holes to shit in anymore, I was starting to become a member of the town. I still helped with little chores, but the bad ones got passed down to a man named Taylor, who had tried to rape one of the women. Taylor was now also a slave, the only difference between us was that people really hated him.

I helped with setting up the decorations for our grand celebration tonight. Sigmund had married a new wife about one season ago, and tonight we celebrated her pregnancy. This was his sixth wife, his previous ones had all died during childbirth, including Ivar's mother.

Though no one thought about that tonight. The life of a child should be celebrated, they kept reminding me. I would agree with them if it didn't cost a life as well.

The celebration was hosted on the town square, which was now lit up with lanterns and candles.

After I was done decorating, I went back to Ivar's house. Slaves weren't allowed to join in on the party, not that I really wanted to. I had no idea what things they even did besides drinking.

There really wasn't a whole lot to do when I didn't get any tasks assigned to me. They didn't have any books, if they did find any they'd use it for fires, nor did they do anything else besides work or talk to one another. It was way too early to go to bed, so I found myself wandering around in the small room aimlessly.

Eventually, I started thinking of home, it was a dark place my mind often went to if I didn't have anything to occupy it with. I thought back to the small room back at home base with 'loyalty, strength, perseverance.' painted on it. Was I even still loyal to the hunters? I wanted to go home, but I had no idea how to. We drove for days to get here, and that was with a car. Even if I manage to steal one, I wouldn't know how to drive it, and they'd surely catch up to me. There were just too many open fields surrounding the town for me to slip away.

Perseverance. That was the keyword. I would get out of here, one day. Even if it was years from now, I couldn't let myself die here. No matter how much I hated the situation I had put myself in, I'd be damned if I died so far away from home.

Ivar burst into the little house, taking me out of my dark thoughts. He looked extremely pissed off until he saw me. "Why aren't you at the party?" He asked me.

"I heard Katlien tell Taylor that slaves weren't allowed to go." I answered.

"Asshole rapists aren't allowed." He said. "Damn you, little bird, I thought you ran."

No, that would have been the smart thing to do.

"Run where?" I gave him a faint smile. He smiled back at me and ushered me out of the house, to the party.

It had been going on for a little while now. The sun had started to set and painted the sky with beautiful pink and purple streaks. Underneath it were the people of Sigholm, freely dancing to the sound of drums, guitars and singing.

The contrast between this party and the one I attended in the capital was great. When I danced with Roderick our movements were precise and controlled. Everything everyone did will be put under a microscope and surely get talked about in hushed whispers later. The royal orchestra is filled with talented musicians, each and every one of them had been absorbed into the tunes they were playing and would be punished if they even skipped a beat.

Here, things were different. The men and women were dancing freely, moving their hips around that would surely be called scandalous if they did it in Vancouver. They danced with multiple people at once and were laughing and singing along to the music.

The musicians here are made out of a small group of the elders. One of them was very gifted on the guitar, yet the other one seemed to be slamming around on it randomly. The drums were the exact same thing, one person set the beat, the other ones just hit along with it.

Whatever they were singing, everyone knew the words to the song. Even Ivar sang along as he pulled me to the small dance floor. I danced with him, with Theodric and even with Don for a little bit, but I never got too close to them.

The night had cooled off the temperature quite a bit, yet I was still sweating like crazy. Dancing like that really burns you up. Ivar and I stopped over at the table for food and drinks.

"What do you think of her?" I asked Ivar, glancing over at his new mother. The girl was around the same age as me, if not younger. She got to enjoy a great deal of wealth ever since she married Sigmund, though Ivar hardly ever spoke about her. Now, she was sitting next to her husband, her hand rested on her flat belly.

"She's better than the last one, worse than the one before it." He just said to me, looking over at her too. "Maybe she's strong enough to actually give him a child."

"The last one didn't do that?" I asked him back. I honestly still did not understand the family relations they had. I thought Ivar was Theodric's uncle, but he could be his brother as well. I really had no idea.

"I had one other brother." He told me. "He died a few months before you got here. All of the other ones died because of their *Vanira*."

Vanira was their word for deformities caused by radiation. Most of the villagers were just normal looking, there were only two with small deformities to their bodies. I looked over at Ivar, he was still glancing at the girl. Did they kill them here?

I knew that in some parts of the world deformities and handicaps were seen as impure. Hell, even inside the Union people treat it like a taboo. Our neighbour gave birth to a girl who missed an arm. The following day the military and doctors took her away. They didn't kill them though, they put them in homes where they could be properly cared for. And studied.

Travellers who had to pass our town to go to Fe San stopped and joined in on the party. Athena had been right, most people outside of the fence just wanted to live their lives. There were only two groups you needed to worry about: Raiders and rebels.

Of course, here they don't call them rebels. I think Ivar called them 'the fighters', though he wasn't particularly interested in what was going on in the rest of the world. He likes hearing about my life inside the fence so he could make fun of it, but that was about it for him.

As the party progressed well into the night, people started to leave. First, it was the kids who got put to bed by their parents, after that followed the grouchy teenagers who thought they were adults already. Most of the elders had gone to bed too, so the music finally stopped.

Sigmund and his wife took their leave also, and soon it was just the blood brothers, their wives, and me. What had previously been the spot for the stage was now the home of a large bonfire. We all sat in a large circle around it, careful not to get burned as the flames danced in the wind. I talked to Ania, who was hoping to start a family with Theodric soon until Ivar stole my attention away.

"Lay on your back." He instructed. The drinks had gone to my head, I was happy to be lying down. I could feel the earth move underneath me, everything was spinning, but when I looked up, I saw why he had told me to do so.

I had never seen stars so clearly. There wasn't one cloud up in the air to take away from the beautiful view, everything was bright. They dotted the sky in weird little patterns, like flowers in a field. It was the best thing I had seen in months.

"Bet you don't have anything like that back home huh?" Ivar asked, after lying down next to me. Though I knew he liked me, he still made sure to keep his distance. He could drink a lot more than I could and still had his head on straight.

"I think we have it also." I said. "But we are all too busy to see."

"Always busy." He said. "But why? Do you get to spend time with your family?"

"So we can live." I told him. "So we won't starve to death." Ivar turned to me, his blue eyes locking with mine.

"And you say this side of the fence is dangerous." He said. I could smell the alcohol on his breath. "You are the little bird who lived in a cage, now you are free."

I was free.

<h1 style="text-align:center">28</h1>

On the following day, our lives went back to normal. I had fallen asleep next to Ivar on the town square but somehow woke up inside his house. My head was throbbing when I woke up, I told Ivar this and he just laughed at me, welcoming me into adulthood.

"Little bird," Ivar said. I had been helping with sorting out what we were going to plant where. The seeds were for apple trees, a new business Sigmund wanted to start. "Come with me."

I followed Ivar further up the hill. Sigholm was built about halfway up the mountain, we could see around the valleys for miles. It was a twenty-minute walk to the top of the mountain, one that we fully did in silence.

I had never been here, I had only heard about it. It was where they had built a small altar to pray to whomever they prayed to. The elders mostly prayed to 'ozed' the sun. The married women prayed to 'the great mother' for fertility. I had never seen Ivar come up here, though his blood brothers went plenty of times.

The so-called altar was a large pile of rocks that was decorated with things like skulls, flowers and pieces of cloth. In front of it were a few pillows that Ivar kneeled down on.

I followed his lead and knelt down too. His arm brushed against mine, as he started mumbling things in the town's dialect. Sometimes I could understand it, it was basically English but they left out a few letters or added more. He prayed for luck which had turned into 'Luky' and for strength which was 'steng'

"Why did you bring me here?" I asked after he was done and had just started staring at the pile of rocks. I wouldn't pray, I had never done it before, so what is the point in starting now? I didn't even know who to pray to. Who would even listen to me?

Ivar turned to me. He reached out with his hand and placed it on the side of my neck, covering up the tattoo with his palm. His fingers brushed over my jaw, as he struggled to find the words.

Words didn't really match up when it came to these kinds of situations anyway. I think he figured that out too. He held my face in his hands as softly as he could and kissed me.

The thought of staying here had popped up in my mind several times already in all truth, but when Ivar kissed me all I could think about were the complications. I felt nothing for him, I doubt I ever would.

"Stop." I said, feeling the panic rise up in my chest. It was like every fibre of my being wanted to move away from him, to scream bloody murder. The only thing preventing me from doing that was being fully aware that I was a slave, everyone would side with him.

"What's wrong?" He asked.

"Not here." I had to quickly think of lies to tell him. "I- I don't think this is smart."

"Why not?" He asked, tugging a stray piece of hair behind my ear. "They saw us come up here, no one will disturb us, little bird."

"No, I mean..." What did I mean? I still needed him to trust me. I couldn't just tell him to piss off. "I'm a slave, your father-"

"Decided to free you on my request." He said, a smile forming on his face. "I know it must be difficult for you here, and that my request is outrageous after the death of your husband." He grabbed my hand and put his over his heart. "But I am flesh and blood. He is not anymore."

"I- I need time." I finally said. His thumbs traced small circles over the back of my hand. I could feel his heart thumping in his chest.

I had felt without a cause for a long time. I had trained to become a hunter. I had gone over the fence to protect my friends and I had lost it all. It was almost tempting to just say yes to Ivar. I'd get to live out my days here in the village, maybe even have some kids. I had never even considered that. I couldn't see myself as a mother and a hunter at the same time.

"Of course." He said, moving away from me. He smiled kindly at me. "Just tell me when you are ready."

The way back down the mountain was quiet too. I had hurt his feelings, I know I had. But I seriously doubt if I was ever able to stop fighting. If I could ever settle here.

Ivar was quiet about everything for a few weeks. He treated me normally, though he refrained from touching me all that much. I had no idea if I was a slave still. It sure seemed like it, every few hours I still had to do a job without getting paid for it.

A loud noise caused me to look up from my job. I was planting the apple tree seeds on a field a little away from the village. They had one loud horn inside the village, that alerted everyone when there were people incoming. I left the seeds for what they were and started running down the hill, back to the village.

The first house I reached was Ivar's. When I nearly broke down the door he just laughed. "It's just the cattle finally showing up. Nothing else."

"Do I need to stay here?" I asked him.

"No, go back to planting." He answered, quickly dismissing me while he clipped my knife to his belt.

I took my sweet time walking back up the hill. Out of all the jobs, working the field was by far the one I hated the most. Maybe it was my factory heritage laughing at me, or the fact that I was now literally doing what I always said I did not want to do. I hated it.

The seeds needed to be planted far apart, so that the trees had space to sprout out their roots. It would take years for them to get big enough, if they even made it that far in the heat and dryness of this area. But Sigmund was convinced that it would help the town greatly, and what he said goes.

I kept my eye on the town as much as I could. The horn had stopped, and I couldn't hear any gunfire, I had to assume everything was fine. Still, the entire Edgo thing did not sit well with me. I wondered if the military already knew about him. If they even knew what happened to the hunters at all.

I heard heavy footsteps come up behind me. "How did it go?" I asked, making sure the seed I was working on was nicely covered in dirt. When Ivar did not respond I turned around, or at least I tried to. Someone blocked me, grabbed my hair and slit my throat.

29

I felt the blood gushing down from the wound, staining the green grass below me. I closed my eyes, hoping to close out the world for my final moments. I would get to see so many people again. I'd see Alder and Ulric, maybe even Katha, I could hardly remember what she looked like anymore.

"Ta was the last un'." The guy said to someone else. The other person laughed and spit on me.

"Shouldn't have deserted." He just said. I heard their footsteps walk away from me and dared to take a small peak. I did not need to see his eyes to know it was the guard from Fe San. He laughed with the other man, slamming his hand down on his shoulder.

I heard the birds chirp, I felt the wind blow on my face and at last, I heard the sound of engines roaring. They had left. I thought that death would be quick. But seconds turned into minutes, and nothing happened.

I needed to survive this, I grudgingly thought to myself. It was easier to just lay here and die. To wait and wait until the blood loss finally becomes death. But I knew too much, I lived too long, I needed to go back home.

I sat up in the grass, the red tainted grass leaving a mark where I once was. My throat was dripping down blood, my hands got stained with it, but It didn't feel nearly deep enough to have cut any arteries.

It was still bleeding though, and I needed to get some help. I made my way down the hill and approached the town.

Everyone was dead. Wherever I went there were more dead bodies piling onto each other.

Some of them had weapons in their hands, others were completely unarmed. I found Theodric with Ania still in his arms. The kids from their neighbour laid dead in the closet, clearly trying to hide.

Everywhere I went I just saw red. Red pools of blood, red clothes. Everything was red. Once again, I was the only survivor.

Maybe it was a curse. Every time I started considering people friends or family, or I started feeling at home, someone died. First, it was Katha, who died without justice. After that the hunters back at the palace and now this town. I was the curse. I brought bad luck.

I found Ivar on the town square. They had placed his body next to his father's. Ivar still had his gun in his hand, but by the looks of it he never really got to fire it. On the ground, before him they had painted a message with his blood

'Let this be a warning to future deserters: Edgo punished those who stray from his glorious purpose. Those who steal his property, and those who lie.'

Stole his property. That would most likely be a reference to me. The guard in the city recognized me from the hunt. I thought he looked familiar, he must have been around when Ivar grabbed me as an extra payment.

I walked closer to his body. They had gotten him good. He got stabbed multiple times in the chest, as well as having his throat slit from ear to ear. I closed the lids on his grey eyes.

I would not mourn him, I tried to convince myself. I grabbed my knife back from his belt and entered the first house I recognized.

It had belonged to the woman with the fierce red hair, Danai.

Her hair now blended in beautifully with the blood that was still pouring out of her, seemingly fatal, wound. I don't know if that meant she was still alive, but I didn't really bother checking either.

I came out of the house in her clothes. For the first time in months I was wearing pants again, clothes I could move around in. I cut up the bottom part of the dress I had previously worn and wrapped it around my throat, hoping that putting some pressure on the wound would stall the bleeding.

I made my way over to the cars, only to find them stolen. Okay, that's fine, I thought. I'll just have to walk. I grabbed some food and stuffed it in a bag.

"The sun comes up in the east and sets in the west." It was like Alder was right beside me, telling me what to do. I had not heard his voice in so long, I wanted to cry. I could not see him anywhere though, no matter how frantically I looked around me.

"The sun comes up in the east and sets in the west." He said again. "You were brought further into their land, which is..."

"East." I said, my throat instantly hurting more.

"West is where you need to go." He said. "Just follow the sun."

"If I go too far down..." My voice really did not want to talk anymore. I felt the makeshift bandage becoming wet with blood. I needed to answer him, he always got so disappointed when I didn't.

"You'll hit Los Angeles." He answered for me. "And you'll die of radiation poisoning."

I heaved the bag over my shoulder and set out. The sun had started its decline, so it was indeed just a matter of following the sun. I had spent most of the day trying to do all of my work somewhere in the shade, it was simply too hot.

I had found out early on that I hated the heat. I grew up with snow and being scared of hypothermia when we could not afford to buy new fabrics for clothes. The heat was much worse though. If I was cold back home I would start running around the house and the field, or I'd simply steal a blanket from my parent's bed. Here it was hot, and if you were hot there was barely anything you could do to cool down.

There was no shade as I reached the valley the town looked out over. Every step I took started clumping together. I felt like I had been walking for hours, and that I made no progress.

The heat combined with the pain made my head race. I felt like everything was watching me. The grass, the trees, even the wind made me afraid that they would bring the attackers back.

It was already pitch black when I finally started getting out of the valley. I felt dizzy, what I could still see from the dark world was spinning around me. Still, I pushed on. Just walk in a straight line, I told myself. Just remember to breathe.

I don't know when exactly the farm came in sight. It could have been minutes since I last fully registered a thought, or it could have been days. I didn't even think about the consequences of it. I could be made a slave again, or they could kill me on sight. I needed to take the gamble, I was bleeding out.

My head was clearer than it had been in months. I felt the sunlight on my face, the soft bed underneath me. There was something else too, it made a squeaky noise and blew a nice breeze into my face.

If I kept my eyes closed, I could believe that I was back home. That I was counting down the minutes until Alder would yell at me to wake up. I'd go downstairs and see Teryn and Athena talking together, though neither of them really liked each other. They did it for me.

My eyes couldn't stay shut any longer, however tempting it may be. I knew I wasn't back home. There were birds singing tunes outside that I had never heard before. I heard the faint sound of people talking, and they weren't speaking English.

It all came back to me, like a crushing wave trying to drown me in sadness. Teryn leaving, the lifeless bodies of my friends at the palace, the explosion which killed Ulric, Alder reaching out for me as I was being taken away.

I opened my eyes. The room I was in was small, with dull grey walls and only really a bed and a fan. Was I in a prison? It didn't look like that. There was a wooden door that was open on a small crack. Behind it was a small boy. When he saw me he looked terrified.

"*Pap! Pap! Shis Awa!*" He shouted, running off further into the hallway and out of my sight. I sat up straight in the bed. Someone had taken my hair out of the braid, and by the looks of it also washed it. For the first time in months, I actually felt clean. I wonder how much scrubbing they had to do to get rid of the layer of dirt that had been on me since the hunt.

A woman came up into my room. She was probably somewhere in her forties, though she already had smile lines edged into her face. Her hair was brown and curly, and her entire body, at least from what I could see, was covered in freckles.

"You look like you have had a rough couple of days." It was clear that English wasn't her first language, but then again it was no one's first language around here.

"More like a year." I said. My throat felt raw, as though I hadn't spoken in months. "Where am I?"

"Well we're not a part of a town, we really don't have a name." She answered. "My husband runs this farm."

The farm, it came back to me piece by piece. I remember seeing it and walking towards it. It seemed like all I could remember was that they had too many fields surrounding them. That I wasn't getting any closer to the actual house.

I brushed my fingers against my throat but found it completely bandaged up. "It was a nasty cut, you were lucky that you found us in time." She sat down on the bed next to me. "You were bleeding out on our tomatoes."

"Thank you." It was really all I could say, though it hardly sufficed, they had saved my life. She could have just left me out there to die, but she didn't.

"You must be starving." She said. "Dinner will be ready in five, join us when you are ready." She squeezed my hand once and took off, ushering the young boy away from the door. He had tried to listen in again.

I got up from the bed and opened the other door in the small room. There was a small bathroom behind it. Though their term of a bathroom was a bit different from ours. They did not have plumbing or anything like that, there was an empty tub that would have to be filled with water from probably a well downstairs. It wasn't what I was looking for though, that was mounted on the wall.

The rear-view mirror had shown me my face, but not the rest. Here I could see myself properly for the first time in months. My bones were poking out through my sunburned skin, I had lost most of the muscle I had been building up with Alder. I thought I looked smaller as well, less threatening. Hell, I hardly looked like I could lift a gun. My hair had become long, too long. It easily reached my lower back now, though it still looked as unmanageable as ever, some things never change.

My ear had healed up long ago, though it still looked kind of odd to just miss the top part. What I was more worried about was the cut on my neck of course. It would be something that I carried with me forever. Radiates don't have the medical knowledge we have. Years ago, the doctors created a cream that could make sure whatever wound we got, did not scar. It was standard to be given to military and the hunters if they got injured inside the fence.

No, I wouldn't be upset about it. Someone tried to slit my throat, and I lived to tell the tale. If anything, it would make me look badass. I already had half my ear blown off, I don't think I was going to win any beauty competitions anyway.

They had given me new clothes, they were simple and grey and flowed over my skin. I was sunburned in most places, but I had gotten used to the feeling after slaving away in the sun for the past season.

"What is your name?" The boy had entered my room again. He clearly found English a lot harder than his mother, though I could hardly blame him for that. He was probably around twelve years old, with curly hair that was threatening to cover his brown eyes.

"Julia." I answered. "What's yours?"

"Tobin." He answered, holding out his hand for me to shake. I smiled at him and shook it. "How did you get that cut?"

"Someone tried to kill me." I answered, closing the bathroom door behind me and sitting back down on the bed so I could put on some shoes. "They failed though."

"Was it scary?" He asked, his eyes gleaming with interest.

"A little bit." I told him. His mother called downstairs that dinner was ready, so after I tied the laces to my shoes, we made our way down.

The house was a lot bigger than I thought it would be. I was almost happy that Tobin decided to stick around, I doubt I would have been able to find the dining room all by myself.

It was a large rectangle room, with one long table occupying most of it. It was clearly made for a full house of people, though that was not the case today. The woman I had met previously was still loading up the table with food. Standing beside it was an older man and a teenage boy. They looked to be deep in conversation, though they stopped talking once they saw me.

"Hello there." The main said with the now oh so familiar accent and shook my hand. "My name is Gerl, what is yours?"

"Julia." I answered. "Thank you for helping me."

"Oh of course!" The man smiled brightly, showing off his yellowed teeth. "Once we saw your tattoo, we knew we had to." They saw that I am a hunter, and they helped?

"You are from the Union?" I doubtingly asked. I knew there was a plan long ago to start making farms outside of the Union, so there could be more houses inside the fence instead of farmland. I also knew that the plan failed because the radiates kept murdering the farmers and their helpers.

"No, we are not." The woman I had previously talked to said, placing a basket of freshly baked bread on the table. "We helped one of your people before, a few years ago."

"And in return, he helped us greatly after." Gerl added. "Gave us seeds to plant, weapons to defend ourselves with. We have been helping travellers ever since."

We sat down to eat. The woman, whose name was Esta, was an amazing cook. She used herbs and spices I had never even heard of and kept on refilling my plate. I had not eaten this much in months, and with every bite I took I found myself returning to my normal self. To the person I was before that fatal night at the palace.

"Who was it that you took in?" I asked with my mouth full of mashed potatoes. The radiates had no laws, and therefore no legal drinking age.

Granted, inside the fence there were only a few social rules that kept young kids from drinking, not any actual government enforced ones. Still, when young Tobin and his slightly older brother started drinking just like the rest of us, I couldn't help but glance over to him every few seconds.

"Norton." Gerl had been drinking slightly longer than the rest of us, the effects had started to show. He did not mind enthusiastically telling me about Norton. "Great man! He came to us bleeding, just like you, nasty gunshot to his leg. Also one in his shoulder I think, there have been so many here since, great man, great man. Do you know him?"

I laughed. "He was the one who recruited me actually."

Gerl and Esta smiled towards each other. "*The cirk ala go roun.*" She said with a smile on her face. "The circle always comes around." She translated for me. "It's a saying around here."

"How is he?" Gerl asked me.

"He is..." I had no idea how to tell them in an easy way. The last I heard of him was at the beginning of my training, where Alder told me that he would be sent to the Darkfort because of choosing me. He was probably killed in the explosion. "Dead, I think. The rebels killed him when they blew up our base."

"Again?" Esta asked, taking a bite from her food. "You'd think after the first time you guys would-"

"What do you mean again?" I cut her off.

"The base was blown up half a year ago." She said to me.

"I know, I was there. No one made it out." I told her. Esta smiled at me and placed her warm hand over mine.

"They did get out." She said to me. "Everyone knows it. It was Edgo's first real failure."

"How?" I could not let myself believe it. I had spent months mourning them. Trying to accept the fact that everyone was dead, that I was the sole survivor of that horrible day.

"I don't know all the details of course," Esta said. "I heard most of them weren't present when the bombs went off."

"No, no." The older brother intervened. "I heard they went to the basement, an old bomb shelter." I looked at both of them in disbelief. Ulric might still be alive, even if Alder and the others weren't. I still had him.

"I need to get back." I just said. I thought there would be nothing for me there. That I could just get my HSC and be by myself for the rest of my life. For the first time in a very long time, I felt hope.

30

I stayed with them for about a week, during which I had both the time to heal up, and time to worry.

I had accepted that all the hunters were dead. It had made me a bit more careless. I did not need to worry about disappointing anyone. I was not worried about what would happen should I ever be able to go back. I wasn't worried about dying.

Now, I was. If the other hunters lived, maybe they got to Alder and Jack in time. Maybe the other cars got away too. I did not dare to hope for a lot, I was too scared to lose it all again.

There was a choice to be made. One that made me pretty unhappy. I could go straight back to the fence. A journey that would take me at least two weeks, if I had a car, and that was even counting on the fact that I would not get into trouble on my way there, something everyone thought was very unlikely. Cars break down, I could run into people, I could run out of provisions.

Then there was the other choice. Only a two days ride to the north was a large city named Denvar. According to Esta, it was the only city still free from Edgo's grasp.

I could find Union workers there and return in their safe military convoy. There was a risk of course. There were no real information outlets, everything was just hearsay. I needed to figure out if I would take the bet or not.

"Julia." Esta disturbed my thoughts. I had been helping her with cleaning up after dinner, though she always tried to refuse. It was the least I could do, my time of healing up was almost done.

"I'm sorry, what were you saying?" I asked her, handing her another clean plate.

"We decided that we'll give you one of the vehicles." She said.

"You guys have already done more than you should have for me," I said to her. "I'll find my own way back."

"We have a bike," she continued like she had not heard a thing I just said. "My husband is too old to ride it and I rather eat sand for the rest of my life than let my boys ride it." She gave me that familiar warm smile. "You can have it."

"I'll make this up to you." I said for the hundredth time. "I know someone in the royal family, maybe I can ask him to allow you guys to be accepted into the Union?"

"We are just fine here, Julia." She said to me. "Just tell Norton we said hello okay?"

Leaving the farm was harder than I had expected to. Little Tobin had not left my side the entire time I was there and started crying when he found out I was leaving.

I had really hoped that they would come along with me. After helping two hunters they would have definitely been allowed, and probably did not even need to work anymore, but they were happy here. I wasn't going to mess with that any more than I had already done.

The bike was something to get used to. Gerl had to walk me through how to use it, and during the first few hours of my journey I took everything a bit slower than I had intended to. The bike was made to go very fast for a very long time. But I felt like I needed to learn how to fully control it first.

I decided to go to Denvar. Even if Edgo was already there, it wouldn't matter. I pretty much looked like a radiate already, and as far as he knew I died when Sigholm was attacked.

I wore Esta's turtle neck shirt, it covered both the bandage and my tattoo, it was perfect for the situation. According to them, it wasn't even that weird to wear around here.

The journey there took me about two and a half days. I hardly slept at all at night, I remembered all of Ivar's stories about night raids, though I hardly had anything worth stealing with the exception of the bike.

Denvar came in sight from miles away. I knew it was hit hard during the Blood War, so I did not expect to see anything left of the previous architecture. Still, the city remained an important place in the area, after the radiation got cleaned up.

The radiates built Denvar from scratch and even made their own little Union inspired wall, which is probably why it was the last to withstand Edgo. When the gates are closed, no one could get in.

But they were wide open today, which made me far more alert. Everything I had heard about Edgo told me that he was not one to just give up. He would not leave this city alone unless they followed his agenda. Especially after his failure with the Hunters.

I parked my bike on the outer edge of the designated parking area, which was still outside the wall and made my way to the gates, alongside what looked like thousands of others.

"What brings you here?" A girl my age asked me. She had blonde, long hair and a kind smile. There was something off about her face though, her nose was pretty much non-existent. Sigholm was lucky that they were so far from any radiation, other towns may have not been so much. I had seen plenty of deformities in Fe San.

"Getting some supplies for my family's farm." I answered her, mimicking the accent I had heard so often now. "What about you?"

"I am meeting up with my brother." She smiled. Everyone around us seemed to be in excellent spirits, which only caused more alarm bells to go off in my head.

It could either mean that Edgo was entirely defeated or that the city fell and I had arrived in the middle of the celebration.

I found my answer pretty quickly. Strung up over the gate were the naked bodies of Union workers. Their blood was used to write 'Edgo' on the sandstone. I could not just turn around and bolt away. I had gotten stuck in a stream of people who were entering the town, not to mention the new city guard, who checked everyone that came inside.

They had set up a checkpoint, where everyone got screened before entering the town. Just stay calm, I thought to myself. I would just play the naïve farm girl. I mean, they tried to kill me twice already and failed. I have the statistics on my side.

"Name." The guard looked bored out of his mind. He was at least thirty already and had half his face covered in tattoos.

"Dalia." I answered. I had heard about it through Ivar. If a baby is found without parents, or the mother died during childbirth, they always named the kid Dalia. It was the most commonly used name across the fence.

"Why are you here?" He rummaged through my backpack. I had my food and my gun in there, as well as some extra coin.

"Just buying some seeds for my family's farm." I answered. The man looked at me kinda funny, and for a moment I thought I messed up. Had I said something wrong? It wasn't weird to send the help to get the seeds. Especially in a city where shootouts happen more often than actual arrests.

"Why-" He started but got cut off by loud gunfire erupting just a few metres next to us. A guard and a civilian had been loudly arguing the entire time, though that was hardly something new around here. What was new was that the civilian had the audacity to pull out an AK.

He shot the guard and went on to aim for the other ones. People got caught in the crossfire and started falling down to the ground, bleeding profusely. Others just started running by the checkpoint, much like myself.

The guard obviously did not stop me, he was too busy getting shot at himself. I figured they'd get the gunman pretty quickly with the amount of guard there, I ran as far away from the checkpoint as possible.

After the adrenaline started wearing off, I checked to see if I got hit. I had some blood on me, but it wasn't mine. Besides, bloody clothes hardly stood out here. The people on the streets nearby heard the gunshots, but no one really acted on it. Even the guards batted no eye.

I needed a new plan. The checkpoint was currently a mess, and it would stand out if I left immediately after the gunfight. People might think I am involved, which I just can't afford.

I wandered around the streets aimlessly. I passed shops and bars, but I didn't dare go in anywhere. I did not speak the rebel language, I had no idea what the people were saying all around me.

The biggest building in Denvar was built right in the centre of the city. It was at least five stories high and definitely stood out against all the other buildings, which were only two stories at most. As I approached it, I realized that it must have been the town hall before Edgo came.

"Here, get this inside." A woman loaded up a basket full of potatoes into my arms. I had gotten too close, they thought I was working here.

I was going to say no, or at least tell her that I wasn't working for them. When I dreadfully realized the opportunity this was. I could go inside the new headquarters of the rebel forces. With a little bit of luck, Edgo might even be in there.

It was valuable information the Union would definitely need. An attack on the palace, the base being blown up, it all showed us one clear thing: Edgo was nothing like his predecessors

"Where to?" I asked her while she loaded a new basket in the arms of a small boy.

"Follow him." She just said. The boy couldn't have been older than eight but seemed to know the layout of the city hall perfectly. He did not speak to me and just kept on walking.

The city hall was built in the simplest way possible, probably to reserve stones for other houses. It wasn't like the royal palace back in Vancouver, that place had been beautifully decorated and was crawling with people of nobility. Here the only decoration was the blood of the soldiers who had died protecting it.

Though the halls were empty, they were not quiet. It seemed like every room we passed had a new set of people in it and a new set of people who were being tortured. I heard the last words of the town's doctor, who had undoubtedly been sent from inside the Union, and the dying screams of an officer.

The boy only really looked back when he noticed that I was no longer following him. If Edgo, or any of his right-hand men, were here they would not be on the ground floor among all the dying screams. They would seek solitude, to create new plans.

"It's this way." The boy said, coming after me as I walked up the stairs. I did not want to get the kid into trouble, he probably already had it rough enough as is.

"Here, this is for you." I said, handing him one of the potatoes from the basket. "You just deliver your flowers okay?" The boy eagerly took the potato from my hand, he looked like they had been starving him out. He just looked at me with big eyes and nodded knowingly, before sprinting around the corner to his destination.

I was right, the top floors were a lot quieter. There were still some occasional pools of blood on the ground, but they had removed the bodies by the looks of it. I got lucky, if I had left the farms a few days earlier I might have arrived in the middle of this.

I found some people on the second floor, but they were all servants. None of them even looked at me, they all kept their heads down and just went their own way. I did not dare ask them where the leaders were. I doubt I could have bribed them with the potatoes as well.

The third floor was different. I heard voices coming through the doors, but I could not make out what they were saying. I walked along the hallway when a man exited one of the rooms. He looked like a guy who could be in charge. He was tall and strong, with long hair that he tied in a ponytail. He let out his female guest with a laugh when he noticed me.

"Taw ode jie ihre?" He asked me. I had no bloody clue what he was saying obviously. He didn't look too happy about me being here though.

"I got lost on my way to the kitchen." It felt like a stupid thing to say, but maybe that was the role I should be playing. The stupid servant girl, not the hunter.

"How many places have you been where the kitchen was on the third floor?" He asked me, grabbing my arm roughly and pulled me inside, the potatoes falling to the ground.

<h1 style="text-align:center">31</h1>

I dodged his fist, my muscle memory taking over. I had not trained in so long. I thought about doing it back in Sigholm, but I was scared that they would catch me and realize I lied. Back at the farm I had tried to, but it all seemed pointless. I had no idea where to even start with the exercises.

He tried to kick me, but I caught his leg and swung it away from him. He got caught off-balance and nearly fell over. The gun was still in my backpack, but my knife was not.

I clipped it off my belt and clenched my fist around it so tightly it hurt. I wasn't the greatest at hand to hand combat, as Alder liked to repeat every time we practised. I sometimes managed to beat people, but that was by outsmarting them, not by being stronger.

This guy was definitely stronger than me, most likely he was more experienced with fighting as well. He tried punching me again and grazed my jawline. His punch opened the window to his chest however, I brought my knife forward and slashed him.

The knife went through the fabric and cut his skin. It started bleeding, but I knew it wasn't a fatal blow. I just needed to tire him out, to do small damage until he eventually got reckless and created a real opening.

That plan of attack relied on stamina, something I did not have anymore. I, however, did not see another approach and kept on dodging his rain of fists as best as I could.

"Stupid cunt." He panted. Eventually, he realized that the punches were not going to do it, and switched over to something that I'll admit, did not see coming.

He charged forward like an angry bull and wrapped his arms around my waist. He did not stop sprinting until my back hit the wall with a loud snap, making me believe that the asshole had broken my spine.

I knew I had to do something, I grabbed my knife tightly and brought it back down into his neck right when my back hit the wall. He screamed in agony and let go of me. Luckily for me, the guy was stupid and pulled out the knife. Blood immediately started squirting out of the wound, painting his clothes with dark red blood.

The knife had blocked the artery and other blood vessels, the moment he pulled it out however, they were open and he quickly started to bleed out. There was nothing to be done, even if I did want to save him.

I had killed before, but it did not register in my mind that I was ending lives. They were far away, inside cars and hidden behind big guns. This time everything happened up close. I could see him struggling to take his last few breaths. I saw the wedding ring around his finger.

No, I would not allow myself to feel bad about this, not here. The mission needed to continue. I would not kill someone in vain, I now needed to get that information even more than before.

My spine was not broken, it was the wall that had snapped. He had thrown me against it so hard it had created a dent.

Upon further inspection, the guy had actually helped me greatly. Sure, my back felt sore and I was out of breath, but he had shown me a way to move around the building without being noticed.

The room had double walls, in an attempt to make it more soundproof. There was a little bit of space between the two walls. It would be a tight squeeze, but it seemed like the safest bet.

I had to make the dent a little bit bigger so I could crawl through it. After I was done, I went back to the guy and got my bloodstained knife from his hand. He wasn't breathing anymore.

I closed the door to the room but left him where he was. I had no time haul his dead body around, trying to find a place to hide him. Besides, the blood had stained the carpet already, only an idiot would not put two and two together.

Instead, I pushed the large wardrobe to hide the hole in the wall. So at least they could not find me after they had discovered the body. Like most radiate furniture they only put the absolute essentials in it and therefore did not put in a backboard. I could just open the closet door, move aside the clothes and go through.

After making sure that the clothes hid most of the hole, in case anyone decided to check the closet for the killer, I started my way through the wall.

I could not move around as fast as I wanted to, I had to go everywhere sideways. It looked like the servants had used this place as a hideout, I found small toys and wrappers hidden away.

I hoped I did not run into any of them and continued to make my way through the walls. The first wall was not built to be strong, which is probably why the guy managed to put me through it, and often had little cracks in it, so the conversations became even easier to listen in on.

I walked by two rooms where a bunch of girls were entertaining two men. They were not really saying anything, and I doubt if they did that it would be any world-changing secrets, I quickly walked passed them.

The further I made my way down the louder my heart seemed to start beating. Had they found the man already? Were the guards inside the walls? They obviously would arm them with guns, and I doubt I could do a great knife throw without being able to lift my arms above my chest.

I past one of the largest rooms in the building and stopped one room over. It looked like this was the bedroom of someone important, and it had not stopped being just that. There was one table in the centre of the room, where six men sat. It had been the first room that I passed where people weren't celebrating, I thought I may have just come across prisoners. That was until they started talking.

"This is a great win for us." Were they speaking English? I peeked through a small crack, and could definitely tell that they were radiates, not captured Union workers. They must have gotten cocky.

"It is." I could not see the man who spoke, he was lying carelessly on the bed. I could only see his legs, which were practically drenched in blood.

"We have completed our goal." The first man said again, clearly trying to strike up the conversation.

"Have we?" The man answered. "We now control the land yes, but do we control the people?"

"They sing your name in battle songs." The man argued. "They use our currency, they are using our language."

"But they are not united." Another man said. He was dark-skinned and put down his uzi on the table as though it was just a toy. The barrel of the gun aimed directly at one of the other men, but he hardly seemed concerned by it.

"Exactly." The man on the bed said. "They can fear me, they can love me. I do not care, as long as they will fight for the cause."

The man on the bed was Edgo, that much was clear. I did not dare move however, I couldn't tell if I got a clear view of him from any of the other cracks. Someone might hear me, I could not risk that.

"Dozens of people have done what we have done, my brothers." Edgo said, still fully relaxed on the bed. "It does not take a genius to capture a city filled with people who won't fight. What we do against the Union, the Stronghold and Vanaheim, that is what will set us apart." I could visibly see the people at the table tense up as he continued talking. "And all we have done against them failed."

I had heard of places that were like the Union, but I never knew any names. In school, we just learned that there were other places, but not where they were. At the hunters, I learned that there were two close ones. One was up north, and one was more down south. Alder told me that their names were not important, they had not made contact with us in decades.

"The Union is strong." One of the men said. He was one of the younger ones and spoke without an accent. "Perhaps we bit off more than we can chew with them. Should we attack Vanaheim first, their soldiers will add to ours, and we have enough to-"

"The soldiers who we allow to live won't fight with their heart. They'll get trampled and will only be in the way." The older man cut him off.

"Vanaheim is led by a child." The boy argued. "Their men yearn for a strong leader."

The boy looked over to Edgo on the bed and gave me a clear view of his tattoo. He had a triangle made of teardrops in his neck, the exact same I had.

He must have been a deserter, I thought to myself. Maybe someone who got cut off and did not want to accept his life at the factory. I could have been in his place, had Jack decided to cut me for being a girl.

"People are too complex, you can never know their desires." Edgo answered. "Vanaheim is more of a secret than the Stronghold. The Union is the weak link. Their people are oppressed by the same system which branded you. Their walls are weaker."

When he mentioned the walls, the men started banging their cups on the table in agreement, each of them grinning widely. Edgo seemed to be enjoying the attention he was getting and added. "They will be much easier to take down, especially with the help of our little friends once Vane breaks them."

So that was their master plan, they would take down the fence. It almost made me want to laugh. He was preaching about wanting to be different from the men who came before him, yet he was doing exactly what they had done. None of them ever managed to get through, only one of them once managed to plant a bomb near the fence and damaged it. I was almost wondering why I was even wasting my time with this. Why I should keep listening in.

"No one ever made it past the fence." The boy seemed to be thinking the same thing that I had been thinking. Maybe Edgo had never seen the fence before and only heard about it. I wouldn't be too impressed by what people beyond the walls call a 'fence' either.

"Well, they did not have this." Edgo threw something at the boy. It looked like it was a roll of parchment, tied together by a little string. When he untied the string, I could practically see his eyes overflow with joy.

"This should do it."

32

I knew the moment the words left his mouth that I needed to bring that roll back with me, or even just get a good look at it myself. I could not do that from my hideout and therefore needed to wait and see.

The roll did not leave the room with anyone, even though the men started leaving one by one. Edgo didn't however and stayed in the bed. He had several more people over, but they all spoke the rebel language I did not understand. That was until a girl, who couldn't be older than twelve, entered the room.

"How are you?" He asked her, finally getting up from the bed. "I heard you were upset." Edgo had black hair that reached his upper back. He had a square face, with a few wrinkles already forming on his skin. The girl was practically a dwarf next to him, he must have been the biggest man I had ever seen in my life. Still, he looked pretty attractive for a monster. That must be why people follow him so easily.

"I wasn't." The girl was clearly lying, she couldn't look him in the eye. She was small, with long, golden hair and pale skin. Her clothes were far too big for her, though she looked well taken care of.

"What did I say about lying?" His voice turned cold, though not as threatening as it had been with the men. The girl kept on looking at her feet and did not answer his question. "Hella, look at me."

He kneeled down in front of her and grabbed her chin, forcing her to look at him. My hand hovered over my knife, even though I couldn't do anything from in here.

Maybe if I made my way back to the entrance quickly enough. "Why were you upset? Was it because of the killings?"

"They were screaming." She whispered. "I heard them."

I would have thought that she was his daughter, but that wouldn't make any sense. They looked far too different to be related to each other. "You need to become stronger. Like your siblings." He said to her on a strict tone.

"Are you going to kill me if I'm not?" Her voice was quivering with fear.

"This world is not made for gentle souls." He did not answer her question, though he did not look at her like he would kill her.

Maybe they were related in some way. I knew there were some cultures out there that took family ties loosely. Though that wasn't the case back in Sigholm. The girl still looked scared, but she did not say anything back to him. Instead, he picked her up in his arms and brought her to the bed.

"It is late, you should sleep." He said to her, tucking her in tightly. Maybe her mother cheated on him and he is just in denial about all of it.

"Goodnight Hella." He said to her, gently removing a lock of hair out of her face.

"Goodnight Eryk." She responded.

Oh.

The pieces clicked together in my head. I thought Eryk had been Athena's boyfriend, or maybe a friendship that went wrong. I had not but Edgo and Eryk together yet. The mentions of their names seemed years apart from each other.

I watched him leave the room, softly closing the door behind him and letting Hella remain in his bed. She tossed and turned around in the bed a bit, before slowly falling asleep.

Athena could have been a bit more specific, I grudgingly thought to myself as I started making my way back to the entrance of the wall. Had she told me the name Edgo instead of Eryk I could have, well I probably wouldn't have done something, but I at least wouldn't have been totally blindsided by it!

I made sure to make as little sound as possible when I exited the wall and entered the closet. The room seemed quiet, so I dared to open the closet door on a small crack.

The man was still lying face down on the floor, completely unmoved. It seemed like no one had gone to search for him yet, the room remained untouched. I had to circle back at least three times to find the room, the city hall looked quite different from within the wall. Finally, I walked through the large room and found myself in front of the correct door.

There were no guards posted outside her door, they were just that cocky. When I entered, she was still sleeping soundly in her bed. I tiptoed my way over to the roll and glanced behind me again. She had turned around, but she didn't open her eyes.

I didn't know the number of people I would encounter on my way back to the fence or just here in the palace. This seemed like the safest place in the entire building so far, I think that even after all of this I could take a twelve-year-old.

I untied the string and let it roll open. The roll had definitely gone through many hands and looked pretty battered. There were stains all over the sides, most of them were blood, and the paper was torn all around. None of this mattered of course, once I started reading what was on it.

I did not know why Edgo hated the Union. I just figured it was why most radiates hated us: We had food and water, and plenty of it. We were entitled simply because we were born inside the fence.

I understood why they hated us for it, I knew that previous warlords had tried taking down the fence so they could share the wealth with their people, not understanding that it would just bring everyone back to the time before the fence existed, but what Edgo as planning was nothing like that. He truly hated us.

The roll was a plan for a missile. One that could take out half the union and leave the rest stuck in radiation. I didn't understand it however, these plans were all terrifying if they were realistic. He would never be able to make a missile like this, he simply did not have the knowledge nor the means to.

The second piece of paper was written by them, not by someone else. It depicted an attack on the southern border of the Union. It was on one of the more unprotected areas because it got too close to the nuclear wasteland that was California. The only people there were the criminals, working to clean up the radiation.

Maybe they were trying to recruit them. They did hate the Union and would die an early death if they kept working there anyway. Still, their numbers wouldn't be a match for our well-trained military.

I heard a small click behind me and turned around. Hella had gotten out of her bed and was pointing a handgun at my head. Her hands were shaking, and she was clutching the gun too tightly to make a steady shot. I knew I could probably get to the gun before she could fire it, but I was not ready to kill a child just yet.

"I'll get my father." She said, keeping the shaking gun on me as she walked to the door. I held my hands up into the air, my mind running with things to say to her.

"Athena." I blurted out when her hand touched the doorknob. She immediately looked back at me. I panicked and it was the only link we had. "She's your friend right? She's mine too."

"She is alive?" Hella asked me.

"She is." I lied. I really did not know. Though I think that if Edgo found his runaway daughter, or whatever she was to him, with the hunters he would kill her publicly. "She told me about you Hella, about how brave you are."

"She did?" She slowly lowered her gun and stepped away from the door.

"Of course," I said. "I am here because she needed some help with something. Can you help me with that?"

"With the papers?" She guessed.

I nodded, lowering my hands. "If these papers stay here... A lot of people will die, Athena will die. I don't think you want that to happen."

"Father will be angry." She said, looking at the papers. He was her father after all. I needed to get more answers, though I shouldn't be getting them from her.

I knelt down in front of her. "You are very brave, Athena told me so. But more importantly, you have your heart in the right place. Do you want to do what is right? To prevent any more killing from happening?" She looked at me with big eyes and nodded. "Then you crawl back into your bed, and never speak of this conversation again."

She considered it for a few seconds and eventually nodded. She went under the covers and squeezed her eyes shut. I quickly tied the string around the roll again and went to leave, but I couldn't just leave like that. She helped me, I would have to repay her somehow.

"Hella," I whispered. "I'll make sure you see Athena again."

With a big smile on her face, I left the room.

The city hall was booming with people, but none of them batted an eye toward me. They were celebrating their victory and thought that I was just another radiate.

Especially after I made my way back to the ground floor the only attention I received came from people trying to party with me. The music was loud and all around me people were dancing. It did not matter that the real party went on in the main hall, the music was loud enough to be heard even in the streets.

I folded the roll in half and hid it on the very bottom of my backpack. There were so many people downstairs that just a few metres took me minutes to cross. I felt like any second now someone might make my cover and I'd be screwed.

I bumped into someone who was going the opposite direction. Radiates aren't known for their good manners, I knew I should not apologise and maybe yell at them a bit. When I glanced up however, I quickly thought of something better.

"Sorry I-" I started saying. Edgo was a giant, I have no idea how I head on bumped into him without noticing. I was so focused on not stepping on someone's toes that I royally screwed myself over.

"It's fine." He held up his hand and cut me off. From up close I could see the little scars that his tattoos tried to hide. He had his right hand, much like Athena's, entirely covered in tattoos. His arm was also covered, but I guess Athena didn't stick around long enough for that part. "Where are you headed beautiful?"

I was considered attractive here because I didn't have any radiation deformities, the missing part of my ear didn't even seem to bother him. "I was just going outside," I said. "It's a bit too crowded in here."

I started to form a, very ambitious, plan in my head. If I could lead him away from his men and be all alone with him, I might get the chance to stop the war before it reaches the Union.

Someone slammed his hand down on Edgo's shoulder and whispered something in his ear. The man had the same nose and the same jawline as the guy I had killed.

The colour of his eyes made me even think that he might have come back to life, they had the same amount of hatred in them.

"My apologies," Edgo smiled at me. I felt my blood turn to ice. "Duty calls."

"Right." I forced myself to smile back. "Good luck."

Edgo turned around and followed the man upstairs. They had found his body. I continued my way outside, my heart beating almost as loud as the music.

When I finally found myself in the cold night air, I calmly walked my way down the street. There were many drunk people still dancing or lying in the gutter trying to sleep. The bars were packed to the last seat. No one would be sleeping tonight.

Logical thinking. It was the core of survival. If I was Edgo, and I found one of my men murdered in his room, what would I do? I would search the room.

Let's say they find the hole, then he would have the walls searched. Someone might go to Hella's room to see if she is alright. Worst case scenario, Edgo realizes that the roll is missing. If Hella doesn't snitch on me then no one knows who to look for. Still, even if they don't find the hole, they'll probably assume that a soldier or Union worker was left alive after the raid. Either way, they'll put the city on lockdown.

It was easy for them to do so. Denvar was a death trap, with only one way in and one way out. I could not afford being locked in here. They'll search my bag and I'll be killed. I had come way too far to just die now.

"Never run while you're on the run." I remembered Alder telling me. "Running is suspicious. Walking isn't." I kept my feet going at a steady pace, and even looked around a bit.

Denvar was built in a rather simple way, there was one main street that let directly to the gate, and about a thousand little back alleys that let to bars, living quarters and the marketplace.

Once I found the main road, all I needed to do is follow it.

I wasn't the only one leaving thankfully, though it wasn't nearly as crowded as it had been this morning. There was a small truck with a bunch of dead bodies still parked at the checkpoint, containing both the body of the soldier who got suspicious with me this morning and the nice girl who I talked to before entering.

Like everything that had happened, I tucked it away in a back corner of my brain that was labelled 'later' and joined the line of people waiting to leave. They did not search any bags, but we did need to talk to them.

"Name." The man said. I could smell the alcohol from where I was standing.

"Dalia." I said again. He wrote it down on a long list of names. I was lucky that most radiates around this area don't have last names, they would never know which Dalia entered and which left.

"Why are you leaving?" It was hard to understand him, he slurred his words so much and nearly fell forward when he tried to get a good look at me.

"Need to get back home before sunrise." I answered. The man nodded and wrote something after my name, though it was so messy that I could hardly read it. Most radiates did not even know how to write, so I am guessing that he was a pretty smart guy when he was sober. I was thankful that he drank too much, only moments later he stepped aside and allowed me to walk past him, the roll still safely tucked away in my backpack.

The parking lot was booming with people who had travelled for hours to make it to the celebration. Most of them rushed to get inside and join in on the party. I found my bike right where I left it, by the looks of it no one had even touched it. My hands were shaking as I turned on the ignition and sped away from Denvar, I was going home.

33

The further the journey took me, the more suspicious I got. During day one and two I could still convince myself that they had not noticed the missing roll. They were probably still partying, or they were getting over a nasty hangover. The following days however I got more and more convinced I could hear the sound of vehicles following me, and I hardly dared to take breaks anymore.

Not properly sleeping for more than a week is really not good for you. The small breaks that I did dare to take were to study the roll and stretch my legs. I had both pages imprinted in my brain top to bottom and fell asleep with them tucked under my backpack, which I used as a pillow.

"Small breaks." Alder reminded me. "No longer than an hour, every three hours."

I had to drive north and avoid the mountain range, after that I would go in as much of a straight line as the buildings and possible radiate towns allowed me to. I knew that Sigholm often housed travellers with gratitude, even feeding them. But I wasn't going to risk it, not with cargo this precious.

Alder had been with me since day seven. I knew that it wasn't really him, he was a hallucination. He looked real enough though, and I could use the company.

It felt much better falling asleep with someone near me to stand guard than to just be all by myself again. I hadn't had company in so long, at least company where I knew I wasn't in mortal danger the entire time. Esta and Gerl were nice people, but if it came to saving me or saving their children, I wouldn't blame them for choosing their kids. I couldn't rely on anyone but myself.

I fell asleep the moment my head touched my backpack. I hadn't even set a timer on the small clock Esta had given me, I slept way past an hour. Thankfully for me, the raiders woke me up after two hours.

The procedure was fairly simple. They took my bike and my backpack, in return my life would be spared. I, however, could not just hand them the roll, and made a fuss about it.

The language barrier made everything an even bigger issue, and eventually, they just ripped it out my hands and pushed the barrel of their gun between my eyes. The two men got on my bike while the rest of them got in their car and drove off. At least they had not found my knife that I had hidden in my shoe every time I slept.

I was left without food or water in the middle of nowhere. At this point I had absolutely no clue how close I was to the fence, I hardly even knew my own name. I watched as the raiders drove off, to mug the next traveller and tried to form a plan in my head.

A plan. Another stupid plan. What good had they been doing to me so far? I planned and I planned, and nothing ever worked out the way it was supposed to. There was nothing to plan here, I would just go.

I followed the sun home. I couldn't just walk in case I was being chased, something my hallucinations had definitely tried to convince me that I am. Instead, I went on a slow jogging tempo. Alder wasn't the only person with me anymore, Ulric was there too.

He wasn't covered in debris or in burns, he looked just like regular old Ulric. I couldn't allow myself to focus on him though, no matter how much I wanted to. I repeated the way the rolls looked in my head over and over again. At least the raiders had found me first, not Edgo's men.

The first thing I recognized was the car. In the far distance, I could see the little town that used to house the Darkfort before it was blown up. The car I passed was where I had last seen Alder, the real Alder. There was still blood in the car from when Jack had been shot, but the rain had washed away any clues that could tell me what had happened after that.

I searched the car for guns, but they had stolen them all. I had not passed any of the cars the other hunters had used, which gave me even more hope that they might still be alive. They could have driven off miles further into the unknown territory or they could have returned to the fence. There was no way of knowing.

My final stretch to the fence was the worst. My throat was dry, my stomach was growling, but I kept up my slow jogging pace. If Ulric could see me now he would have laughed at me. All my stamina was gone, as well as any muscles that I had built up during my year with the hunters.

Loyalty.

I had to repeat the words in my head. For the first time in my life, I felt them give me strength. Alder told me that the loyalty we had made us family, and I'd do anything to get back to them.

Strength.

I was strong. Maybe physically I had taken a beating over the last few months, but I was still strong mentally. I could get over all the things I saw, I could go back to the way things were.

Perseverance.

I would make it back home. I would persevere over the hunt, over Sigholm and even over Edgo. I was going home.

There was no way to describe the feeling I had when I finally saw the fence break over the horizon. I could explode with happiness, as well as collapse in agony. So much had happened, would I even be able to just go back? I brushed my fingers over the long scar that had started to form across my neck.

A bullet hit the ground near my feet. The fence had dozens of military snipers on it, to stop any radiates from sneaking in. In some places the fence was more heavily guarded than others. I was approaching the busiest checkpoint: the eastern gate.

I rolled down the turtleneck and looked to the side as I started to approach them. To make sure they really got the message I also lifted my hands high above my head. I did not have any guns anymore, I didn't even have my backpack. All I had was my knife.

I did not look at the fence. I looked to the left. If they had snipers, they had scopes. If they had brains, they saw my tattoo.

In the distance, I heard the gate opening.

Epilogue

I was put in a large, military SUV. I heard people talking all around me, but nothing really came through. My head was stuck in a fog of sadness and being so tired that even my hallucinations finally left me. I wondered if I would be trading them in for the real people any time soon.

No, I heard a sergeant explain to me that they would take me to Vancouver, not home base. Back to where the nightmare began.

We took some of the backroads. Eventually, I recognized which ones. We drove by my old school, by the local doctor's office, and eventually, we drove by my house.

The kids were playing outside, under the watchful eye of my father. He should be at work right now, he must have quit. He looked like he had aged twenty years in the time that I hadn't seen him. Dawson was off by himself, he was clearly training. He would be next to take the interview, though it would be in two years. The girls were playing tag. One of them fell and started crying.

There were two gravestones on the hill behind them.

Acknowledgements

First and foremost, a big thank you to my parents for not only bringing me to life but also managing to keep me that way. Mom, thank you for being the shoulder I cry on during my downs and the person I laugh with during the ups. Dad, thank you for always sharing your infinite wisdom with me, and your cooking of course.

Thank you to my sister Lisa. I struggled the most with writing a thank you note for you, because you have both influenced me as well as changed me so much as a person, that I can't even begin to describe it. Thank you for telling me how to properly use punctuation, for being my number one supporter when it comes to writing but most of all, thank you for being the best big sister I could ever have.

And finally, thank you. Thank you for going through countless books and deciding that this is the one you want to read. Publishing a book has been my dream ever since I could dream, and to have it become a reality is more than I could have ever hoped for. From the bottom of my heart, thank you.

Thank you so much for reading my debut novel *Beyond the Walls*. If you'd like to stay updated on any of my future writing endeavours, you can follow me on Instagram and Twitter @AliceWestcreek